I Only Read Murder

I Only Read Murder

Ian Ferguson &
Will Ferguson

HarperCollinsPublishersLtd

I Only Read Murder

Published by HarperCollins Publishers Ltd

First edition

HarperCollins books may be purchased for educational, business or sales promotional use through our Special Markets Department.

HarperCollins Publishers Ltd
Bay Adelaide Centre, East Tower
22 Adelaide Street West, 41st Floor
Toronto, Ontario, Canada
M5H 4E3

www.harpercollins.ca

Library and Archives Canada Cataloguing in Publication

Title: I only read murder / Will Ferguson & Ian Ferguson.
Names: Ferguson, Will, author. | Ferguson, Ian, author.
Description: Series statement: A Miranda Abbott mystery ; 1
Identifiers: Canadiana (print) 20230145396 | Canadiana (ebook) 2023014540X
ISBN 9781443470766 (softcover) | ISBN 9781443470773 (EPUB)
Classification: LCC PS8561.E7593 I26 2023 | DDC C813/.54–dc23

Printed and bound in the United States of America

23 24 25 26 27 LBC 6 5 4 3 2

CHAPTER ONE

A Postcard from the Past

An actor dies. The audience reacts.

Not with applause, but confusion. Fear and bewilderment take hold. Death is stalking the stage, hovering in the footlights. The rest of the cast look to each other, not knowing what to do, trapped in their uncertainty. They are waiting for their cue. But the cue never comes.

An actor dies onstage. Two hundred witnesses and no one saw a thing.

Six weeks earlier . . .

Name the worst day in history. The Fall of Rome? The eruption of Mount Vesuvius? The ill-advised launch of New Coke? For Miranda Abbott, actress extraordinaire, star of stage and screen, the worst day began with her agent, Marty Sharpe. Of course it did. She always knew Hell would be an agent's office.

Miranda had swept in with a fling of her scarf—green satin to set off her red hair and celebrated cheekbones—and a breathy "Hello, darling. It is I."

Marty looked up from his needlepoint and sighed. Not her. Not this. Not now.

He was working on one of his Movie Stars of the Golden Age portraits–Marilyn Monroe or maybe John Wayne, it was hard to say; most of them ended up resembling some sort of amphibious creature. A frog or a salamander.

Round-bellied with necktie permanently loosened, Marty had represented Miranda since before she was famous–and long after she no longer was. He seemed decidedly unthrilled at seeing his longtime client waltz in unannounced, as was her habit.

"What have I told you about making appointments, Miranda?"

"I don't make appointments, darling, I keep them."

She had a way of speaking in aphorisms that sounded profound but rarely made sense–except, perhaps, in the emotional realm. Miranda was all about *emotional* intelligence. Trivialities such as making appointments or paying bills or filing her income tax on time didn't enter into it. Nothing she did was ever about the money. Which is probably why she had lost all of hers, several times.

Moments later, her long-suffering assistant Andrew Nguyen appeared, trim and tailored, looking frazzled even if impeccably dressed.

"Sorry. I was putting money in the meter. They still have meters down here, can you believe it?"

They had driven in Andrew's Prius, Miranda's BMW having been recently repossessed, or, as she described it, "taken into the shop."

Andrew's parents had fled Vietnam in an overcrowded leaky boat, had struggled and scrimped and saved so that he could pursue the American dream. Which, in his case, meant managing the affairs of the mercurial Miranda Abbott. On LinkedIn, under "current position," he'd been tempted to enter "babysitter to the stars."

But that wasn't entirely accurate. Not the word *babysitter*, the word *star*.

Andrew took a seat next to Miranda, handed her a bottle of Aquafina. She looked at it with mild confusion and then handed it back so he could unscrew the top for her.

"Thank you, Andrew darling, at least there's one person who cares for me and takes care of me." With a single sip, she was ready. "I warn you, Marty. It's Monday morning, and I am in a feisty mood." She passed the bottle back to Andrew, who just as dutifully screwed the lid on again.

"You're always in a feisty mood," said Marty.

"That reality series you promised me? Where is it? Why has nothing materialized?"

"*The Real Has-Beens of Beverly Hills*?"

She winced. Miranda hated the title. Would talk to the producers about that. Something more dignified, *The Queens of the Silver Screen*, perhaps, or *Real Ingénues of Hollywood*. Beverley Hills was so passé.

"Well?" she said.

"I pitched."

"And?"

"I pitched. They passed."

Miranda fell back in the leatherette chair, a hurt look on her face. Her assistant, Andrew, knew that look. Behind the facade, there was a pool of sadness.

"I'm not even famous enough to play a has-been?"

"No, no, no," said Marty. "You're plenty famous. You're just not"—he searched for the right word—"crazy enough. You're too . . . normal."

Andrew raised an eyebrow.

"Here's the deal," said Marty. "Producers of reality TV are looking for flamboyant unstable delusional narcissists."

"And?" she said.

"Don't get me wrong. You're plenty narcissistic."

"Thank you."

"But not narcissistic *enough*."

Andrew raised the other eyebrow.

"Hang on a sec," said Marty, shuffling through some papers. "I may have something for you. A commercial."

Ah, that was more like it! Tiffany diamonds? Saks Fifth Avenue? The Céline Dion Living Legends Line?

"Metamucil," he said, as he pulled out the script. He slid it across to her.

"Metamucil?" she said. "The fiber supplement?"

"C'mon. There are no small parts, you know that. This isn't simply a commercial. It's a tender and touching dramatic scene: three generations of women, a grandmother, her daughter, and granddaughter in summer dresses at a picnic discussing their digestive issues. I circled your lines."

She flipped through the pages.

"The *grandmother*? You circled the grandmother's part?" She was aghast at the sheer effrontery of it. "Surely, you mean the mother. Or, with the right lighting, the daughter."

"She's a youthful grandmother," Marty assured her. "And she has the best lines. *Life is too full to feel full.* That's gold, Miranda! Think of the layers of nuance you can add to that. Think of the residuals."

She was livid. "I am NOT playing a grandmother! I am nowhere near that age."

"Well," said Marty, with a shrug, "when it comes to actresses, after forty or forty-five, it all starts to blur."

Andrew braced himself for what was coming. *Five . . . four . . . three . . .* He used to start the countdown at ten, but Miranda's fuse had gotten shorter lately.

"May I remind you," she said, blood and voice rising, "that I was Pastor Fran on *Pastor Fran Investigates*, investigating crimes as Pastor Fran, for six years, Marty! I was the lead character on a top-ten network TV show for six years!"

"Five," said Marty. "The ratings tanked at the end, remember? The DUI and that drunken brawl at the Golden Globes? Tarnished the image of you as a woman of the cloth, as you'll recall. And anyway, *Pastor Fran Investigates*, that ended, what, fifteen years ago?"

"I was a star, Marty!"

"And you still are. You're just in a bit of a slump, that's all."

"What kind of slump lasts fifteen years?" Her scarf had slipped down, and she flung it back with renewed purpose. "If you are not going to bring me worthwhile roles–"

At this, Marty rankled. "Don't be too proud to take the work that comes your way. Metamucil pays the rent." He would have said "mortgage," but that hadn't been true with Miranda in a long, long while.

"I had my own line of action figures!" she shouted. "I had my own glow-in-the-dark doodle poster! I was on lunch boxes and iron-on T-shirts. I had my own Bedazzler, for god's sake! And now you want to have me advising young girls to eat more fiber so they can shit better?"

"Miranda, calm down."

In the history of the universe, has telling someone to calm down ever actually made them calm down? Miranda rose from her seat, arms wide in full theatrical mode, hitting every word like a driven nail. "I. Am. Beloved!"

"Was," said Marty.

"What did you say?"

"Was beloved, *were* beloved. You're in a slump, Miranda, so you've got to be strategic in what you do, now that you've entered the–" He caught himself just in time.

She glowered down at him. "Say it," she said.

Andrew tried to intervene. He got up from his chair but was swatted aside with an imperious wave of her hand.

Her eyes remained locked on Marty's.

"Say it, you rat bastard."

"Look, Miranda, it's just a commercial. A bit of work to get you through. That's all."

"Say it. I dare you! Now that I've entered 'the suicide years.' That's what you were going to say." Her face was as red as her hair at this point.

Her assistant Andrew pled for decorum. "Please. Maybe we should all take a moment to–"

"No! I will not stand here and be insulted. I made you, Marty! Suicide years? No. These aren't the suicide years. These are the murder years. These are the don't-give-a-damn years! These are the 'stab your agent in the eye with a salad fork' years!"

A strange look came over Marty. The feigned warmth and feigned friendship, the practiced flattery and the ingratiating mannerisms drained away, replaced by a harder and, it must be said, colder gaze.

"Get out," he said.

"Fine!" she replied with a final fling of the scarf. "Come along, Andrew." Then, to Marty, "I warn you. The next time I visit this meager kingdom you call an office, I shall be expecting something more than a grandmother sharing the intimate details of her bowel movements."

"There won't be a next time," said Marty. "You're done. I'm firing you, as of today."

"You can't fire me. You're my agent. If anything, I should be firing *you*."

"By all means," he said. "If that makes it easier for you. You fired *me*. But either way, you're not welcome in this officc. You are no longer my client. And I am no longer your agent."

She stormed down the stairwell with young Andrew trailing behind.

"Maybe we should go back," he said, all but begging. "And apologize."

"Never!"

She burst out into the muggy heat on Sunset Boulevard, muttering invective.

The front tire of Andrew's Prius had been clamped. Miranda stood staring at it as though it were an odd bit of flora.

"I told you!" said Andrew. "I said, we can't park here. And you said, no one cares."

"Well," she said, "take it off so we can go."

"Take it off? How?"

"I don't know. You're the personal assistant. Make some calls."

"Calls? To who?"

"Whom," she said. "Make some calls to *whom*. Can you still drive it?"

"It would tear away the fender."

"Yes, but can you still drive it? I'll pay for the fender."

"With what? I haven't received any reimbursement for the last three months. I'm basically an unpaid intern at this point."

Andrew had been hired by Miranda long after her fall from stardom. She had paid well—at first. She'd even covered his kid brother's college tuition, a gracious gesture that she never dwelled on. "That's what money is for, darling," she'd said. But since then, her funds had evaporated and so had Andrew's patience.

"Have you not been paid?" she said, genuinely puzzled. "Well, you should rectify that, Andrew. You're in charge of the money."

"The nonexistent money."

"I'm between gigs, that's all. As for this ridiculous clamp that the city has seen fit to attach to your vehicle, if we can't drive out of here, that's fine. We'll take a bus. Here's one now."

She stepped out into traffic and raised her hand. The bus rumbled past in a cloud of exhaust.

"You can't flag down a bus like it's a taxi," said Andrew. "There are rules."

"Rules don't apply to me," she said. "I apply to rules." And with that, she headed off, skirt and heels and green scarf fluttering, down Sunset toward the Hollywood Hills.

Andrew watched her leave.

"I can't do this anymore," he said.

But he couldn't leave her on her own, either. He hailed a taxi and picked up Miranda as she strode through the heat haze of an LA morning.

"To the Hollywood Hills," she informed the driver as she slid in.

"I already gave him the address," said Andrew. He leaned up to make sure there was no misunderstanding. "It's in the *lower* hills, just above Santa Monica."

"The Hills are the Hills," said Miranda. "Anything above Santa Monica is still in the Hills. And I am above Santa Monica!"

"Barely," said Andrew under his breath.

He had decided that after he got her home, he would hand in his resignation. He'd had enough. His parents had watched *Pastor Fran Investigates* faithfully, religiously, every Friday, had learned their English from that show, had been proud beyond words when he got the job ferrying the Star Herself around. "Is she like her character?" his dad would always ask, and Andrew would always lie. "Yes, Papa. Exactly like the character."

But he was done lying. Was done running interference. Was done, done, done. He had always been loyal to her. But even loyalty cannot survive penury and magical thinking.

The De-Lux Arms looked like a motel, though it was in fact apartments. Green stucco, sun-faded to pastel, with outdoor stairwells wrapping around a cement pool, cracked and usually dry. A few palm trees out front swayed in the heat, listless and limp.

Above the De-Lux rose the grandiose homes of the Hollywood Hills, cantilevered in ascending steps above the lowly less-famous below.

Miranda Abbott had once lived in those hills, in those homes.

As she and Andrew walked the stairs to her second-floor apartment, a ruddy-faced man in coveralls approached with a warm smile, beaming at her. "Hi there! Ms. Abbott?"

"It is I."

Always happy to meet a fan.

He had a clipboard. "Can you sign here?"

She took his pen with a flourish. "Certainly. And who should I make it out to?"

"The furniture company, I guess."

She looked through the document. "You're taking my dining room set? That is genuine Moroccan rattan! Do you have any idea how much that costs?"

"About $781.50, I would imagine," he said, tapping a finger on the overdue amount.

"I should never have bought that on layaway."

"I tried to warn you," said Andrew. "When expenses incurred are greater than income received . . ."

But she wasn't listening. "Fine," she said, scrawling her name across the bottom. "But I better not see that on eBay."

She didn't know exactly what eBay was, but she'd heard that

certain celebrities were selling their autographs on it. She assumed it was some sort of memorabilia store.

As the ruddy man whistled down to his crew to come up and begin hauling away the dining room furniture, Miranda sighed and, tempting the gods of literary irony, said, "I don't know how this day could possibly get any worse."

When she went to let the repo men in, she found an eviction notice taped to the door.

"They spelled my name wrong," she complained, pulling the notice down and stepping aside as the movers bullied past. "Two b's and two t's. How hard is that to remember?"

A Murphy bed, opened and unmade, a wall of photographs, once framed but now thumbtacked to the faded paneling, a messy stack of gossip magazines, the latest edition of *Variety*, unread. A closet stuffed with Pastor Fran memorabilia.

Miranda Abbott's last stand...

Andrew picked up her mail from where it had fallen and then been trod upon by work boots. His final duty as her personal assistant.

He took a steadying breath. It was time.

"Miranda," he said. "There's something I need to tell you. Something I need to say." But the goodbye got caught in his throat.

She waved in the general direction of the icebox.

"At least they didn't take the fridge. Small mercies. Andrew, darling, there's a fresh jug of lemonade in there. I made it just for you. I know how much you like it."

A simple recipe: lemon juice and two pounds of sugar. Andrew had made the mistake of complimenting it once, and now she prepared it for him every time she knew he was coming over. It broke his heart, bringing it out onto the balcony, with the wisteria and the view of the Hills beyond. Lemonade and foot-trodden mail.

Bills mainly, and a postcard. There was a time when she would have received hundreds of letters a day.

Not now.

"Miss Miranda," he said, taking a seat next to her for a final glass of the world's worst lemonade. Even the bees in the wisteria gave it a pass. "You were always so kind to my parents. You knew how much your show meant to them, and I appreciate that and, well, I just wanted to say . . ."

"You see that house? The red one, halfway up. That used to be my house. Did you know that?"

He did. She pointed it out every time they were on the balcony, or driving by, or looking through her photo albums.

"Sometimes, the sounds of the parties will drift down at night, when I'm trying to sleep." She took a deep drink from her glass. "They say they will remember you, but they forget. They forget." Eyes shining, trying to smile away the pain, she asked, "What was it you wanted to say, Andrew?"

"Just that. Thank you."

She laid her hand on his. "And your boyfriend? He's well?"

"My fiancé, yes."

"Such bright young men, both of you."

"Hey. A postcard," said Andrew, trying to stem the overwhelming melancholy of this day. "Maybe it's from a fan!"

He handed it across to her. It was a forested harbor scene with mountains cloaked in mist, and when she turned it over, the message read:

It's been fifteen years, Miranda.
I think it's time.

"Hmm," said Andrew. "A bit cryptic. What do you think it means?"

But Miranda knew exactly what it meant. And for the first time in a long, long while, a smile burst across her face. She looked happy. She looked relieved. She looked . . . beautiful.

"Andrew," she cried. "Pack the valise! I have been summoned."

An actor dies.

The audience reacts.

CHAPTER TWO

The Bus to Happy Rock

The overnight coach from Los Angeles to Portland, Oregon, took sixteen hours and thirty-seven minutes.

"That seems oddly specific," Miranda said when Andrew told her.

"It costs $156 one way."

"But what about the express option?" she asked.

"That is the express option. The regular bus takes even longer."

"Sixteen hours?" she said, aghast at the thought of it.

"And thirty-seven minutes," said Andrew.

They were at the San Fernando bus depot, across the freeway from Holy Cross, Miranda having insisted they cab it all the way out here in the heat to avoid boarding a Greyhound anywhere near the Hollywood Hills, lest someone see her and call those vultures at TMZ.

With her scarf pulled over her head and oversized sunglasses in place, she looked exactly like a celebrity who was trying not to draw attention to herself. She had already decided, if anyone should ask or, god forbid, a fan spotted her on the bus, she would tell them she was "researching a role."

"Sixteen hours and thirty-seven minutes," she moaned. "I could fly to Cannes and back in that time."

"Yes, but we can't afford Cannes," said Andrew. "And we can't afford a last-minute flight to Portland, either."

He said "we," but he meant "I." The cost of the bus ticket, like the cost of the cab, was coming out of his hypothetical and most likely nonexistent future wages. The same imaginary wages that would pay to have his car rescued from the impound lot. Miranda had assured Andrew that since his Prius had already been booted, it was like having a "free parking spot." But when Andrew had returned to retrieve the car, it had been towed. Of course it had been towed. Miranda described the world how she thought it ought to be, not how it really was. And in the world of Miranda Abbott, cars never got towed and TV stars never took an overnight bus, unless it was "for a role."

After purchasing a ticket for her, Andrew walked Miranda to the loading bay, where he handed her a final bottle of Aquafina. The coach doors opened with a hydraulic hiss, and the other passengers began to file on.

"I shall return in triumph," she assured him.

"I know you will," he said, and he almost believed it. Almost, but not quite. He wasn't entirely sure why she was going or what was waiting for her, but he was sure he wouldn't be here when she got back. If she got back. He tried to let her know that this was goodbye, but the words once again got caught in his throat.

"When they take everything from me, can you save at least one Pastor Fran action figure? As a memento. Will you do that for me?"

He promised he would, and with that, Miranda Abbott picked up her valise, squared her shoulders, and marched up the steps–into the Greyhound and away from him. Andrew waved, but the windows were tinted and he didn't know where she was. Not anymore.

As the bus rolled out of the bay and onto Laurel Canyon Boulevard, Andrew stood on the sidewalk, still waving. He was surprised by a sudden wash of emotion; he should have been relieved, happy even, to see her go. He touched his fingers to his eyes and thought, What is this? Am I crying?

No. Not crying. Weeping.

Inside the bus, Miranda clutched the postcard in her hand and watched as the city fell away. Onto the interstate, picking up speed, in and out of scrubland forests and arid hills, they cannonballed past the Santa Clara studios where they'd filmed the first two seasons of *Pastor Fran.*

Our Lady, who arts on the mean streets of Crime City! Hallowed be her fists. Crackin' wise and solvin' crimes. It was an iconic opening, up there with *The Six Million Dollar Man* or *Hawaii Five-O.*

The highway rolled on. The sun went down, and as the darkness gathered outside, the bus windows slowly became a mirror. Miranda stared through herself at the fading landscape beyond.

When a character died on *Pastor Fran*, it was always at the midpoint, just before the commercial break. In the first half of the episode, viewers were trying to guess *who* would be murdered; in the second half, they would be wondering *why*. They never wondered whether Pastor Fran would solve the case, though. That was a given.

If only life followed such a comforting pattern, thought Miranda. If only I could say with certainty, in the second half everything will be resolved. But this wasn't an episode of *Pastor Fran*, this was her, alone on a Greyhound, heading toward a postcard–and a promise of better days to come.

Night had fallen by the time they pulled into Sacramento, the only stop on the express route, and she ate, huddled over a cup of herbal tea (lukewarm and weak) and a croissant (dry and flavorless) at the bus depot cafeteria. She really should complain to the chef, she thought, but was mortified at the possibility someone might recognize her.

Instead, she rehearsed her alibi.

Why am I dining alone in a bus depot? Research, darling. Research. Why, yes! It is the return of Pastor Fran. Thank you for asking. All hush hush, of course, so don't say a word; the studios want to make a splash when they announce it. And yes, I would be delighted to take a photo with you. Always happy to meet my fans.

But no one recognized her or, if they did, they were too intimidated to approach. Miranda finished her tea and then pulled the scarf tighter as she reboarded the coach, keeping the sunglasses on even though it was now night. More passengers had joined them, but no one sat next to Miranda in the dark, and she fell into a deep slumber, forehead resting against the glass.

She dreamed of red carpets and a golden Lab . . .

Woke up feeling fuzzy-headed and cotton-mouthed as the bus pulled into Portland. The sun was softer up here.

She knew she had to change coaches when she got to Portland, and there was a moment of panic and confusion as she searched the timetable posted out front. Gladstone? Was that the name of the town?

Sunglasses still firmly in place, she approached the young man at the ticket counter with a haughty air, saying, "The town of Gladstone. That's on the ocean, yes? With forested hills and sailboats?"

"Not really. Gladstone's a suburb of Portland. You're probably thinking of Happy Rock, out on Tillamook Bay."

Glad-*stone*. Happy *Rock*. "Why on earth would there be two towns with such names?"

"They translated it from the same Native American word, is what I heard. But used different dictionaries. Probably for the best.

Wouldn't want there to be two Happy Rocks." He grinned. "One is plenty."

"And how do I get there?"

"Just keep going till you run out of road. It's the last bit of land before you reach open water. If your feet get wet, you've gone too far."

It was another hour and a half to Tillamook Bay inside a glorified school bus with broken suspension. Miranda was tossed about like a die in a cup, the driver hitting every pothole along the way–intentionally, it seemed to her. Bounced her scarf clean off, in fact, as she gripped the seat in front of her, trying her best to remain insouciant. Fortunately, Miranda's death-wish driver seemed too intent on charting his slalom course along narrow, twisting roads to notice who he had on board.

There was only one other passenger that day: a green-haired, nose-pierced goblin of a girl in ratty jeans who sat across and up from Miranda. The girl had slung a camera onto the seat next to her and opened a heavy ring-bound manual of some sort, and had then almost immediately fallen asleep, head back, snoring. That someone so petite could snore so loudly! Feeling curious–a camera always made her curious–Miranda peered across at what the girl had been reading. Could just see the title on the bound pages: *Toxicology Report: Portland Coroner's Office*. Strange reading, thought Miranda. Maybe she's researching a role? Miranda felt that most people spent their lives researching a role, practicing the parts they hoped to someday play. And she wasn't entirely wrong.

The road to Tillamook Bay wound its way through forests of pine and Douglas fir, across rivers running clean and clear. She remembered this road. Remembered the harbor that eventually opened up, the protective peninsula that curved around it, the mist-infused hills beyond, and the cluster of sailboats below. The candy-striped lighthouse at the end of the bay. And that grand dame of a hotel out front, ivy-clad and facing the water.

She was back.

It had taken fifteen years, but she was back. Miranda Abbott had returned to Happy Rock.

She climbed out of the bus, bruised but undefeated, alighting in front of the staid glory that was the Royal Duchess Imperial Hotel. The Duchess, for short.

Crisp air and cold water.

"I'm here!" she said. She wanted to twirl like Mary Tyler Moore, throw her scarf in the air, but it was an expensive scarf, and she was still in disguise.

Now. Where was it?

She remembered a narrow lane, up a hill, a mansard roof and a widow's walk. Victorian twee, the best kind.

She walked along the harbor in the sunlight, dragging her rattling valise behind her, past the expansive lawn of the hotel, looking for lanes leading uphill. Everyone moved slower out here, more leisurely, as though time were less pressing. It was a watercolor come to life. A doily of a town, with marigolds and flowering begonias spilling out of streetlamp baskets. Happy Rock hadn't been built; it had been crocheted into existence. Miranda was sure of that.

But still she couldn't find the lane she was searching for.

Past the Duchess Hotel was the stately Opera House with its marquee out front, and Miranda crossed the street to read the poster:

The Happy Rock Amalgamated & Consolidated Little Theater Society

PRESENTS

for the 10th consecutive year in a row!!

"Death Is the Dickens"

a whodunit for the ages!

Miranda ignored the 8 x 10 glossies that were posted of last year's cast, zeroed in on the namc of the playwright instead. It was listed at the very bottom of the poster: *Doug Dirks.*

Whew.

She had never heard of Doug Dirks. With this reassuring piece of information, she turned, still not sure which way to go.

"Aha!"

Miranda had spotted a patrol car coming along the harbor toward her, and she stepped out, directly in front of it, flagging it down the way one might a valet driver. Startled, the vehicle swerved to the side of the road with a single whoop of the sirens.

"Happy Rock PD! Ma'am, are you all right?"

The officer who'd clamored out of the police car was a rounded fellow with a worried look on his face. Everything about him was slightly overinflated, from his ample belly to his smooth, plump cheeks. A kindly soul, she could tell. And Miranda Abbott was a good judge of character!

She folded her scarf and tucked her sunglasses into her voluminous carry-all bag. No need for such a ruse now that she was under police protection.

"I am lost," she declared in the same way one might announce that they had conquered Everest.

"Um, sure. I can help you with that. I'm Ned. Ned Buckley, like the cough syrup." He gave her a smile, which was returned, unopened.

"Well, Officer Buckley—"

"Chief," he said, almost embarrassed to admit it. "I'm actually the, ah, Chief of Police here in Happy Rock. Truth be told, there's just the three of us, and Carl, he's part-time, and Holly, well, she's got a little one on the way, so when the old chief retired, that pretty much left me."

"Not a lot of crime in Happy Rock, then?"

"Well, no, not that you could speak of." He chuckled. "Most recent was the Case of the Missing Pocketbook. A lady called in, convinced someone had stolen her pocketbook. Strange thing was, no one had tried to use her credit cards or ID while it was missing. So I asked her, 'Are you sure it was stolen?'"

There was a long pause.

"And?" said Miranda. "Did you solve it?"

"The missing pocketbook? I suppose. Closed the case, anyway. It turned up a few days later, right where she'd left it."

"So . . . not stolen. Misplaced."

His chuckle turned into a chortle. "Oh, that's not how she tells it. She's still convinced someone took it. That's Happy Rock for you, I suppose."

"Well, Chief, I have another case for you to crack. I am looking for a certain building on a certain street."

"Could you narrow that down a bit?"

"A beautiful building with soft light across the front, a gentle breeze and a soothing glow in the early afternoons."

"Um."

"Victorian latticework. A garden."

"That's half the homes in Happy Rock."

"It would have been a bookstore."

He frowned. "There's no bookstore in town. Except, the murder one."

"Murder?"

"Thrillers and killers and such. A specialty shop. Only sells mysteries. It's behind the Duchess, up on Beacon Hill."

"That's the one!"

Leaving the Chief of Police to fetch her valise, she climbed into the back seat of his patrol car as though he were indeed her personal chauffeur.

"Um, okay," he said.

He followed with her luggage. Put it in the trunk and came around to the driver's side.

"Won't take long," he said, pulling on his seatbelt. "It's just up the hill." He angled the rearview mirror to study her. "First time?"

"In a police car?"

"In Happy Rock."

Miranda looked out the window to the sailboats in the harbor. The curve of the bay, the rising steam. A floatplane coming in had left a spreading V of waves in its wake. It was as beautiful as she remembered. Maybe more so. Beautiful–and suffocating.

"I was here," she said. "Once. Many years ago."

"Just the once? Well then, welcome back, I guess." He signaled and pulled out, shoulder-checking the lack of traffic behind him.

It was all coming back to her now: the lane behind the hotel, angling upward to the top of the hill. A view of the harbor below, like a postcard. And there it was: the same gingerbread trim and stained-glass transom over the front door, the same widow's walk up top. A front garden lush with peonies.

Above the front door, in classic Garamond font, was a sign that read: I ONLY READ MURDER.

"Strange name for a bookstore, right?" said Chief Buckley as he brought his police car to a slow stop out front. "Was originally called Tillamook Books–that's the name of the bay–but the new owner changed it after a comment from one of the customers, a sweet little granny who pooh-poohed the suggestions the staff kept making. 'I only read murder!' is what she said. From that came the idea of specializing in mysteries and mayhem."

"Well," said Miranda, "I thank you for the ride. It is very much appreciated."

But the chief didn't respond. He was watching her from the rearview mirror more closely than before, and when she tried to open the door, she couldn't. No handles on the inside, bars on the back window, and eyes in the mirror.

"Excuse me, Officer. I mean, Chief. Can you let me out?"

But still he said nothing. Stared at her in the mirror.

"I'd like to get out now."

The doors remained locked. She was trapped in the back of a cruiser with the engine still running.

When he finally spoke, his voice was calm. "Maybe I should just arrest you now, get it over with."

"I beg your pardon?"

He turned, leveled his steady gaze upon her. "I mean, everywhere you go, bodies do seem to pile up, don't they?"

She fumbled in her bag for her can of mace. Never would she have imagined she would need to use it in Happy Rock. Hollywood, perhaps. The De-Lux Arms, certainly. But not Happy Rock. She would wait until he opened the door, whenever that might be, and . . .

But then the most remarkable thing happened. He smiled. A warm smile. Very warm. You could roast marshmallows on that smile.

"I mean, you are Pastor Fran, right?"

She relaxed her grip on the mace, let it fall back into the uncharted depths of her bag.

"Indeed," she said. "It is I."

"I knew it!" His smile grew even bigger, if such a thing were possible.

Miranda Abbott felt a wave of relief wash over her. Not a psycho. A fan. Though even she had to admit, the two categories often overlapped.

When a character died on *Pastor Fran*, it was always at the midpoint of the story. So she was safe—for now. Except, of course, this wasn't an episode of *Pastor Fran*. This was something else entirely.

CHAPTER THREE

Into the Murder Store

"Sorry about locking the car door on ya. Standard police procedure," he said jokingly, motor still running and door still locked. "Had to make sure you didn't try to disarm me."

"I thought I already had," she said, "with my smile."

His round cheeks bunched up, almost blushing. Pastor Fran, flirting with the chief.

"Well, I am single," he said.

"I'll keep that in mind."

He sat there bobbing his head and grinning at her like a schoolboy. He reminded Miranda of a bobblehead. A friendly bobblehead–but a bobblehead, nonetheless.

There had been a Pastor Fran bobblehead, too, once upon a time, though it hadn't sold nearly as well as the Season Three action figure. And no wonder. That one came with built-in karate-chop action. You pressed a plastic lever on the back of Pastor Fran, and the arm came down with its patented Sinner-B-Gone™ chop. She'd always had trouble with the *Haii-ya!* that she was required to shout whenever they filmed a fight scene, so they'd had to bring in another actress to dub those over. Miranda's voice was too sultry, too raspy, couldn't hit the sustained high note required for a decent *Haii-ya!*

Meanwhile, Chief Bobblehead was still grinning away at her from the front seat of his cruiser.

"The door?" she said.

"Oh, right." He pressed the unlock button, but before he got out to come around and release her, he said, "I know who you should see while you're in town!"

This gave her pause. How much did he know about her? And how much did he know about her reasons for coming back to Happy Rock?

But he wasn't referring to the bookstore, he was referring to–had she heard him correctly?–Bees Bees and Bees? BBB? Better Business Bureau?

"Bea," he said. "She runs the B&B down by the harbor. A cottage-style house. Nice view from the porch. Bea is your biggest fan. I know people always say that, but with her, it's true. Really, it is. She has all of your shows on VHS. 'Pastor Fran Fridays.' I bring the popcorn, she brings the Fran. Caramel popcorn," he explained. "Bea likes caramel. She's practically memorized all of your lines. Can recite entire episodes by heart."

Oh great, thought Miranda. Just what I need now. A *Misery*-type superfan.

"Bea Maracle. That's her name. Lost her husband a while back. Runs a B&B. Bea's B&B. That's her place. Real comfy, though I imagine a Hollywood star like you, you've probably rented out an entire suite at the Duchess. But if you get a chance, stop by, say hello to her. She'd be thrilled. Like I said, I wouldn't expect you to actually stay there, at Bea's. Although–here's an idea!–you could make an appearance at our next Pastor Fran Friday. Only if you wanted to, of course. Only if it wasn't a bother. I would hate to impose."

Miranda's smile had grown strained. She made a list of things she would rather do than attend a Pastor Fran Friday in Happy Rock: a root canal on rough seas, a blindfolded chainsaw juggling competition on a trampoline, a Metamucil commercial for an extra-fiber diet.

But...

If this really was some sort of weekly event, might it not be a good way to get her name in the public eye again? Hadn't Jerry Lewis been heralded as a genius in France? Wasn't David Hasselhoff a star in Germany? Why couldn't Miranda Abbott be equally celebrated in Happy Rock?

"And how many are usually in attendance at these 'Pastor Fran Fridays'?"

He frowned, thought a bit. "Just Bea and me, really."

Great.

"I should be going, Mr.–" She almost said Bobblehead. "Vicks, was it? Or was it Robitussin?" It had already melted away. She had a memory for faces, not names. Unless those names were above the title, of course.

"Buckley," he said. "Ned Buckley. Like the–"

"Yes. The cough syrup. Well, Ned, I should be going. It's been an absolute delight, but–" She gave the slightest of nods in the direction of the bookstore. "I am expected."

"Are you? Geez." His face clouded over. "You know the owner, do you?"

"I do."

The frown returned. "Tread carefully, okay? He's... an odd one."

"The owner? Why do you say that?"

"Surrounded by murder all day? Gets my police instincts up. Who knows what someone like that is capable of?"

"Ah. The Case of the Missing Pocketbook. You suspect the owner of the bookstore, do you?" She was teasing, but he took it seriously.

"Haven't ruled it out."

Small-town police officers, so lacking in guile.

Chief Buckley, suddenly remembering his manners, climbed out to open the rear cruiser door for her. If he'd been wearing his police cap, he would have tilted it to her.

"You take care, ma'am. Like I said, the owner of the murder store is a bit of an oddball." Then, quickly, apparently not wanting to speak ill of people, he added, "But not without charm."

Oh, I know, thought Miranda. A deadly charm. A disarming charm.

Miranda tried to tip the chief for his help, but he waved it away, embarrassed by the offer. Which was probably for the best, because Miranda was down to her last few dollars. (She hadn't yet found the fold of twenties that Andrew had slipped into her bag before she left. He might as well have thrown it into a well, such was the maw of Miranda's carry-all.)

But not to worry! She wouldn't need money, not for a while anyway, not once she walked through those doors.

Miranda entered on a jingle of a bell. The air inside was liquid and warm. Bookshelves lined the hallway and she followed them down, along a carpet prismed with light spilling through the front transom in a multihued glow. A house of books. And at the end of the hall, in what must have been the Victorian-era living room, oak shelves flanked the walls, floor to ceiling. Wheeled tables were layered with the latest hardcovers. Lurid books with DEATH and KILL and MURDER in the title.

A massive oak desk with a roll top took up one entire corner.

Beyond this main room, in what must have once been the dining area, a handwritten sign above the arch read *Used & Beloved, This*

Way. Here were the secondhand Agatha Christies and the Penguin perennials.

Miranda recognized the handwriting on that sign. The awkward ampersand, the flowing *s*. Jazz was softly playing over speakers hidden among the tomes. Count Basie and his orchestra. She recognized that, too.

It was only when Miranda returned to the main room that she noticed the diminutive woman who was on duty behind the massive desk, all but hidden by it, lost in a book and surrounded in a halo of light. She was as faint and ethereal as the lace curtains behind her.

A creak in the floor gave Miranda away.

"Oh, goodness. I'm sorry," said the tiny lady. "Was deep in my cozy. Didn't see you."

Deep in my cozy? Was this some sort of quirky Oregon expression?

"Cozy?" said Miranda, assuming the lady was referring to the chair, or perhaps the bookstore itself. But no, she held up the cover: *Mrs. Petunia's Perfect Caper*.

"The latest."

"Oh, and how is it?"

"Not as good as the first forty-seven in the series, but better than the last twelve. *Mrs. Petunia's Penultimate Puzzle* was the best, though. I like a good puzzle cozy."

So *cozy* was a type of book.

Noticing the look on Miranda's face, she said, "I don't like the gore of thrillers, or the endless details of a police procedural, or anything involving serial killers. I like a good amateur sleuth, preferably female, and a small-town setting. No graphic murders. And you, my dear? Where does your taste in murder lie?"

Miranda pondered this strange question. Her taste in murder?

She thought about her own character. Pastor Fran was an amateur sleuth, true. The murders were shown on screen, but only up to a point. They usually cut away to a woman screaming or a teacup shattering at the very moment the deed was done. But the show also featured car chases and explosions and at least one karate chop per episode. And the producers were always trying to get her into a miniskirt or a bikini. *Pastor Fran goes undercover at a sexy disco! Pastor Fran goes undercover at the bikini warehouse!* That sort of thing. A little risqué for a cozy, no?

"I'm not exactly sure," said Miranda. "Is there such a thing as an action mystery thriller cozy?"

"Second shelf on the left," said the lady. And sure enough, there was a category labeled Action Mystery Thriller Cozies.

There was another shelf labeled Animal Cozies. Another swath was labeled Period-Piece Mysteries, with stories stretching from Ancient Rome to Jazz Age flapper detectives. There was a shelf called Hardboiled, featuring two-fisted men, bombshell blondes, and lurking thugs. One bookshelf was simply labeled Detective, and next to it, Historical Detective, the difference between "period-piece mystery" and "historical detective" being a mystery in itself. Which brought it all back around to Cozy Detective. It was enough to make her head spin.

A table in the center of the store was slab-high with Thrillers (International), right next to Thrillers (Domestic). Ah, finally! A straightforward division: international thrillers would take place in exotic locales like Bali or Paris, Venice or Vienna. Domestic thrillers would be set in the States, or whatever country the author was writing in. But no! As Miranda discovered when she read the descriptions, international thrillers were exactly that, but *domestic* thrillers meant murders within marriages. Spouses setting up partners, catching them in a web of deceit. She tried to think this through. So a murderous marriage . . . set in Venice . . . would be a DOMESTIC THRILLER INTERNATIONAL? The mind boggled.

A bookshelf for younger readers was labeled YA SLEUTHS and featured Nancy Drew, Encyclopedia Brown, the Famous Five, and the Brothers Hardy. Farther down was TRUE CRIME, lurid and lascivious. And above that was a shelf weighted with CLASSICS, the Holmeses and the Sergeant Cuffs, which were apparently *not* historical detective stories because *at the time they were written*, they were contemporary. Boxes within boxes. How many ways could you possibly divide a single genre? There were none of the *Pastor Fran* TV tie-in novelizations, though. At least, not that Miranda could see. Those would no doubt be in a discount bin somewhere in the back. Or filed perhaps under "period piece." Or "vintage."

They'd never sold well.

Which was a shame, because it was the author of those very novelizations whom she had come to see. *It's been fifteen years. It's time.*

"Is the owner in?" Miranda asked, returning to the lady, interrupting her once again from Mrs. Petunia's latest.

"Edgar? He hasn't come down yet. I open the store, he closes. It works well. I'm an early bird. He's a night owl." She looked to the ceiling. "He lives upstairs, above the store."

"Alone?" Miranda asked, a little too quickly.

"That depends," said the lady, placing her paperback to one side, having carefully inserted a bookmark first, "on what you mean by alone."

At which point, a muffled thump could be heard upstairs, followed by the sound of footsteps above, the clattering of claws on a floor, the whirr of a can opener–and Miranda's heart leapt.

The pale lady tilted her head as she looked at Miranda. "How do you know Edgar?"

"I'm Miranda," she said, as though that should mean something, but apparently it did not.

"And I'm Susan," she said. Neither of them extended their hand. "But you didn't answer my question. How do you know Edgar?"

"Miranda *Abbott*," she said, and now the proverbial penny dropped.

"Oh," said Susan. "I see. I thought you'd vanished."

"I did. I had. But I'm back!" She couldn't help it, she was beaming. Everything would be okay now. Pastor Fran would return. So would the joy. The house in the Hollywood Hills. "It's a new day!" she said.

"It is, indeed," said Susan. She was whatever the opposite of beaming was. Perturbed, perhaps. And clearly protective of Edgar. "Does he know you're coming?"

"He invited me." She would have said "summoned," but Susan's face had grown sour, and Miranda's confidence was beginning to falter.

Miranda rifled through her bag but couldn't find the postcard. And that was when she realized she'd left her valise in the trunk of Chief Buckley's car.

"Never mind," said Miranda. "He's expecting me."

The creak of a door above, heavy footsteps coming down equally creaky stairs, the whistling of a tuneless tune—all these years and he still hadn't learned to whistle properly!—accompanied by the exuberant *thump-thump-thump* of a companion. Man's best friend.

A golden Lab came galloping in, happily uncoordinated, waving its tail like a baton.

"Oscar?" said Miranda.

The dog ran over and let her scritch behind the ears, then circled around and came back for another scritch.

"Oh, Oscar. I missed you so much." Miranda's eyes brimmed with happiness.

"Hello, Miranda."

She looked up and there he was, blurry through her tears. Older, but still Edgar. Trim, as always. Jeans and a plaid shirt. Graying at the temples now, and softer of jaw, but with those same warm sardonic eyes, impossibly blue. A face creased with sun—and kindness.

"I can't believe how spry Oscar is," she said, fighting back a sob.

"That's not Oscar, no. That's Emmy, daughter of. I had to put Oscar down. He was so old and in so much pain. At the end."

And now the sob did escape. It wasn't Oscar. Of course it wasn't Oscar. Time hadn't stopped while she'd been gone. Dogs got old and passed on here in Happy Rock, just as they did anywhere else.

Edgar came over, laid his hand on Miranda's shoulder, firm and gentle at the same time, the way he always had when she'd needed comfort, when she'd needed to know she wasn't alone.

"You came," said Edgar. "All this way?" Like he could hardly believe it. He turned to his bookstore clerk and said, "Susan, this is Miranda Abbott. My wife."

Not ex-wife. Wife.

"We've already met," said Susan, her voice icy.

"I came as soon as I got your postcard," Miranda said. The words tumbled out through the tears. "And you're right, Edgar. You're right! It's been too long. It's time for us to be together again, to be a couple again. Hollywood has been so unkind to me, but I'm here now. I'm your wife, and we're going to get through this. You will write again, and I will act. Together, we'll relaunch ourselves into an even higher orbit than before."

He was clearly taken aback by this. "Relaunch?"

She missed the question mark hanging off that word. "Exactly! A relaunch, Edgar. Bigger, better, stronger than before. I've had so many thoughts on the way up. Remember the series finale?"

"There was no series finale. They pulled the plug without warning, remember? We didn't have time to wrap anything up. It was left in limbo."

"Exactly! There was no closure, Edgar. There I was, Pastor Fran, pushed off a cliff, *again*, and the image froze with me in mid-air–I was always good at falling–and then those horrible words: *To be continued.* But there was no continued, Edgar. Pastor Fran was left there, falling, never landing. Well, I was thinking, we could pick it up right where we left off, same cliff, me catching a vine or landing in some water or something. Mind you, it would have to take place today, fifteen years later, so we'll need to update my wardrobe."

"Long fall," he said. "Fifteen years."

"Well, maybe not mid-fall then. But a gritty reboot, nonetheless. Those are all the rage now, as I understand it. The main thing is, I'm here, Edgar."

Susan was watching all of this unfold with a concerned look.

"Miranda," said Edgar. "I think there's been a misunderstanding. It's been fifteen years, yes. But I didn't mean it was time for us to get back together. What I meant was, it's been fifteen years; it's time for us to finally get a divorce."

And with that, Miranda Abbott's world fell apart.

CHAPTER FOUR

Parrot P.I.!

This wasn't the first time Miranda's world had imploded. When NBC yanked *Pastor Fran Investigates*, unceremoniously and without warning, leaving her—quite literally—hanging in mid-air, Miranda had felt numb, overwhelmed. Crushed.

She had imagined people whispering maliciously when she entered Dan Tana's, clerks snickering behind her back when she shopped on Rodeo Drive, attempting, in vain, to staunch the pain through some high-end retail therapy. And when she was clearing out her dressing room for the last time, all those years ago, she'd overheard a pair of stagehands gloating about her misfortunes.

"Talk about a swan dive!"

It still stung.

And then the real dagger. "Loved that final tumble, though. Eyes all buggy, arms pinwheeling. The stuntman had trouble matching it, is what I heard. And you know it's bad when you're overacting more than a falling stuntman."

Falling stuntmen tended to vaudeville it all the way down, something that drove directors to no end of distraction.

Being canceled had left Miranda reeling. But not Edgar. For Edgar, it had been a blessing of sorts. He saw it as a chance to catch their breath, re-evaluate their priorities.

"Let's take that honeymoon we always talked about," he'd said.

Their lives had been so hectic for so long that getting pulled off the air had afforded them that rarest of opportunities for a Hollywood couple: time together. Just the two of them.

Edgar Abbott had been a scriptwriter on *Parrot P.I.!,* a series about a cigar-chomping private eye and his parrot Buster Jones who was always helping him "crack the case" by squawking out key phrases at key moments.

Hard to imagine now, but this had been an actual fad for a while. Humans with animal sidekicks. *B.J. and the Bear* had featured a truck driver with a chimp (named, inexplicably, "the Bear"), which in turn had been inspired by the orangutan Clyde in the *Every Which Way But Loose* films. The back lots were rife with such critters. There had been jocular talking dogs and magical talking cats and, of course, the granddaddy of them all, Francis the Talking Mule. And then there was *Parrot P.I.!*, featuring the only animal who could legitimately talk. (True, Baretta had a pet cockatoo, but it didn't help him solve crimes.) Unfortunately, Buster Jones had been a miserable creature who pecked and harried its human co-star on *Parrot P.I.!* constantly. More than one episode featured the mustachioed investigator sporting bandages on his fingers and a terrified look in his eyes. Parrot PTSD, as it were.

Edgar Abbott had been hired out of the theater scene in New York, plucked from a successful Off-Broadway run and called to lotusland to head the writing team on *Parrot P.I.!* A temporary gig, he was sure. A California lark to pay off some bills and get back to where his art was. He had assumed that *Parrot P.I.!* would tank, and he would take his "walking away money" and return to the world of the stage, flush with cash.

But California has a way of lulling even the most resistant souls into submission, and when the show became a hit, Edgar Abbott found himself practically chained to a desk in the writing room.

He first met Miranda at a table read for an episode called "Where Angels Fear to Tread," on Season Five of *Parrot P.I.!*, the exclamation point being part of the registered trademark. This particular episode had featured a secondary character named Fran, a youth pastor who was caught up in trying to rescue a teenager from the grips of a marijuana gang, and Miranda had been cast in the part.

She was funny and vivacious and thoroughly engaging, and Edgar fell for her, hard. He'd always had a weakness for redheads, but more than that, she was fearless. If she had to run across train tracks and rescue a girl from the nefarious clutches of unwashed villains, Miranda Baker was up for it. Which was how she was credited at the start of that episode, "Introducing Miranda Baker," in what was supposed to be a one-off appearance. But the plucky young female pastor had proven immensely popular, and Miranda was brought back again. And again. And by her third appearance, she was Miranda Abbott.

They'd had to postpone their honeymoon when word came down of a spin-off. Miranda would be given her own series! And Edgar would come with her. *Pastor Fran Investigates* was born, and they never did find time for a honeymoon.

When *Pastor Fran* ended, Edgar had suggested a marital getaway to the Pacific Coast of Oregon. He'd chosen the place almost solely for its name: Happy Rock. The notion that something as inanimate as a rock could still have emotions appealed to his sense of the whimsical. Plus, they had a luxury hotel, "right on the water."

Miranda was from Minnesota originally. The thought of forests and lakes didn't attract her, but Edgar had insisted.

"That's why I *left* Minnesota," she said. "To get away from that. Lakes? I prefer a nice spa and a glass of Dom Pérignon."

"Not a *lake*, a bay. On the ocean. A harbor with sailboats. Majestic scenery. Quaint shoppes–with two p's and an e, no less–and the chance to enjoy a world-class dining experience at the historic Duchess Hotel."

"You're just quoting from the brochures now," she'd said with a laugh.

So they had gone, and the salmon had indeed been world class, the lovemaking even better. It was while they were walking up Beacon Hill for a view of the harbor that Edgar had spotted the bookstore. He always was a sucker for a good bookstore. It was dusty and musty inside, and the owner was about to retire and was looking to sell.

"We could do this," Edgar had whispered to Miranda as they walked through it. "We could move here, open a bookstore. Or a theater."

She thought he was joking, but he wasn't.

"This," he said, waving his arms to the bookstore and the lane and the harbor below. "*This* is life. Hollywood is some weird, warped version of it."

Their holiday came to a close, and Edgar didn't want to leave.

"But what about New York?" she'd pleaded. "What about LA? They are waiting for my return, I am sure! We have to set up meetings, get back in the game."

"But don't you see? That's just it. It is a game. That's all it is. This? This is real. I never realized how *tired* I am, Miranda, till I came to Happy Rock. Can you give me just two weeks? That's all. Let's rent a room in town, get to know the place. See if we want to stay."

She left the next day.

She left while he was sleeping, tangled in cotton sheets in the drowsy light of their room at the Duchess. She placed a note on the dresser and let herself out.

I'm sorry, but I have to go back. I'll never forgive myself if I don't at least try. Enjoy your rest. You've earned it. I will send for you.

But she never did.

And now another note had brought her back, a postcard from the past, and a misunderstanding on her part. Not a husband-and-wife reunion. A divorce.

They were above the bookstore now, in Edgar's modest but comfortable quarters. It was the second floor, but felt like the attic, with low ceilings, a small dining nook, and a table to one side with a computer and printer and a stack of paper beside it.

"Third floor's mainly storage," he said, almost apologetically. "Rooms full of boxes. Boxes full of books. I stay here on the second. Easier to get down to the store. Not fancy, I know. But it suits me."

We had a house in the Hollywood Hills, she thought.

Or rather, *Miranda* had had a house in the Hollywood Hills. She'd purchased it, down payment in cash, when *Pastor Fran Investigates* was picked up for a third season, had entertained the crème de la crème of the industry in it while Edgar hid in his room, stabbing away at his keyboard. The electric typewriter had given way to a word processor, she noted, but not much else had changed. He was still Edgar. For better or for worse.

Till postcard do us part.

"Tea?" he asked. "The kettle's still warm from this morning."

She joined him at his comically small kitchen table while he poured her a cup of chamomile. *Chamomile.* That was her. She had done that. He had been a coffee-drinking caffeine slinger before he met her. The smell of flowers in a cup. Herbal tea and a warm bath. Together. That had been their last night as a couple...

Today? Chipped china and mismatched saucers. And Edgar Abbott staring down at the table.

"You didn't need to come here," he said, and were there ever crueler words spoken? And crueler all the more for the tenderness in his voice. "We could have done this over the phone. We just needed to sign some papers, that's all. I could have mailed the forms to you."

"But I did come, Edgar. I'm here. And I want us to be together. It's been too long."

He agreed. It had been a long time. "Far too long to simply pick up where we left off, Miranda."

Another shiv in her heart.

She took a sip, the way one might test the waters before a leap. Lukewarm, but still chamomile.

"Come back with me, Edgar. Just for a while. Marty will–" And then she remembered that Marty had fired her. "*I* will set up some meetings. Personally. And if you decide to pass, I will return here with you. I promise. One last kick at the can, that's all I'm asking."

"We can't reboot *Pastor Fran*," he said. "That ship sailed a long time ago, Miranda."

Cans that were kicked and ships that had sailed.

"But it hasn't sailed," she said. "The ship has turned, Edgar. Don't you see? Nostalgia is in again. Wait long enough and everything comes back around. If they can give Archie comics a gritty reboot, they can sure as hell give Fran one, too. What is it they say? 'The older it is, the newer.'"

"No one says that."

"Well, maybe it was the other way around. But the time is ripe!

Not just for Pastor Fran, but for us. Maybe a romance?" she said, and it wasn't clear if she meant the two of them, or a possible TV show.

"A romance?"

"My gay assistant reads them. I'll have him send some up." She had slipped the gay part in rather artfully, she thought, so as to assure her husband that no hanky-panky was involved. She wasn't some cougar preying on young men.

But Edgar just smiled. "Romance? I only read murder, remember?"

"Will you think about it, Edgar? That's all I ask."

"I have. For fifteen years."

"Okay. If not Fran, how about *Parrot P.I.!*? It's had a resurgence lately. They've been showing it on YouTube. That's what Andrew, my gay assistant, tells me. It's considered 'ironic' among young people, he says. And I believe him, because he's young. And gay. Very gay. Parrots live, like, two hundred years. We could even get the original Buster Jones to reprise his role. As for the private eye who works with him, I was thinking..."

"I know what you were thinking. You. Right?"

She shrugged as though the notion had just struck her. "I suppose I could be talked into it."

"You don't want it, Miranda. Trust me. That parrot was one mean son of a bitch. And anyway, I burnt out writing that show. It was more work than you'd think trying to figure out scenarios week after week where the bad guys would explain their plans in front of the parrot enough times for the parrot to repeat it later on. I was glad to be moved to *Pastor Fran*. And even gladder when *Pastor Fran* ended."

Miranda was trying not to cry, was trying not to raise her voice. She didn't want Susan in the store below keeping tabs. She'd enjoy that, wouldn't she?

"I'm living off syndication checks, Edgar. I'll be up late, clicking my way through the channels, and come across an episode of *Pastor Fran* playing on some golden oldies 'where are they now?' show, and I will think, Yes! Another $2.49. Three more and I can just about afford a carafe of cheap plonk."

"Do you need money?"

And oh, how easily sadness turns to anger. A flash of rage. Green eyes and a red-headed temper.

"Certainly not! You think I came here to beg? Well, I did. But not for money. For my husband. I want us to be a team again. Like we were when we were young."

"But we're not young, Miranda. Not anymore. We've aged."

"Speak for yourself!"

"Do you have a place to stay while you're in town?"

"I had assumed I would be staying *with my husband*!"

"I can make up the couch. It folds out."

Would the cruelty never end?

"I did not come sixteen hours and thirty-seven minutes by bus, and then change onto another smaller bus, and then flag down a doughy policeman, to sleep on a fold-out couch!"

"I'll take the couch, then. You can have the bed."

"I am your wife, Edgar! And you are still my husband."

He swirled the tea in his cup as though trying to read the leaves. "I haven't been your husband for a very long time, Miranda."

"That's not true," she said, and her voice began to break.

"What did you think we had, exactly?"

"A marriage, interrupted. That's all. But I'm back, Edgar. We can start again. Start fresh."

"I'm only your husband in the legal sense."

"Have you been cheating on me? Is that what this is, Edgar? Is there some trollop you want to be with? You thought, Oh, better ditch the ol' ball and chain?"

"There was someone. Yes."

"A fling! I knew it!"

"A fling? You could say that. We were together for three and a half years."

"And where is she now?" Miranda looked around as though expecting to find some woman in her underwear hiding behind the lampshade.

"She left. Said I was holding on to the past. She's married now, living somewhere else. Not with me."

He was alone, then. Somehow that only made it worse.

"Fine!" she said (yelled). "I know when I'm not wanted!"

Miranda stormed out, down the stairs and through the bookstore, schlepping her bag and trying, but failing, to slam the door behind her. Past the peonies and judgmental geraniums. (She didn't know why, but she always felt geraniums were judgmental, just as peonies were shy, marigolds a bit pompous.) She was halfway down the street when a voice called out, "Wait!"

Not Edgar. Susan.

She caught up to Miranda, out of breath. "I'm so sorry, Mrs. Abbott. I care deeply about Edgar. I was rude and I shouldn't have been. Everyone deserves to be treated with respect and consideration. You have to understand, Mr. Abbott is hurting. He just won't admit it." And then, voice dropping, "He speaks about you all the time."

"He does?"

"You were the love of his life. That's why he couldn't let go. It's why it took him so long to send that postcard. At least, that's how I see it."

So the match wasn't over. Not yet.

"Thank you, Susan. I appreciate your kind words." And with that, Miranda Abbott spun, head high, and began the long march down the hill toward the harbor.

"Do you know where you're going?" Susan hollered.

"Indeed I do!" Miranda called back over her shoulder. I do indeed.

BEA MARACLE OF Bea's B&B was finishing up a pie when a sharp rap came at the front door of her cottage.

"Hold yer horses."

Wiping floury hands on her apron, she went to see who it was. She didn't have any bookings till the weekend, wasn't expecting any guests.

So Bea opened the door, and standing there, jazz hands in a ta-da! pose, was the last person she would ever have imagined showing up at her doorstep.

"Yes! It is I. And I understand that someone here is my biggest fan."

Bea's jaw dropped. Oh. My. God.

CHAPTER FIVE

The Golden Age of the Rotary Phone

Wednesday morning. One month and twelve days to the murder...

Miranda Abbott rolled over in the down comforter, feeling languid and lazy. She was on that edge of awareness between sleep and wakefulness when you don't want to open your eyes and ruin it by returning to the real world.

For a moment–just a moment–everything in Miranda Abbott's world was perfect. She was nestled deep in a suite in the Roosevelt Hotel on Hollywood Boulevard, with Edgar at her side. Room service (which Miranda used in lieu of wake-up calls or alarm clocks) would soon be tapping gently on her door to announce, with quiet dignity, that an array of succulent fruit, freshly squeezed orange juice, French press coffee, and oven-warmed scones had arrived on a silver tray.

Miranda sighed with contentment and–

A loud pounding on the door pulled her out of her reverie as an impossibly cheerful voice on the other side shouted.

"Morning! I've got oatmeal a'waiting!"

Groaning, Miranda peered with a bleary gaze at the ancient clock parked on a prehistoric nightstand. A brass clock. A faux-Bavarian nightstand. Not that either of them could actually be called antiques. They were just . . . old.

Happy Rock, she thought. I'm still in Happy Rock.

Not cuddled up in the Roosevelt with Edgar, but on the set of *Misery* with Bea What's-Her-Face outside her door hollering about oatmeal.

Miranda stretched, looked around her. The bedroom was chock-a-block with bric-a-brac and quilted throw cushions, a too-big-for-the-room dresser and threadbare Queen Anne chairs next to an ornate lamp. It was as though an overzealous set decorator, tasked with creating the boudoir of an elderly aunt, "quaint and snug," had gone hog wild.

The best room in the house . . .

It wasn't the first room that Bea had shown Miranda, taking her through the cottage.

"I can't believe it . . . Pastor Fran at *my* B&B . . ."

She'd shown Miranda the four rooms available, and Miranda had dismissed each out of hand. A shared washroom? Down the hall? No thank you. An attic? What am I, hiding from the KGB?

It was only when she passed the second-floor bedroom, noting the large, downy bed, the view of the harbor, and the en suite bath, that Miranda had said, "This one is adequate. I'll take it."

"That's, um, my room," said Bea.

"Very well, make it up for me. I will be back shortly."

With that, Miranda had left Bea to prep the room for her—with bath balms and fresh peonies, no doubt—as she strode off, along the harbor. She was on a mission.

Miranda had spotted the police station on her trudge down from the bookstore. It was a modest brick building with a HAPPY

Rock PD sign in blue, just past the town's unfortunately named grocer, TB Foods (*T.B.* for "Tillamook Bay," she hoped). The police station, like the food store, was located on the harbor. Of course it was located on the harbor. All of Happy Rock was located on the harbor, or so it seemed, Edgar's bookstore on Beacon Hill aside.

Miranda swept into the cop shop, dinging the bell and asking for the chief.

Start at the top, she figured.

Miranda could have had Bea send someone to the police station to fetch the valise for her, but the valise was merely a pretext. If Miranda was going to win back her husband, if she was going to convince Edgar to recant and see the error of his ways, she would need allies. It was no different than auditioning for a role: the more people involved in the production who were on your side, the better the chance the director would be swayed to cast you.

Miranda would need a team behind her if she wanted Edgar to cast her in the role of Repentant but Loving Wife, Returned. She needed a Team Miranda, as it were. Susan, certainly. Bea, absolutely. And Chief Ned, most definitely. He was easily charmed, easily beguiled.

But he was also absent.

A stupendously pregnant officer waded out to greet Miranda instead.

"Ned's on a call. The Opera House. A window in the back was open, so he's checking to see if there's been a break-in. A regular Hercule Poirot, our Ned. Should be back soon, though."

So said the officer in the stretchy maternity pants and unbuttoned uniform. This was Officer Holly, and when Miranda asked after the valise, the one the chief had inadvertently whisked away in the trunk of his patrol car, Holly called to the other officer on duty.

"Carl! Did Ned say anything about a valise?"

"What's a valise?" came the glum voice from the far desk.

"It's a suitcase, Einstein."

A sigh so loud Miranda could hear it from the front desk, and then Officer Carl appeared, looking gaunt and ill-humored, as though they were distracting him from some Very Serious Police Work. Perhaps a hot tip on the latest misplaced pocketbook, thought Miranda. He reminded her of the pitchfork farmer in the painting *American Gothic* as he wheeled Miranda's valise over.

"You'll need to sign for it," he said.

That was ridiculous. "But it's my valise."

He gave her a baleful look. "Have to be sure, ma'am."

"Of course. I could be some sort of valise thief, moving town to town, stopping at local police stations in case someone left a valise behind so I might snatch it up with a suitably diabolical laugh."

"Maybe," he said.

So she signed with a flurry and said, "Well?"

But instead of rolling her suitcase around to her, he studied her signature instead, as if for a possible forgery.

And then he said something that seemed particularly odd and ill-humored. "Casting call has already been posted, just so you know."

Casting call?

"*Death Is the Dickens.* They've already set the auditions. It'll be too late for you. Chief Ned mentioned you were some sort of actress. You are an actress, right? I mean, Ned didn't tell me your name and"—he looked again at her signature—"it's hard to tell what exactly you scribbled down."

If she wasn't seething before then!

Miranda didn't deign to respond, but stomped out, pulling her rattling valise behind her. Well, that was one name that was definitely NOT going on the Team Miranda roster!

She followed the harbor around, stopping to calm herself on one of the benches that faced the water. The benches sported the giant face of a real estate agent, which only irked Miranda more. At times like this, everything irked her. Ads on benches. Ads *with faces* on benches. Ads with faces on benches *for realtors.* Who thought that was a good idea?

Still seething, she dined on mussels and sipped Spanish coffee at a bistro on the harbor with an impressive view of the ivy-clad Duchess Hotel, wishing she were in a suite there instead. But Miranda knew she had to be frugal.

"Another Spanish coffee, and perhaps another round of mussels. You can send the bill to the cottage," she said with a vague wave in the general direction of the B&B.

"Oh, Bea's? Sure. I know Bea," said the owner of the bistro when the waiter brought him over. "She's good for it."

And now here she was, nestled in a comforter as Bea thumped on the door. She thought of the events of the last forty-eight hours as though it were a dream. Images of that green-haired goblin girl reading the coroner's report, the Chief of Police eyeing Miranda in the mirror, Edgar's bombshell, and that long walk of shame down the hill.

But today would be better! It could hardly be worse. Today would be better, because Miranda had a plan. She wouldn't be retreating, tail between her legs. She would be assembling Team Miranda!

She had a long soak in Bea's tub, scattering potpourri in the water. She ignored the entreaties from the hall about the oatmeal "gettin' cold" and then traipsed through her room, leaving her towels strewn behind her and wet footprints across the hardwood–it was good to have a housekeeper again–and flung open her valise to retrieve her silky green dressing gown (one must maintain certain standards, even in a lowly cottage). And that was when she noticed. Someone had been in her valise. She was sure of it.

But who? Bea, when she was asleep? Someone at the station? A rogue cop? She had encountered enough of those as Pastor Fran.

Snoopy bastards. What were they up to? Planting drugs? Searching for pornography or bondage paraphernalia? Snapping scandalous photos to peddle to TMZ?

Ha! There was nothing incriminating in her valise for them to find. She had left her bondage paraphernalia back in LA. (Really just a set of fur-lined handcuffs an admirer had given her with the note *Pastor Fran! Arrest me next!*)

Wrapping her robe around her, Miranda Abbott descended to the parlor below, where a nervous Bea was waiting, starstruck as ever.

"I shall breakfast on the veranda," Miranda informed her.

"The veranda?" said Bea, as Miranda swept past. "You mean . . . the front porch?"

"Yes," said Miranda, calling back. "Champagne and orange juice, and whatever fresh fruit is in season."

The veranda, or "front porch," as it was known in the local vernacular, was rickety, with splinter-ridden Adirondack chairs lined up. The paint on the porch was peeling, but not in a quaint or picturesque way, and the garden out front was overrun and tangled up, what might otherwise be known as "English" style. (The way gardeners who lost control of their hollyhocks and vines dubbed their arrangements "an English garden" and were done with it.) Must talk to the gardening staff, thought Miranda.

There had been no key to her bedroom, either, and the front door, she noted, was left unlocked. Anyone could sail through, at any time. Had Miranda had any stalkers, she would have been concerned. Instead, she had to worry about TMZ slipping in. She made a mental note: Must talk to the security detail.

Bea appeared with a glass of SunnyD and some melba toast and marmalade.

"Out of champagne, I'm afraid, and as for fruit, marmalade is always in season, right?"

"Has the lunch menu been prepared yet? If not, I will reserve whatever the catch of the day is." Miranda cast a glance around the dusty, peeled-paint porch. "Perhaps I will take lunch indoors, instead of al fresco."

Bea didn't know how to approach it. "Lunch? But this is a bed and *breakfast*."

Miranda gave her a sliver of a smile. "Well, then, let's just call it brunch, shall we? Split the difference. Trout, salmon. I'm really not picky. As long as it's poached, not pan-fried nor–god forbid–deep-fried. And no tarragon in the Béarnaise sauce, please." She lowered her voice as though confiding a deep secret. "Gives me indigestion, you see."

"I guess I could stop by the morning fish market before it closes for the day . . ."

"That's the spirit! Like I said, I'm not picky. Add it to the bill for my room. Can you bring me the house phone? My mobile phone doesn't seem to be working. Add the cost of the call to my bill."

"Oh no, I couldn't charge you, Pastor Fran–I mean, Miss Miranda. You're a personal guest, not a customer."

"But I insist. I will call my gay assistant"–just in case Bea spoke to Edgar later or, even worse, TMZ; wouldn't want rumors of a May-December romance swirling around her–"and he will arrange the proper remuneration. Now. About that house phone?"

Bea had an actual landline (speaking of antiques) in the sitting room (ditto).

"It's a rotary," Bea warned, as Miranda followed her through to the aforementioned sitting room.

"My dear," said Miranda, taking a seat on yet another threadbare Queen Anne chair, next to the clunky phone. "*Pastor Fran* was launched during the Golden Age of the Rotary Phone. In fact, I seem to recall one episode—"

"Yes! Season Two. Episode Seven. 'Death Takes a Dial.' You figured out the phone number of the killer by the sound each number made as it was being dialed. Longer clickety-clicks for seven, shorter for two, and so on. You were hiding in a confessional, listening in. Good thing there was a phone in that church, and so close to the confessionals!"

"Well, there you go. I am a master of the rotary phone."

Bea watched in dismay as Miranda dialed . . . and dialed . . . and dialed.

"That's, um, a really long number," said Bea. "Long distance, is it?"

"Hollywood, darling," she said, then cupped her hand over the receiver. "A private call."

"Oh, right. Of course." Bea retreated, but not entirely. She hung back, just around the corner, in case she was needed.

Miranda had texted Andrew the day before to let him know she had arrived, though really it had just been a litany of complaints about the ride up. "Honestly, the coach you booked for me was smaller and less comfortable than the motor home we used on location during *Pastor Fran*. And don't get me started about the local bus to Happy Rock!"

Andrew had no desire to. Instead, he texted back: "The mysterious writer of postcards? Have you managed to track him down?"

In a flurry, Miranda had attempted to reply using emojis for full emotional impact, but that only confused Andrew more.

"Big Hat Monkey Toast? What does that even mean?"

But before Miranda could elaborate, her phone had gone dead. That was yesterday. She was now sitting in the aptly named room, receiver to her ear, as the line rang and rang and rang.

When Andrew finally answered, his voice was uncertain. "Hello?"

"It is I!"

He hadn't recognized the number.

"My mobile phone has ceased to function," she explained.

"Yeah, they tend to do that when you don't pay your bill."

"Well, as my assistant–"

"Former assistant."

"Former? Pfft, nonsense. I will leave it for you to sort out the phone, Andrew."

There was a long pause. "I'll see what I can do. Maybe if I make a partial payment, you'll still be able to use it, for emergencies. But don't run up the minutes!"

When Andrew asked again about the postcard, she cried, "It was the ol' bait and switch! My husband doesn't want me back, he wants a divorce."

And she burst into tears. Not theatrical tears, real ones. She sniffled and wiped them away, tried to calm the quaver in her voice.

Andrew (thinking): Huh. I didn't know she had a husband. Andrew (speaking): "Are you sure? How do you know he really wants a divorce? What did he actually say? Sometimes you jump to conclusions." (Andrew said "sometimes," but he meant "always.")

"I read between the lines!" she said. "It's all in the subtext. Any actor worth their salt knows that."

"But what did he say *exactly*?"

"He said, 'I don't want you back. I want a divorce.'"

"That would do it."

"It's been an absolute ordeal, Andrew. It truly has. I was taken in a police car to my husband's bookstore. A police car! They are out of champagne, the mussels were mediocre at best, and I fear that someone went through my valise when I wasn't looking."

"Come now. Why would you think that?"

"Because," she said, "my items were more neatly folded than they had been before."

Only Miranda could have a break-in where the robbers left the place tidier than they found it, Andrew thought.

Rather than try to fix things, because they seemed unfixable and he wasn't sure what help he was able–or could afford–to offer, he suggested she try to reconcile with her husband.

"When Brett and I had a fight, and he moved out–"

"Your boyfriend?"

"My fiancé. When he left, I thought it was over for good. But I fought to win him back. I didn't give in, and I didn't give up. This isn't the time for pride, Miranda. This is a time for humility."

"But how?"

"That, I couldn't tell you."

Miranda could hear muffled voices in the background on Andrew's end.

"Where are you?" she asked.

"A golf course in Burbank."

"Oh! How wonderful! Scouting locations? Networking on my behalf?"

"Folding towels."

"Why on earth would you be doing that? Ah! Is it for a mystery set on a golf course? Perhaps you're researching a role for me," she said–hopefully. Hope and desperation being two sides of the same coin.

"No, the only mystery is how this is considered a sport. What is it they say about golf? A good walk spoiled. I'm employed here, Miranda. This is my job."

"But as my assistant–"

"Former assistant."

"–I have an important question to ask you, Andrew."

"Yes?"

"Will I be all right? Will everything be okay?"

It was the one question he couldn't answer.

"I'll see what I can do about your phone. I have to go." And now he was holding back tears, as well. "Goodbye, Miranda."

CHAPTER SIX

Pastor Fran Rides Again!

An actor dies. The audience reacts.

After she hung up the phone, Miranda tried her best to stem the tears, using the sleeve of her dressing gown. But satin is not particularly absorbent, and the tears continued to spill.

Bea had been listening in, not because she's a snoop, certainly not! She was just awfully concerned about this lengthy and emotional and possibly very expensive long-distance call. At least, that was what she told herself as she crept back around the corner with a tissue box in hand.

"I always knew," Bea tutted. "Even if he refused to admit it."

Bea Maracle, in her middle years, with gray hair in a bob cut, sturdy hips and sunny eyes, looked very much like one of the secondary characters in *Pastor Fran Investigates*. The wise widow, say, who gives Pastor Fran crucial but evasive advice at key moments in the show. *I'd keep an eye on the ol' fishin' hole if I were you...* That sort of thing. They were always so coy. No one ever came right out and said, *Just so you know, the local smugglers are stashing their moonshine under the dock at the local fishing hole.* No, there was always a sidelong glance and enigmatic clues. It had bugged Miranda at the time, and she'd complained to Edgar about it, but as he explained to her, if it weren't for those sidelong glances and enigmatic clues stretching things out, each episode would have been over in about eight minutes.

As for Bea, who knows? Having immersed herself in the show for so long, perhaps she had adopted some of the mannerisms.

"You always knew what?"

"I always knew that Edgar was your husband. When you showed up on my door, I figured Edgar must've had something to do with this. You being here. Whenever I try to speak to him about Pastor Fran, he clams right up. Won't even stock the novelizations in his bookstore. It's like he wanted to put it all behind him, like he wouldn't even admit you were real."

Why would he do that? thought Miranda. Susan at the bookstore had said the exact opposite: *He talks about you all the time.* Yet Bea told a different story. She claimed Edgar refused to speak about her, practically denied Miranda's existence. Why would Edgar give two completely contrary impressions to two different people?

Bea sat down beside Miranda, folded her hands on her lap. When she spoke, her voice was soft. "In moments like this, I always ask myself, What would Pastor Fran do?"

"Karate kick him in the chest?"

"I was thinking more on the investigative side, dear. She would *investigate* him. Find out the truth."

"I know the truth. He doesn't want me anymore."

"Maybe he just *thinks* and *feels* and *says* that. That doesn't mean it's really the case. Maybe he doesn't *know* what he really feels. Or thinks. Or says."

"You're right," said Miranda, feeling the vim return. "Maybe he just *thinks* he knows what he *says* he's feeling."

"That's right," said Bea. "You go get changed. I've got a call to make."

"To whom?"

Bea blinked. "Why, the police."

If Miranda thought that Bea was going to have Edgar arrested on emotional cruelty charges, she was sadly mistaken.

When she swept back downstairs in a silky green dress, which clung to her only slightly less than the silky green dressing gown had–Miranda was never one to hide her curves–she was met, not by a tactical squad, but by the Chief of Police, Ned Buckley.

"Well, hello there!" he said. "I brought popcorn and a dead fish."

He held up a blood-stained paper-wrapped package in one hand and a plastic tub marked *Candy Shoppe* in the other.

"I'll try not to get the two mixed up," said Miranda.

"Oh. Well, the popcorn is in the candy container," he said, missing the joke.

Bea appeared, out of her apron now, in a flowered skirt and–was that? yes–a smidge of lipstick. "Thank you, Ned. I'll take that. Salmon," she said with a smile to Miranda. "Coho. Fresh from the market. What do I owe you, Ned?"

"Just some peach cobbler."

Bea's peach cobbler was famous. At least, to hear Ned tell it.

Miranda was scooted into the living room, where Ned popped the lid on the caramel-coated treats and settled back in the sofa. Bea, having placed the salmon aside in the kitchen pantry, joined them, sliding open the cabinet beside the TV to reveal a wall of VHS tapes.

On Miranda's confused expression, Ned explained, "Pastor Fran Friday."

"But it's Wednesday," Miranda protested.

"No never mind," Bea said, selecting one of the tapes to push into the machine. "Pastor Fran Friday can be any day of the week. Even Wednesday. Could hardly miss the opportunity, now that the real Pastor Fran is in attendance!"

"Amen to that," said Ned. Then, to Miranda, "Popcorn? It's caramel. No? Okay. More for me then!" And he laughed. Oh how he laughed.

I'm trapped, thought Miranda. This isn't a B&B. This is a hostage taking.

Bea settled in beside them, VCR remote in hand. Dimmed the lights. Pressed play. The opening credits began with those iconic lines ringing out: *Our Lady, who arts on the mean streets of Crime City! Hallowed be her fists.*

"I thought I would choose an apt episode for today. Very apt." She turned to Miranda. "Season Six. Episode Nine."

This meant nothing to Miranda, so Bea elaborated.

"The episode titled 'Sin City.'"

Still nothing.

"Pastor Fran goes undercover in Las Vegas?" said Bea.

"Ah yes. I remember that one. They wanted to dress me up as a chorus girl."

"That's exactly right! My, weren't you plucky, though," said Bea. "You were trying to infiltrate a marijuana gang."

"I was always trying to infiltrate a marijuana gang."

"You were tracking a killer."

"I was always tracking a killer."

"Well, in this one, the killer joined a theater company in order to murder the leading man, a rival in love. You can see what I'm getting at?"

Of course she couldn't.

Ned cut in. "One thing I could never figure out. Why you wore a priest's collar, even when you were undercover. And do pastors even wear a collar? I mean, you took it off at the beauty pageants and when you were in a swimsuit, but before that, even when you were working as a lumberjack. Always with the collar."

Miranda had hoped that Bea might shush him, but Bea had questions of her own.

"In Season Five, Episode Twenty-One, 'Death on Trial,' you were sworn in under the name Frances Marie Lamb. But in Season One, Episode Eight, 'Death in the Fast Lane,' they show your driver's license briefly when you're renting a hot rod and, when I paused the image on my VCR, the name on your ID–it's blurry, but you can make it out–reads 'Francine Lamb.' Why is that?"

"I am sure I have no idea," said Miranda. "Those wouldn't have even been my hands in the close-ups anyway."

Bea shook her head in amazement. Not her hands! Who would have thought?

"And is 'wandering pastor' really a thing?" asked Ned. "Going from town to town, church to church, giving sermons, preserving the faith. Does that really happen? Every episode seems to end with you hitchhiking down the road to a new town. And I still don't know how they never arrested you. I mean, every time you arrive someplace, someone gets murdered right away. Seems suspicious, no? I say that as a law enforcement official, you understand. Not as a fan. I mean, god knows, I would never accuse Pastor Fran of being a serial killer, but others might."

But all she was thinking as she watched herself high-kick yet another gun out of yet another mobster's meaty fist–in stiletto heels, no less–was how young she was back then. Young and lithe and so full of life.

The years erode us, she thought. The years erode us and the credits roll.

The closing theme song was playing now, the harmonica low and mournful. *Maybe down this next road, I'll find a place to call my own. Maybe this time, I'll rest and find a home. Maybe this time, the Lord won't let me roam. Maybe this time...*

A long silence, and Bea said, "Well, I think you can see my point?"

Ned was silent, the caramel popcorn had hardly been touched, and Miranda felt wistful and alone. Point? What point? That we age? That youth fades and the plucky young woman of yesteryear becomes the spurned wife of today?

"And what would that point be?" she asked, in a tone laced with warning.

Bea looked to Ned, and he took out a folded paper from his uniform pocket, opened it up, and laid it on the coffee table, flattening out the creases with his hand.

It was a playbill from the Happy Rock Amalgamated & Consolidated Little Theater Society.

"*Death Is the Dickens*," said Ned, somberly.

Bea nodded, just as somberly. "The lead role is up for grabs this year."

"And?"

"Well, think of Pastor Fran. The man she was tracking joined a Las Vegas theater troupe just to be near his lost love."

"And to kill his rival, remember?" said Miranda. "With a sandbag. From the rafters."

"Yes, but let's not focus on that part. Let's focus on this." She tapped a finger on the name of the theater company. "Our company was formed ten years ago when the Happy Rock Little Theater, the Tillamook Bay Dramatic Society, and the Peninsula Players amalgamated and then consolidated."

"Before that, it was dark days in the little theater community," said Ned.

"We were splintered," said Bea. "Divided, competing for casts and venues."

"I was with the Tillamook Bay Dramatic Society," said Ned.

"And I, the Peninsula Players." It was as though Bea were discussing a feud between Highland clans. "Our casts and budgets were so small we could never mount a proper production. We staged Chekhov's *Two Sisters*. And *Eight Angry Men*. And for the kids' matinee, *Snow White and the Four Dwarves*."

"And it was no better for us," said Ned.

They hung their heads in sad recognition of those divisive times.

"But one man brought us together," said Bea. "He saw where the infighting and the divisions had taken us, and he united us, creating one single, overriding little theater. That man's name was Edgar Abbott."

This set Miranda back.

His words returned to her, across the years, what he'd said on their honeymoon after they'd stumbled upon the place on Beacon Hill: *We could move here, open a bookstore. Or a theater.* Not or. Both. He'd managed to do both.

"Edgar is always heavily involved with the production," said Bea. "If someone were to be cast in the play, as the lead, say, that someone would spend a lot of time with Mr. Abbott. *An awful lot of time*." She hit that last line with extra force.

Team Miranda to the rescue!

Except–

"But that dour cop, the one at the station. He said auditions were already closed." Not that Miranda would need to audition. A star sweeps in? She would be cast by acclamation. But still.

"Officer Carl? Well, technically, yes. Carl was correct. You would need to speak with the theater's secretary first."

Bea and Ned exchanged glances.

"It's tricky," said Bea. "But it can be done. Miss Lladdwraig is a stickler, you see. A kind heart, but a real stickler."

"Welsh," said Ned, as though that explained everything. "She handles all the memberships, all the scheduling, prompts the actors during the play, collects the fees, writes up the receipts. You would need to be on her good side."

Miranda flipped the playbill over and held out her hand. A pen materialized and she jotted this down. "And how do you spell her name?"

"Pretty much like how it sounds," said Bea.

The more people involved in the production who are on your side, the better the chance the director will be swayed to cast you. Miranda would need to make sure Edgar didn't block her.

"Who else matters? So to speak," Miranda asked.

"Well, I help strike the sets and put them up," said Ned. "And Bea volunteers with the tickets and seating. As for the others . . ."

Bea leaned in and began ticking off the elite of the Happy Rock community theater scene. "Judy Traynor, she's the director. She's very good. The shows always start on time. Very punctual."

"And mean as a snake in a sack that's been shook," said Ned.

"She's not mean," said Bea. "Not exactly. She's . . . *professional.* Our productions always look so professional, everyone says that. 'It's so professional. Very professional.'"

"She's mean," said Ned. "Husband left her. No wonder."

"Ned! He died in a car accident."

"Yeah, well, I always figured, he saw that hairpin turn, thought about what was waiting for him at home, and cranked that wheel."

Bea ignored him. "Graham Penty is the murderer."

What?

"In the play. Every year, Graham is cast as Lord Buckingham, the male lead. The prosperous business owner who is also the murderer. I hope I didn't ruin it for you. Graham himself is a drama teacher by trade." Her voice dropped. "Went to Yale."

"I've always wondered why a graduate of the Yale drama school ended up teaching high school in Happy Rock," said Ned.

"Well, his wife is from here."

"Yeah, but didn't he go to the same classes as Sigourney Weaver? Or maybe it was Jodie Foster. Which one fought the aliens?"

"They both did, I think."

"Well, *I* didn't go to Yale," said Miranda, feeling prickly at the mention of actresses who were, after all, only slightly more successful than she was. "I am a student of life. Just as life is a student of me. Carry on, please."

Who else?

"Doc Meadows. He plays the role of the avuncular doctor. That's what it says in the play's notes: avuncular doctor."

"Wait," said Miranda. "His name is Doc? They cast someone named Doc to play the doctor?"

"His real name is Murray, but everyone calls him Doc."

"And what does this... Murray... do when he's not treading the boards?" Miranda had a feeling she already knew.

"He's the town doctor."

Of course.

"I'm surprised he signed up this year," said Ned. "I hear he's having marriage problems."

"Teena Culliford, she's a sweetheart. A young thing. Helps out on crew. A star volunteer. She was one of Graham Penty's most promising students. He was always very fond of her."

"Yeah, no kidding," said Ned under his breath.

"She starred in every production through high school," Bea explained.

"Oh, and don't forget Burt," said Ned, perking up.

"Burton Linder," said Bea. "He builds the sets and does the lights."

"And he's a spy!"

"Allegedly," said Bea.

Ned gave Miranda a knowing look. "Retired–*allegedly*."

She was confused. "Allegedly retired?"

"Allegedly a spy."

Miranda looked down at her cheat sheet.

Judy Traynor - *director - mean - husband died*
Graham Penty - *leading man - drama teacher - Yale*
Murray "Doc" Meadows - *Doc the doctor - marriage problems?*
Teena Culliford - *general helper - Graham's former protégé*
Burt Linder - *stage, props, lights - not important*

"There's plenty more," said Bea. "But that's a start."

Miranda smiled. The route back to Edgar had opened up again. "They sound like an absolutely lovely group of people. I can't wait to meet them."

This took Bea's breath away. "So does that mean . . . does that really mean . . . ?"

"Yes! I'll do it."

Pastor Fran, performing in Happy Rock!

"Heck," said Ned, pulling on his police cap. "Let me run you over right now. We can see Miss Lladdwraig in person. She's in most afternoons."

"Give me five minutes," said Miranda, "to put on my face." She made it sound as though she were preparing to don a mask, and perhaps she was. "Five minutes and no longer, I assure you."

Ned and Bea exchanged worried looks, but relented.

Forty minutes later, and following several fretful knocks on the bedroom door, Miranda Abbott was being whisked away in Ned's patrol car, around the harbor and past the Duchess to the Opera House, home of the Happy Rock Little Theater. (It was all Ned could do not to put on the siren and clear traffic, should any appear.) He walked Miranda up the side of the building, pounded on the stage door, then stood back, grinning.

Miranda straightened herself, adjusted her scarf, and–when the door opened–was greeted by a familiar smile.

"Mrs. Abbott!"

"Susan?"

CHAPTER SEVEN

Burt the (alleged) Spy

Susan held the heavy door open for Ned and Miranda.

"I was expecting you!"

"Bea called?" said Ned.

"She called everyone, I'm sure." And, with a warm smile to Miranda, said, "She's your biggest fan."

"Yes, I think she may have mentioned that," said Miranda with a wry smile of her own.

They followed Susan down a narrow hallway.

"Why the side door?" asked Susan, leading them to the room that was the Happy Rock Amalgamated Whatsit office.

"We didn't want to come through the lobby," Ned explained, "for fear of creating a hubbub." Ned lived in dread of hubbubs. Hullabaloos, as well.

The office was small but tidy, much like Susan. She took a seat at her desk and waved for them to please sit down, too. A small cashbox was arranged just so, with a mauve receipt book beside it.

"Don't you worry," said Ned. "Susan will sort you out. You still have"–he checked his watch–"twenty-seven, no, twenty-*six* minutes."

"Until cutoff?"

"Until auditions."

"Wait. What? The auditions are today?"

"That is correct," said Susan. "The schedule is set, but we can fit you in. *If* proper procedures are followed."

Miranda could hear the murmur of voices and footsteps passing outside the office. She'd assumed there was a town meeting or a matinee of some sort. But no. *Death Is the Dickens* was being cast right here, right now. No time to prep. No time to set Team Miranda in motion.

"It was on the playbill," Ned whispered, referring to the paper he'd given her earlier, the one she'd written down the list of key players on. "At the very bottom. Auditions. Today, at one. It's almost one now. Good timing on that, right?"

Miranda was never one to read the fine print. That's what Marty was for.

So. No time to perform vocal warm-ups or deep breathing exercises or yoga stances.

"Will, ah, Mr. Abbott be in attendance?"

"Not this year, no," said Susan. "I called the bookstore just before you arrived to ask him that very question. He has decided it's best if he doesn't come down for it. He did say one thing, though, which struck me as strange. He said to tell you—what was it he said?—he hopes you 'sprain your thumb.' Though I'm not sure what that means."

Miranda held back a smile. She knew exactly what that meant. It was an inside joke between the two of them, something Edgar always said to her before shooting began, a gentler spin on "Break a leg!" which was the usual actor's wish in lieu of the jinxed "Good luck!" *Break a leg*. After Miranda had almost done just that, falling off a speeding horse as Pastor Fran, he'd amended it first to "Twist an ankle" then to "Bruise a knee" and finally "Sprain a thumb."

Ned looked at his watch. "Twenty-*one* minutes."

"Oh right," said Miranda. She turned to Susan. "Where do I sign up?"

"First, there's the issue of your membership." She slid a clipboard across to Miranda for her to fill in. "You can list Bea's as your address. I already called and checked with her, and she said that's fine."

Miranda could hear the murmurs growing outside the door as more and more people filed past. The clock was ticking. "Can't I fill this in later?"

"I'm afraid auditions are only open to *paid* members of the Happy Rock Amalgamated & Consolidated Little Theater Society." She emphasized the word *paid.*

"And, ah, how much is the fee?" Miranda was thinking of the exorbitant rates that the Screen Actors Guild charged.

"This year's annual membership is set at $43.87."

But Miranda wasn't sure she had that to spare, either. She made a show of digging in her bag. Maybe she could postpone the payment until after her audition...

"That seems an oddly specific amount."

"Well," said Susan, "when the theaters in town amalgamated–"

"And consolidated," said Ned.

"The annual dues were set at $35 a year, to be adjusted annually for inflation and the rising in the cost of utilities, of course."

"Of course."

"And that's what I have done, year in and year out, using the federal year-end rates, of course."

"Of course."

"Fortunately, you don't need to worry about the fee."

"Waived?" said Miranda.

"Paid," said Susan. "By a third party." She laid a regretful hand on her mauve receipt book. "Unfortunately, I can't issue you a receipt, as that would compromise client privacy. I've been the Administrative Treasurer and General Secretary for the past ten years, and do you know the most important thing I've learned in that time?"

Miranda had no idea. "I have no idea."

"Not to fill out a receipt book ahead of time. You wouldn't believe it, but every year we get at least one no-show, and it can really throw the record keeping off. But rest assured, your annual membership fee *has* been paid in full. You wouldn't be allowed to audition otherwise. It wouldn't be fair to the rest of the cast."

It was Edgar, thought Miranda. That's who paid for her. It had to be! A gesture of reconciliation? Love, even?

Susan handed over Miranda's membership card, written in precise cursive. Susan had clearly mastered the Palmer Method. Even better, Miranda's name was spelled correctly.

"Eighteen minutes," said Ned.

Susan pulled out a large leather-bound book labeled *Rules & Regulations.*

"There is one last thing..."

She began looking through it, page by page.

A knock on the door and an older, gray-haired gentleman in loose jeans and plaid flannel came in. He was compact and wiry, with a bristled brush cut and a work belt heavy with tools.

"Fixed the window latch, like you asked," he said. Then, with a nod to Chief Buckley, "Ned."

"Hey, Burt!"

Ah, thought Miranda. Burton Linder, aka "Burt." Celebrated Spy of Happy Rock. Lights, sets, and skullduggery, apparently.

He did look ex-military, Miranda thought. In his bearing and posture, and his clipped manner of speaking. Ned was giddy. Miranda could recognize a man crush when she saw one. Any sense of urgency the chief had shown about the auditions vanished with Burt's appearance.

"So, Burt, have you been up to anything?" Ned asked–then dropped his voice. "That you can talk about."

"Nope. Just that window latch. Ever figure out who broke it, Ned?"

He hadn't. The Case of the Broken Window Latch remained unsolved.

"I guess some things will always be a mystery," said Burt. Then, with a half grin to Susan, he asked, "Atticus sign up this year?"

This was meant as a mildly mean-spirited joke and was received as such by Susan.

"Of course he didn't. You know he didn't."

Ned leaned to Miranda. "Atticus Lawson. Terrified of public speaking. Absolutely petrified. He had to give a speech at LOJIC once, passed out. Fainted dead away."

"Logic?" said Miranda.

"Loyal Order of Joyous, Igneous & Cretaceous Bricklayers. It's a service club. They have meetings once a month in the theater."

Susan Lladdwraig had finally found the page in the regulations that she was looking for.

"Hmm," she said. She was frowning.

That can't be good, thought Miranda as the minutes continued to tick away. How on earth could she possibly prepare? She couldn't rush the stage. Or could she?

Burt still hadn't acknowledged her presence. Starstruck, no doubt. Instead, he chuckled and said to Ned, "I hear Carl is trying out again this year."

"No! How much rejection can one man take?"

Carl? thought Miranda. Wasn't that the creepy cop who made her sign for her valise?

"Going to audition for the part of Reginald Buckingham," said Burt.

"The lead? Carl?" Ned turned to Miranda. "He's a good officer, but as an actor? Usually Carl trics out for the part of the butler. Never gets cast." And then to Burt. "And now he wants the lead? What's he thinking? That part always goes to Graham Penty."

"The high school drama teacher?" said Miranda.

"Every year, like clockwork. Really just a formality, having Graham audition for it. As for Carl, well, I guess he figures he's ready to not be cast in a *speaking* role this time."

Burt nodded. "Yep. Carl is an odd duck, all right." There was a pause, thick with meaning. "Fifty years old and still living with his mother. A very odd duck, indeed."

Miranda looked at the clock on the wall behind Susan. They were now ten minutes away and counting...

I know everyone moves a little slower out here, but really, thought Miranda, this is ridiculous.

"Here we go," said Susan, reading from the pertinent passage in the theater's regulations and rules. "'New members must be voted in by a majority, making up a quorum of no less than two-thirds of said membership.'"

"Oh, there's no time for that," said Ned. "Can you waive it?"

"As Administrative Treasurer and General Secretary of the Happy Rock Amalgamated & Consolidated Little Theater Society, I *can* waive this requirement–"

"Good!" said Ned. "Glad we cleared that up for Pastor Fran–I should say, Miss Abbott."

"–with board approval."

They were back to square one, with nine minutes to go.

"But," said Susan, reading a sub-clause to the sub-clause, "'a new member *can* be admitted on payment of fees *if* they are vouched for *in person* by a fully paid member of the board.'"

Good grief, thought Miranda. This is more complicated than getting into Actors' Equity.

"No problem. I'll vouch for her," said Ned. Then, to Miranda, "We should probably go in. If you're late, you may not get to audition. Director's discretion at that point."

The murmurs outside the office had gone ominously quiet. Everyone must already be in their seats.

Susan shook her head sadly. "I'm sorry, Ned. But you're not on the board. You're on the steering committee."

"There's a difference? Well, what about you, Susan? You could vouch for her."

"Unfortunately, no. That would put me in a conflict of interest."

How? thought Miranda, trying not scream. How is that a conflict? How?

She should have paid attention–to everything. The fees, the casting, the complicated nature of the process, even the number of chairs that were placed onstage. It. All. Mattered. But that's the problem with clues; they only look like clues in hindsight.

Seven minutes.

And then, an unexpected savior. "I'll do it," said Burt. "I'll vouch for her."

"Didn't know you were on the theater board," said Ned.

"Lifetime member," said Burt.

"Done!" Susan stood and turned to Ned. "Why don't you bring Mrs. Abbott through to the auditorium. I'll make sure Rodney puts out an extra chair." And then, looking into Miranda's eyes with heartbreaking sincerity, she said, "You will do fine. I know you will."

It was the kindness that threw her. Miranda Abbott was not used to this. Awe, perhaps. Envy, undoubtedly. But kindness?

"You're going out of your way to help me," said Miranda. "Why?"

"Because," said Susan, "I know how much you mean to Edgar. And I know how much Edgar means to this community."

"But Bea said he doesn't even acknowledge my existence."

This surprised Susan. Her lips pursed. "Now, why would Bea say that? I know Edgar. He speaks of you all the time. That's very strange that Bea would say such a thing."

Ned had his arm on Miranda's elbow. "We gotta go."

He led her out the door. And as they left, Burt called out, "Good luck!"

Jinxed! Damn you, Burt, you old coot! Or was he a codger? Both, she decided, as Ned hurried her across the lobby. A cooty old codger. A codgery old coot. Jinxing me like that!

They made it in with only moments to spare. The volunteer usher, a big lumpy kid in a too-tight turtleneck, was closing the doors, and Ned and Miranda had to slide through the gap like a scene in a heist movie.

The lobby of the theater had been beautiful but faded. Like me, Miranda had thought as they passed through it. But now, stepping into the auditorium itself, she straightened her shoulders and threw back her head. She would enter as a star.

If she was expecting applause, she received none. Which was strange, because the place was packed. The entire first six rows were filled. Surely these couldn't all be actors trying out for a part?

Ned slipped into a seat at the back, leaving Miranda on her own. "Good luck," he whispered.

Et tu, Ned Buckley?

She wasn't sure whether to make the long walk down to the stage or wait for someone to call her name. Up onstage, a dozen folding chairs had been arranged in a semicircle facing the audience, with a large leather wingback chair in the center.

The houselights dimmed, and as she waited for her eyes to adjust, a voice said, "You're new."

Miranda turned to find a young woman smiling at her. A tumble of chestnut hair and wide trusting eyes.

"You're in the wrong place," the young woman said in a stage whisper.

You're telling me, thought Miranda, and she didn't just mean the theater.

"You're going to volunteer, right? Or are you here to watch the auditions?"

Nothing about that sentence made sense to Miranda.

"People come to watch . . . the auditions?"

"Oh, yes," said the girl. "It's wonderful. They watch the auditions and then they watch the rehearsals and then the dress rehearsal and opening night, too."

Of the same play. Not a lot to do in Happy Rock, she was guessing.

"I'm Teena, by the way."

"Miranda. Miranda Abbott."

"First Victim," she said.

Miranda could feel a migraine coming on. These people kept speaking what was obviously English to her, but she didn't understand a thing they were saying.

"That's the part I'm trying out for. First Victim. The one who dies in the opening act. I'm a little nervous, so I'm hanging back here till my butterflies settle."

Miranda still hadn't answered her question.

"So . . . are you here to watch?" Teena asked.

"The auditions? No. I am here as an actress."

"Cool! Which role?"

"I can't recall. The female lead, whoever that is."

"Do you have a script?" Teena asked. "No? Here, you can have mine. No, really. Take it. It's okay. I only have the one line and I've pretty much got it memorized."

"First Victim?"

"Yup. That's me. The maid. The one who gets murdered. I've

always wanted to play that, but, well, you know how it is."

"I don't."

"Holly Hinton gets the part. She's really good at dying. The audience gives her a round of applause every time. Sometimes they cheer and even whistle. But Holly is pregnant this year, like, really, really, really pregnant, so . . . fingers crossed."

"Holly? The police officer?"

"You know her?"

"Sort of."

"Well, I really hope I get the part this year. The character has a really good death scene, right at the end of Act One. Then you get to enjoy the play from the wings, and you don't have to do anything until curtain call. Holly used to put her uniform back on and go on patrol, but she always made sure she was back in time to get the applause at the end. Well, except that one time when she had to, like, help out a stranded motorist or something."

Onstage, the lumpy young man from earlier was setting out another folding chair. That must be Rodney, Miranda thought. Dressed all in black, he looked like a large stack of garbage bags that had somehow gained sentience and learned how to walk.

Miranda began flipping through the script, but it was too dark for her to see what role she would ask for.

"The other actors are in the first row," Teena whispered. "That's where we're supposed to wait till they call us up. Follow me."

Teena and Miranda made their way down to the front of the auditorium, joining a row of people who were waiting in various stages of nervousness and anticipation. Some were positively cool about it, though. Case in point: the well-turned man in his early forties wearing a cardigan and hipster bow tie, and sporting a neatly trimmed mustache. He looked up as they sat down next to him.

"Hello, Teena," he said.

A smile played across her lips. "Hello, *Mister* Penty."

"We're not in school anymore, Teena. It's just Graham. No such formalities are needed, okay?" He crooked his head at Miranda. "And you are?"

Ah, she thought. The local drama teacher and leading man. The one who went to Yale. Allegedly.

As with Burt the Spy, she was beginning to have her doubts. Happy Rock seemed more and more like the sort of place people came to reinvent themselves. Or to hide.

CHAPTER EIGHT

The Eighth Deadly Sin

In a darkened auditorium, it was the closest thing to a voice from on high: the static of the PA, and an announcement. "Will the actors auditioning for this year's roles please make their way onstage."

Miranda went up last, swanning across the boards to a rousing round of indifference. Must not have recognized her under the tungsten glare of the lights, she decided.

She took the large comfy chair in center stage, turning to look benevolently upon her fellow would-be thespians. Only one folding chair was empty. Someone must have missed the cutoff.

But then Teena tapped her on the shoulder and said, "That seat's reserved."

Oh. Of course.

Miranda rose and made her way down to the one remaining empty chair, trying her best not to feel slighted.

Bags were placed on the floor, scripts unfolded from sweaty hands, reading glasses discreetly dug out of shirt pockets, and water bottles fumbled with. The actors turned their scripts to different sections, and that was when Miranda realized what was going on.

She turned to the man next to her. "Excuse me. Sir?"

A laconic smile and thick dark hair salted with gray. He gave Miranda a friendly nod. "Ma'am."

"Are we all going to audition together? At the same time? In front of an audience?"

"Oh, yes," he said. "That way, everyone knows that the best actor got the part and there's been no preferential treatment. Murray," he added. "Murray Meadows. That's my name, but you can call me Doc. I'll be trying out for the part of–"

"The doctor."

"That's exactly right. How did you know?"

"Lucky guess."

Applause rippled through the auditorium and Miranda thought, Finally! They've recognized me. The ovation grew stronger.

But it wasn't for Miranda.

It was for a woman who, at first glance, appeared to be the female villain from a low-budget superhero movie. She was short and wide and dressed in scarlet and fuchsia, sporting a floppy wide-brimmed hat and a shawl draped over nonexistent shoulders, much like a matador's cape.

She looks like a Technicolor fireplug, thought Miranda.

The lady walked to center stage and removed her hat with a dramatic swoop, acknowledging the applause and revealing the sort of shiny black dye job that other women talk about when they go to the washroom.

"Welcome!" she said. "Welcome, one and all."

More applause.

This, Miranda thought, has to be the director.

"As you all know, I *am* Judith Traynor." She paused for more applause. "And it is my"–she pressed her hands to her ample bosom—"exquisite pleasure to be asked to direct this year's production of *Death Is the Dickens* for the tenth time, for this, our special ten-year anniversary show, marking a decade of Dickens and death."

Judy settled herself into the wingback chair, a clipboard and vibrantly colored pencil case in hand.

"I thank those of you in the audience for coming to watch these auditions. It's very exciting for us, because several roles in this year's production will be played by first-timers. Tabitha has moved to Tacoma, and I know we all wish her well and thank her fondly for the stellar work she did in seven of the last nine productions."

There was applause from the actors onstage for whatever this was supposed to be. It certainly didn't resemble any audition Miranda had ever experienced.

"That means, of course, that the lead part—our prized *rôle principal*!—of Mamie Dickens has opened up and will be played by one of these brave, brave actresses in attendance today." Judy gave a slow look around the semicircle, noting those few who were courageous enough to try out, giving Miranda a puzzled tilt of the head as she did so.

"Furthermore," Judy said. "As many of you may know, our beloved Holly Hinton is currently with child, which is a huge, *huge* disappointment."

The audience nodded and mumbled in agreement. Very disappointing.

"I know that one of the highlights for everyone is Officer Hinton's death scene at the end of the first act."

More disappointed grumblings from the audience.

"I have pleaded and I have begged, I have even asked, but I have been unable to change her mind. She was simply unwilling to participate this year, even though I was fully prepared to change her part from that of 'maid' to 'pregnant maid.' Regrettably, she was unable to find her way through to putting the needs of the theater above those of her own."

Doc Meadows leaned in and whispered to Miranda, "I was the one who told her not to. She could pop any day now."

"Is that the proper medical term for a delivery?"

He chuckled. "It is up here."

The director cast a mildly disapproving look their way, asking with her eyes for silence. She continued. "Officer Hinton felt she would not be able to perform her death scene with her usual gusto due to her unfortunate condition. It is a shame, truly. But life goes on! And we must soldier through it. I forbid–absolutely forbid!–any of you to hold it against our dear Holly."

The audience expressed their begrudging agreement.

"Before we get to the *theatrical* auditions, let's start with our volunteers, shall we?" Judy stretched out her magnanimous arms to symbolically encompass everyone sitting in the house. "We couldn't do this without you! What is a queen without her pawns? A king without his footmen? Well, still a queen, still a king, but far less robust! We, and here I speak for myself, truly appreciate your dedication and participation. Give yourself a round of applause, all of you, whilst patting yourself on the back!"

How one would clap while simultaneously patting oneself on the back was not clear.

Again with the applause. Miranda was beginning to wonder if there was anything that wouldn't inspire this group to flap their hands like seals. *Ladies and gentlemen, we have just discovered that the sky is indeed blue!* Rapturous applause. *And rain falls down. Down, not up!* Cheers and whistles. It was as if she'd wandered into some sort of revival hall meeting.

"Let's begin auditions for the volunteers." Judy peered under her hand to the darkened auditorium. "Who would like to start?"

"Auditions? For *volunteers*?"

"Mainly by acclamation," said Doc Meadows.

A silhouette stood up in the third row. "Okay. I'll start."

Miranda recognized the diction.

"I'm Burt. You all know me. Set and lights." He paused. "Not sound."

Judy, scanning the audience, said, "Does no one else wish to vie for Burt's position? No?"

This elicited a further chuckle from Doc Meadows. "Just as well. Burt could probably kill you with his thumb." Then, in case Miranda had missed his point. "A spy. Retired."

"So I've heard."

Burt sat down to more applause; they clapped when you stood, they clapped when you sat. Sheesh.

A voice in the back.

"Hello, everyone. It's me, Denise, and I–"

"Please stand up, so we can all see you."

"Um, okay." A tall woman, mostly in shadow. "I teach music at HRHS, and I would like to volunteer this year to do the sound and music, unless–" She sent a questioning look Judy's way. "It hasn't changed, has it? The music will be the same as last year?"

Judy Traynor nodded.

"Okay! Then I'd like to volunteer to do the music again. And the sound effects. Those haven't changed, either, right?"

"No," said Judy, with a saintly look. "Same as last year."

"Excellent!"

Denise sat back down to the usual response.

And so it went.

The local pharmacist would be doing hair and makeup. The local hairdresser would be in charge of designing the programs. And the local graphic design company would arrange the necessary first aid certification.

The Happy Rock Winery announced that they would donate "five of our finest boxes of wine," and a pair of elderly ladies–Mabel and Myrtle, or some such–would "whip up" the food for the opening night reception.

"Mabel used to work the school cafeteria circuit," Doc Meadows confided. "Still has plenty of connections in the food supply business, if you know what I mean. Can get us access to some top-notch cuisine. And Myrtle? She works the breakfast grill at the Cozy Café. Can crack an egg with one hand, and almost no shell in it. When it comes to food, what Mabel can't get us, Myrtle can. Or–wait. Is it Myrtle who ran the school cafeteria?"

Mabel and Myrtle. What absurdly old-fashioned names, thought Miranda–whose name was, of course, thoroughly modern.

Tanvir Singh, owner of Tanvir's Hardwares & Bait Shop, offered to assist with building the set, and he received a courteous nod of acknowledgment from Burt.

Tanvir's wife, Harpreet, stood with a wave to everyone. She was dressed for summer in a light tunic in teal green, a loose headscarf, and billowing trousers cuffed at the hem. A fashionable woman, Miranda noted. And no wonder. Harpreet was the finest seamstress in Happy Rock. She offered to do costumes because she "had so much fun last year and the year before and the year before that."

"*And* the year before that," said Doc, approvingly. "Does a bang-up job. Brings an exotic touch to it."

"Exotic?"

"She's from Portland, y'see."

"Just let me know if you've gained weight," Harpreet said, addressing the actors onstage. "Or lost some."

Chuckles from the crowd. No one *lost* weight in Happy Rock.

"Let me guess," said Miranda. "The same costumes every year?"

"Pretty much," said Doc.

By the time the last volunteer offered their services–and every position was indeed by acclamation–Miranda had become dizzy. She'd stopped trying to remember names and felt a pang of sympathy for Susan Lladdwraig, whom she spotted in the wings, jotting it all down.

Ned Buckley had volunteered to strike the set and put it up, "though not in that order." He also volunteered Bea, who wasn't able to attend the auditions, to run the box office again. "With Rodney, of course!"

Bea would be Head Usher and Primary Ticket Taker. Rodney would be some sort of second-in-command.

"I'd like to help out with the lights, too," Rodney mumbled from the side aisle.

Burt assented to that, as well.

Onstage, in the last chair on the left, one of the would-be actors was watching Miranda. She almost didn't recognize him out of uniform. But there he was. Officer Carl, staring at her.

She looked away, thought again of his dour *American Gothic* features, and wondered if he had a pitchfork stashed away somewhere.

The ever-formidable Judy Traynor now stood, regal as she was righteous–short, yes, but regal still–and clapped her hands, once, to get everyone's attention.

"Is that everyone? Good stuff. Well done. Well done, indeed." She looked offstage at Susan Lladdwraig. "Have we filled all the necessary volunteer roles?"

Susan was going through the list to make sure, and the delay irritated Judy into a tight smile.

"Come on, now," she said. "Miss Lladdwraig, one mustn't dawdle. We can't waste time while you check your paperwork. May we move on to the real auditions or not?"

"Yes, you may."

"Very punctual," said Doc Meadows with a sage nod to the director.

Poor Susan. Miranda decided then and there to offer a sympathetic ear to her next time she saw her, unless she forgot, or was feeling too tired, or if her own audition didn't go well, in which case she would be the one in need of sympathy.

Not that Miranda's audition would be anything but spectacular!

She hadn't had time to prepare a reading from the script, true, but Miranda had several set pieces locked and loaded that she could unload on a director like a howitzer, if need be.

Judy turned, first to the right, then to the left, and addressed the dozen actors who were assembled onstage. Thirteen, with Miranda.

"There are nine parts. And twelve–sorry, thirteen–people vying for them this year. Worrisome odds, I know! But I also know, in my heart of hearts, that all of you here today are ready to offer us your very best. Some of you may be hoping to get a bigger part than you've had previously. Some of you may be trying out for the first time–"

Was that a look she threw Miranda's way?

"–but remember the credo of Thespis. There are no small parts, only small actors! Don't look at this as an audition; look at this as an opportunity *to act.* Let's start with the leads. The ones who, for want of better phrasing, truly matter." Judy took her seat again and, consulting her clipboard, saw an unexpected name. "Officer Carl? Really?" She flipped back, checked if it was a mistake, but no. "Please," she said. "The floor is yours."

Carl rose with a throat-clearing cough. More of a hacking gasp, really. A hack of nervousness. His script was clutched in his hands.

"Carl, sweetheart," said the director. "Normally, you would be trying out for the butler."

"Yes, ma'am."

"But this time, you would like to read for the male lead. Am I understanding this correctly?"

"Yes, ma'am."

"Very well."

"Uh-oh," whispered Doc Meadows.

"Uh-oh, what?" Miranda whispered back.

"She's taking out her ruler."

Sure enough, the director had retrieved a clear plastic ruler and had placed it on her clipboard, ready and waiting.

"Judy'll make a large checkmark next to the name of someone who does well," Doc explained. "It'll be real obvious when she does that. And if she doesn't like 'em, she draws a straight line, crossing out their name. Also very obvious."

"Carl, sweetheart, can you turn to page nine, Scene Three? About halfway down."

"The part with the bottle?"

Carl found the page and read from the scene where Reginald Buckingham the Third snatches a glass vial the butler has discovered, taking a careful sniff of the contents. The scene ends on a dramatic revelation.

"'The smell of bitter almonds,'" said Carl in a flat monotone. "'Oh my god it's cyanide or my name isn't Reginald Buckingham you are correct doctor she was murdered yes murdered I tell you she was completely murdered and someone is to blame.'"

His voice didn't rise or fall once, nor did he seem aware of the purpose of punctuation.

He sat down to a smattering of polite applause. Judy smiled, took her ruler, and drew a line across.

"Thank you, Carl. That was wonderful. Absolutely wonderful. I'm just curious, though. Would you still be interested in trying out for the butler, if, say, you aren't cast as the lead? I believe Everton has retired from that role, so . . ."

"Didn't retire," said Doc Meadows. "Doing five-to-ten for embezzling church funds. Damn shame."

"I imagine."

"Yeah. It was real bad. He was good as the butler. Died really well offstage."

How on earth would someone die well *off*stage?

"The butler, that's a demanding role," whispered Doc. "Third victim. Doesn't have any lines, and you spend the play pouring drinks for everyone and you never get to sit down. But somehow, old Everton made it work. Can Carl pull it off? I don't know. Those are mighty big shoes to fill. Bar's been set pretty high."

Carl himself was waffling over it. "Play the butler? I could, I guess. If you ask the playwright if I could maybe get shot onstage this time?"

"I'll bring it up. Susan! Take a note." Then, with lathered voice, Judy turned and said, "Now then, Mr. Penty?"

The drama teacher was whispering to Teena, but he looked up at Judy with a smile.

"Yes, my love?"

"How many times have you performed the role of Reginald?"

"Every. Single. Time."

He said this with a smile. Or something resembling a smile. Perhaps it was a trick of the light–stage lights do tend to cause a glare, in every sense–but Miranda caught a flash of annoyance, even anger, in his eyes. So quick, she wasn't sure she saw it.

But before she could dissect this look further, the doors to the auditorium slammed open, light from the lobby fanned across the crowd, and a woman strode down the aisle, heading straight for the stage.

"Lord, love us," said Doc. "It's Annette."

Miranda may not have known it, but the real star of the show had arrived. Envy was one of the Seven Deadly Sins. Murder, strangely enough, was not.

CHAPTER NINE

Enter Annette

They killed.

That's what they say when an actor nails a performance. Less often said was "they *were* killed." Killed and killer, two sides of the same performance, yet a gulf as large as the sea lay between the two.

The woman who entered the auditorium had clearly come to kill, not be killed.

Not striding, Miranda realized. Gliding. The woman was *gliding* through the auditorium, down the aisle, as though parting the Red Sea. A murmur of excitement followed her up the stairs and onto the stage. When she reached center stage, she pivoted as though at the end of a catwalk, and she smiled. It was a smile that was beyond radiant. It was fluorescent. A beam that washed over the crowd.

"Hell-*lo!*" she chimed. And the crowd had no choice but to burst into applause.

Doc Meadows leaned into Miranda.

"Pride of Happy Rock," he said.

Legs up to here, as they say, with a tight wraparound skirt and dark hair, loosely coiled, spilling across her shoulders with an artful abandon. She was tall. She was confident. And she was here.

"Annette was the cohost of the KGW morning show in Portland for years," Doc Meadows said. "Even had her own segment there for a while."

"I know her," whispered Miranda.

She had seen her before, though not on TV. But where?

"Well, she is one of the most successful realtors in the Greater Tri-Rock Area."

That was where! It was *her* face that had been plastered on those benches along the harbor.

The buzz of excitement was dampened only by a calming gesture from Annette Herself. "Please," she said. "You're too kind."

"Oh my," stammered the director, flustered and tickled beyond belief at this turn of events. "This is most unexpected. Ladies and gentlemen, the one and only *Annette Baillie!*"

Miranda had to stop herself from joining in on the adulation. She literally sat on her hands to avoid gushing. Stars do not gush. They are the gush*ees*, not the gush*ers*. This was the First Rule of Celebrity.

And still Annette hadn't taken a seat, and still she was facing her adoring public with that high-beam smile.

"When I," she said (and her speech was peppered with I's and me's), "heard that Tabitha had moved to Tacoma, I said to myself, I am from Happy Rock, and I have always considered this theater *my* home. I must come, I thought. I really truly must."

"So . . . ," stammered Judy the director, blushing now. "Will you be trying out for . . . ?"

The possibility hung in the air.

Annette turned to the crowd with a mischievous twinkle. "When I saw the part was open, I said . . ."

And the audience answered for her. *"You bet, Annette!"*

Judy was thrilled. Annette wagged her finger at the audience in mock admonishment.

"You know me too well! That is precisely what I said. I said to myself, Self, said I, can I help the Happy Rock theater? And I told myself, *You bet, Annette!*"

Cheers from the cheap seats as Miranda whispered to Doc Meadows. "Let me guess. Her segment on the morning show was called 'You Bet, Annette!'"

"Yes! That's exactly right. How did you know? You certainly are a sharp cookie, Miss . . . ?"

She hadn't introduced herself yet.

Here we go, she thought. "My name is Miranda Abbott."

"No kidding! Any relation to Edgar, who runs the murder store?"

But before Miranda could squirm out of that question, the director had joined Annette at center stage. The Fireplug Arises! thought Miranda.

A head shorter than Annette, Judy gestured to her own coveted wingback chair. No mere folding chairs for Our Annette. No sir!

"Please," said Judy.

"Oh, but I hate to impose."

"I insist!"

"Oh, I wouldn't want to cause any disruptions. I'm just here to audition, like anyone else."

Such modesty!

But she took the director's seat anyway, forcing Rodney to scramble onstage with yet *another* folding chair, this one for Judy. He struggled to open it, with Judy hissing "Hurry *up*."

Annette waited as the director sorted out getting the extra chair and then said, in the most munificent manner, "Please carry on. Don't change your schedule on account of me."

And there it was again, that flash in Graham Penty's eyes. Fleeting, but unmistakable. Miranda had caught it, stronger than before. It was a look of pure hatred, there and gone in a heartbeat.

Graham smiled at the director. "I believe I was about to read next."

"Oh yes, that's right," said Judy, still a tad flustered. "Let's proceed. Graham, could you turn to the final scene, Act Seven?"

"Has the play changed since last year?"

"No, it's the same as always."

And with that, he turned the script over, facedown on his lap, took a breath, closed his eyes, and recited the lines perfectly. "'Why did I do it? Why did I kill her? You need only look in the mirror, Miss Dickens. I have long lived in your shadow. But I shall not live there any longer...'"

When he was done, he opened his eyes to a fulsome ovation. Miranda was impressed, in spite of herself. He could act. That was good. Very good. But was it Yale good? She still had her doubts, but she also knew that if she wanted to find out, she could. Hollywood was crawling with Yale drama grads. Someone would have heard of a certain Mr. Penty, surely.

Judy made a large checkmark on her page after Graham was done, and Annette turned her head like a gun turret, leveling her gaze at him. She smiled, but not with her eyes.

"I thought that was splendid, Graham. I truly did. And how is everything at the high school drama club? This year's production. *Under the Yum Yum Tree*, is it?"

Graham Penty smiled back. "You know it is."

Doc Meadows explained, speaking low to Miranda to avoid Graham hearing. "Every darn year, his students do the same exact play. *Under the Yum Yum Tree*, every darn time. It's getting tiresome. The wife and I almost didn't go last year."

Miranda considered this dark-haired doctor with the laconic features. Too old to have a child in high school. But too young to have a grandchild there, either.

"So . . . you and your wife go to the high school drama productions?"

"Oh, sure. They sell out every year."

Not a lot to do in Happy Rock, thought Miranda–not for the first time. Or the last.

"Next, we come to the coveted role of female lead. The amateur sleuth, Mamie Dickens!" Judy flipped the page over. "Now then. Miranda, is it?"

Miranda had been trying to keep track of the various roles in the script–the butler, the maid, Reginald Buckingham the Third, Strongman Seth, the doctor, the Earl of Wussex, the Great Oracle Olivia–and through the process of elimination had determined that Mamie Dickens was her part.

Miranda stood, her moment of glory finally at hand. She waited for the inevitable gasp from the audience as they realized who she was. None came. Struck dumb, no doubt!

"I have a prepared passage," said Miranda, and with that she began . . .

She spoke and the crowd went quiet.

Miranda's voice rose, then broke with emotion, by turns harsh and defiant, and then soft and vulnerable, as she carried the scene forward, from heartbreak to heartbreak, all the way to its cathartic end.

"'You think I have been defeated? I have not. I am bruised and broken, I am tired and forlorn, but defeated? No. I have tasted bitter wine and that sweet poison of disappointment. I have reached for the stars, only to fall. Only to reach anew, only to fall again. But I have not been defeated. You can cage these arms, this body, but you cannot cage the spirit that flutters within it like a bird yearning for the wind. Like a single drop of rain against a window, misted with memory. Defeated? No. I am victorious. You need only ask your partner, Buster Jones, and he will tell you, repeatedly. Not defeated. Not defeated.'"

This had been her favorite monologue from *Parrot P.I.!* It was this monologue, in her third appearance on the program, that had convinced the producers she could carry her own show.

Miranda sat down. There was a moment of absolute silence—and then the audience erupted.

The energy swept through, turned into a wave, and the wave crested into a standing ovation. Tears and applause in equal measure, the actor's greatest reward. And in that moment, Miranda was hurled back again to Minneapolis, as an understudy at the Orpheum, and to LA, those long nights in the theater, the joy and the exhaustion, the euphoria of it all. In the days before *Pastor Fran*, before any of this.

Judy placed a large—a very large—checkmark beside Miranda's name.

"Geez," said Doc Meadows. "You're good. You should be a real actor."

She looked at him warmly. "I am a real actor."

At the back of the auditorium, Miranda caught a slash of light as the door opened and someone slipped out in the shadows. A reporter? A talent scout? Whoever it was, they hadn't stuck around to see the next actor in the queue.

All eyes now turned to Annette, whose smile was frozen in place.

"We're ready for you, Ms. Baillie," Judy said. "You will also be reading for Mamie Dickens, I presume."

But Annette remained seated.

So Judy said, "By way of introduction—though I'm sure Annette needs none—Ms. Baillie is one of the finest amateur actresses in the Greater Tri-Rock Area. She has appeared in the History Society's musical, *Happy Rock, Ho!,* and I'm sure we all remember her in that commercial for Otto's Auto Pilot services."

As Judy was reciting Annette's CV, Miranda whispered to Doc Meadows, "They keep saying that. The Tri-Rock Area. What is that?"

"Oh, that's Gladstone, Happy Rock, and Jolly Pebble."

"But—Gladstone is a suburb of Portland, I thought."

"It is. The Tri-Rock Area stretches from there to here, and then up along the coast to the beach at Jolly Pebble. Can't get there by road."

"So, not really a cohesive geographic area? More just based on the similarity of the names?"

"Exactly right. You're catching on."

And god help her, it was almost starting to make sense.

"It's from the word *tillamook,*" he said. "That's Salish. It means 'Land of Many Waters.' Somehow that got changed to 'Good Waters' and then to 'Happy Waters' and then, somewhere along the way, 'Water' became 'Rock'—it never was clear to me how that happened; I mean, the two words are completely different in Salish—and then those got mistranslated, as well."

"Three different times? Three different ways?"

"Yup."

"Wasn't Gladstone a British prime minister or something?"

"Maybe. But he wasn't Salish, I can tell you."

"Shh." Another glare from Judy and then, sweetly, back to Annette. "Ms. Baillie, we await your words."

And now, at last, Annette rose. She lay her script to one side and faced her audience.

"I," she said, "am so grateful, I truly am. I am grateful and I want to express to you just how grateful I am, and that I always will be. Grateful, that is. Happy Rock is where my heart is, and I know it always will be. For me."

She's stalling, thought Miranda. This is good.

"Who is Mamie Dickens? I asked myself that on the way in, and I can honestly say that she *is me.* I am Mamie Dickens! I feel her in my bones, I know her in my heart. I have traveled with her through many a night on my own. Oh, how I've missed her! As you know, I've played Mamie Dickens in the past, I have, and I look forward to playing her again in the future, I do. Indeed, I am honored and I am humbled to be asked. Thank you."

And she sat down!

Miranda was stunned. Annette hadn't even read for the part! They couldn't possibly cast Annette now, she thought, no matter how much she'd tried to tug on audience sentiment.

This was great news! Miranda would spend the next weeks of rehearsal in close contact with her husband; she would make him see that he was wrong. Wrong about her. Wrong about them. Their marriage had not died, it had only been put on hold. Paused during playback.

The auditions went on, but Miranda was too elated to follow much of it. Two more read for the role of Mamie Dickens; one mumbled, the other shouted. Both ends of the Goldilocks equation. These were followed by two more sharp lines drawn along Judy's ruler.

Two different actors tried out for the Earl of Wussex, one of whom had side whiskers and was thus all but guaranteed the spot.

Teena Culliford, however, was the only one auditioning for First Victim (aka the maid). Considering she was, essentially, a shoo-in, she still gave it her all with a gurgle, a gasp, a clutched throat, and a heaving spasm as the poison kicked in, followed in quick order by a twitch, a moan, a shiver, and that immortal single line, "Alas, I have been poisoned! *Gawwck!*"

Polite applause. Everyone was clearly still thinking of Holly in that role. As Doc Meadows might have said, those were mighty big shoes to fill.

The role of the groundskeeper with the suspicious limp seemed sure to go to the actor with a prosthetic leg, which gave him a distinct advantage. And with that, the *Death Is the Dickens* tenth anniversary auditions came to a close.

Miranda was so overjoyed at being back in the game that she had failed to notice the even bigger checkmark the director had ticked off when Annette sat down.

The houselights came up and the stage lights went down. Rodney began folding the chairs back up. Everyone gathered their scripts and assorted water bottles–Annette's was gaudy with rhinestones, Miranda noted; who does that?–and then shuffled out of the auditorium toward the lobby.

"Staying?" Doc Meadows asked.

"For what?"

"The wrap party."

They had a wrap party for auditions? Of course they had a wrap party for auditions. This was Happy Rock. Nothing here made sense.

As Doc and Miranda made their way up the aisle, coming in, through the crowd and against the current, was someone Doc recognized.

"The press is here," he said.

Dammit! Miranda pulled her carry-all bag closer. Too late for a scarf and sunglasses. Bloody paparazzi.

"Quick. Is there a back door?"

But it was too late.

A sullen young woman appeared with a camera slung over her shoulder, pen and notebook in hand. Green hair and a nose piercing.

"What brings you to the auditions, Finkel?" Doc Meadows asked.

Who names their daughter Finkel? Miranda wondered to herself.

"I got a tip someone was in town. Boss sent me."

Doc introduced them. "Miranda, this is Finkel Erdely with *The Weekly Picayune*."

"I know you," said Miranda.

The girl looked at her through heavy-lidded eyes. The personification of I Don't Care. "Everyone knows me. This is Happy Rock. The wonder would be if you didn't know me."

"I mean, I saw you. On the bus. Yesterday, from Portland."

A hard stare. "You're mistaken. I wasn't on the bus from Portland."

"But you were. I'm quite sure of it."

"Wasn't in Portland. Wasn't on that bus. Got it?"

And with that, she pushed past Miranda. "Ms. Baillie! Finkel Erdely, *The Weekly Picayune*. Can I get a photo?"

CHAPTER TEN

The So-Called "Wrap," So-Called "Party"

Rolled ham with fancy toothpicks (i.e., toothpicks with frilly plastic ends). Cubed cheddar and boxed wine, and a generous bowl of mints for dessert. Such was the largesse of the Happy Rock "wrap" party.

"But we haven't *wrapped* anything," Miranda said. "We've barely begun."

"Any excuse for a party," said Ned Buckley as he popped a cube of cheese into his mouth.

He offered her a Dixie cup of wine. "That was a good month," he said approvingly as he studied the side of the box, but Miranda waved it away.

She wasn't here to socialize, and she certainly wasn't here to drink whatever form of local kerosene they were passing off as plonk in these parts.

No. She was scanning the crowd in the lobby with a sniper's gaze, looking for targets, looking for allies. If she was going to assemble

Team Miranda, she would need to start here, with the cast and crew.

Doc Meadows was certainly on the list. She needed to ask Ned about him.

"You gave a good recital," Ned said, popping another cube into his mouth. "Standing O, no less." This was followed with a swish of wine and a satisfied sigh. "That was from *Parrot P.I.!*, right?"

"It was, yes."

"Good show, that one. They should bring it back."

"Audiences loved that parrot. I knew we were in trouble in Season Six of *Pastor Fran* when they brought the parrot in for a cameo. They were trying to boost our ratings, and it worked for about two weeks, and then, well, the swan dive followed."

"I remember that episode of *Pastor Fran*!" said Ned. "Bea played it for me a couple of weeks ago. The parrot kept saying 'Polly wants a cracker,' and you figured out that Polly was actually the childhood name of the woman who had been kidnapped, and that the cracker was actually a Ritz, which in fact referred to the hotel the criminals were holding her in." He thought a moment. "I never did figure out how the parrot knew that the name *Ritz* is both a cracker and a hotel."

"Well, he was a pretty smart bird." And a son of a bitch on set. But enough of Buster Jones and his avian antics. "Tell me about Dr. Meadows."

"Doc? Good man. Plays the doctor really well. Does a terrific job."

"Every year?"

"Every year, except that one time he was on a fishing trip and Owen McCune took over. We were all happy when Doc was available the next year. Nothing against Owen, he's a fine mechanic, but he didn't do near as good a job."

"Owen McCune?"

"The mechanic. That's him over there, yakking to the doc."

Glorious sideburns on our Owen.

"Ah," said Miranda. "You mean the Earl of Wussex."

Ned frowned. "Not officially. He hasn't gotten the part, not yet. But–Owen has been growing those whiskers since March, so there's that."

Annette Baillie, having finished her interview with the press, was now holding court in the theater's ornate lobby in a comfy chair next to Judy. Partygoers were approaching them practically with hat in hand like 'umble peas'ntry.

Definitely not Team Miranda material.

"Deadly duo," said Ned. "That's what we call 'em, anyway."

Ah, she thought. Now we're getting somewhere. Dirt on the supposedly revered Ms. Baillie? Were there dark undercurrents against her?

"Who's *we*?" she asked innocently. "Everyone?" she said hopefully.

"Just me and Bea. I've seen Judy reduce young actresses to tears on a set. Like I said, mean as a snake."

Miranda next zeroed in on Graham Penty.

"He seems, ah, very close to his former students," she remarked.

"You mean Teena? She was a favorite of his, for sure. Naturally. I mean, makes sense. She was cast as the lead in every production of *Under the Yum Yum Tree* in high school."

Graham and Teena were once again entwined in conversation.

"And his wife?" Miranda asked, trying her best to sound nonchalant. "Not here?"

"Mrs. Penty? Oh, that's her over there."

It was Denise, the music teacher, looking awkward and unsure of herself at the far side of the lobby.

"Not good at small talk," said Ned. "But a fine woman."

The world seemed to be divided into Good Men and Fine Women

in the eyes of Ned Buckley—the deadly duo excepted, of course.

"Mr. Penty's audition was very strong," Miranda admitted.

"Always is. Did you know he went to—"

"Yes, yes. Yale, I heard." She thought of the daggers Graham had shot Annette's way earlier.

"Edgar sure likes what he does. Says Graham Penty is an 'actor's actor.'"

Does he now? Definitely future Team Miranda material in Mr. Penty, then.

Ned gave a sour look in Annette's direction.

"Not a fan?" said Miranda, returning her attention to her rival.

"Nope," said Ned. "Treats people badly. Smiling away, but don't be fooled. There's ice in those veins. When Judy's husband died, Annette tried to blame Owen McCune, the mechanic. Hubby drove off the road, you see. Annette started a whisper campaign against him, lasted for years. Damn near ruined Owen. Heck, his business is barely hanging on, even now."

"But you don't believe that?"

"I examined the brakes myself, right after the crash. That car went off the road is all. Easily done. You fall asleep or aren't paying attention."

"Look at you," said Miranda. "Checking out brake lines and investigating suspicious deaths. You're a regular gumshoe."

He blushed. "I'm no Pastor Fran. But I can follow the clues as well as the next person, amateur or otherwise. And sometimes a hairpin turn is just a hairpin turn."

"I see."

"Judy is bad enough," Ned said. "But Annette? That's a whole other level of mean. Was glad when she stopped auditioning. Was just as wary when she showed up today, forcing her way into the proceedings. But that's just me. Lotta people love her. Sort of a celebrity, you see. Closest thing we have to a bona fide star out here."

Ouch.

"I will keep that in mind," said Miranda. "And now, I really must go and mingle with my fellow thespians."

He looked at her.

"It means *actors,*" she said.

"Oh, right. Not that you need to explain anything. Not at all. Everyone is welcome here in Happy Rock, even, ah, thespians."

Miranda Abbott picked up a Dixie glass of wine, more as a prop than a beverage, and sailed across the lobby to Graham Penty. Edgar is a fan, well then, so am I.

He was talking with Teena. They had their backs to her, and before Miranda could announce, "Yes! It is I," Whiskers McGee stepped in between her and Mr. Penty with a bellowing "Cousin Graham!"

Graham sighed. "Owen, how many times do I have to tell you? You don't need to call me cousin or mister or 'the professor.' None of that."

"But you are my cousin," Owen said. He looked at Teena. "On the wife's side, anyway."

"Please. It's just Graham, okay?"

"Fair enough. What did you think of my audition? Figure I'll get the part?"

"Well, you do have the whiskers for it," said Graham.

"Hoo-ha! That's what I thought, too, Cous–" He stopped himself. "Graham."

Doc Meadows joined them, congratulating Miranda again on her fine audition.

Graham agreed. "It was stupendous." Then, with a cackling smile, he added, "Annette must be terrified."

"Come on, *Graham,*" Teena said. "Be kind."

"You're absolutely right," he said. "The fact that Annette will be denied the coveted female lead, which in turn means I don't have to kiss her in Act Two or wrestle the poison out of her hand in Act Three, is reward enough."

Kiss?

Miranda considered the mustache and the sweater and thought, I've kissed worse.

"I was surprised to see her," said Doc Meadows. "Considering how many bridges she's burned in this town."

"She's still on the Tri-Rock Regional School Board," said Graham. "I can't escape her even if I try." He grinned at Miranda. "A realtor, a school board trustee, *and* a former cohost of a local TV show? That's what we call a triple threat in Happy Rock."

He extended his hand to Miranda.

"I don't believe we've met. Formally, that is. I know your work."

Ah. A Pastor Fran fan.

"I saw you perform as Blanche DuBois in the Fifth Avenue Theater production of *Streetcar* in Seattle. You were sublime."

That was after Pastor Fran, but before being turned down for *The Real Has-Beens of Beverley Hills.*

"Alas, the theater backers thought otherwise," she said. "Those who produced the play pulled the plug early. They had thought I would bring in bigger crowds than I did."

"Well, they're fools. It was fantastic. They should have had faith in it. It would have found its audience."

Maybe he did go to Yale, thought Miranda, thoroughly flattered. He certainly appreciated the finer arts. Or was he just buttering her up? And if so, to what end?

Her suspicions were further aroused when she saw his expression shift again. Looking past her, he seemed . . . not annoyed, exactly. Fatigued.

"My wife," he said. "I better go rescue her from herself."

"Be kind," Teena reminded him, more sternly than before.

"Of course, of course. It's just– She hates going to these things, but still comes anyway. Ta." He headed across the lobby with a "Denise! Honey. Why so glum?"

Teena said, "I suppose I should be going, too. It was so great to meet you, Miranda! I really hope you get the part."

A gracious nod from Miranda. "As do I."

Teena left, and now it was just Miranda and Doc Meadows, which suited Miranda fine. The doctor would be a key player in Team Miranda, she was sure.

"Tell me, Dr. Meadows–"

"Doc. Please."

"Do you know my husband? Edgar Abbott?"

"Edgar's your husband? Well, shoot. I should have figured."

"Oh," she said, a little too eagerly perhaps. "He's mentioned me?"

"Nope. Your last name. What are the odds, right? Not a lot of Abbotts in this area. Tons of Meadowses, all up the coast. Throw a stick and you'll hit one of my relations. But Abbotts? You and Edgar are about the only ones, I think."

"Well, married we are," said Miranda, before remembering that one way to get people on your team was to pretend to be interested in what they do for a living.

"GP?" she asked.

"That's right. Family medicine. Like my dad, and his dad, and his dad before him, and so on. We've been in the medical profession going back, oh, fourteen generations or so."

More nonsense from the denizens of Happy Rock. First it was a spy, then a supposed Yale grad teaching high school drama, and now an ancient line of sawbones. Fourteen generations of doctors would take you back to the Elizabethan era.

"Fourteen?" said Miranda, giving him the opportunity to amend his statement. "Are you sure?"

"Maybe more. The record gets a bit foggy before that."

"Here in Happy Rock?"

"Yup."

"But the plaque on the front of the hotel says FOUNDED IN 1887." She'd seen it on her walk over yesterday.

"That's right."

"And the town itself began as a Victorian holiday resort. It began with the hotel."

"More or less."

She could feel another Happy Rock migraine coming on. She was relieved to see Susan Lladdwraig appear. The Administrative Treasurer and General Secretary of the Happy Rock Amalgamated & Consolidated Little Theater Society had exciting news.

"He was here," she whispered. "*In the audience.*"

Ah! The scout or reporter that she had spotted earlier, the one who had slipped out after Miranda finished her monologue.

"Edgar," said Susan, giddy. "He was here, in the audience. I told him he had to come and he said no, all gruff–you know how he gets–but he came anyway. He closed up the bookstore, snuck in the back, watched you perform, and then left before anyone noticed him."

"But... Why wouldn't he tell me he was coming?"

"Didn't want you to know, I guess. Was worried it would throw you off, that's what I think. Didn't want to give you stage fright, that's all."

"I've never had stage fright in my entire life." Quite the opposite. Miranda had "*not* being onstage, *not* being on camera" fright.

"But don't you see what that means?" said Susan. "It means he cares. It means he still has feelings for you."

"Not to hear Bea tell it."

Doc Meadows had wandered off to get more hors d'oeuvres–if cheese cubes and toothpick-skewered rolls of ham could be called hors d'oeuvres–but Susan still glanced over her shoulder to make sure no one could hear.

"I don't understand why Bea is saying that," said Susan. "It's not like her. I know Edgar. I've been volunteering at his bookstore for years and–"

"Wait. You *volunteer* at the bookstore?"

"Yes, so that he can sleep in, keep the store open longer. I Only Read Murder is an important part of our community, a hub of sorts, but he can't afford to hire extra staff. So I help out. He pays me in cozies."

"Cozies?"

"As many as I can read. May I confess something? Sometimes"–and again her eyes flitted around the room–"if it's a hardcover, when I'm finished, I slip it back on the shelves. And not in the used section! Edgar said that's okay, but it still feels a little . . . naughty?" She laughed. "As for Bea . . ."

It really bothered Susan, Miranda could tell.

"I wouldn't worry about it," Miranda said. "Maybe she misunderstood what Edgar was saying."

"Maybe," said Susan, but she didn't seem convinced.

"Certainly Chief Buckley didn't seem overly concerned about what Bea was claiming," said Miranda.

"Ned?" Susan scoffed at this. "I wouldn't put too much stock in anything he says."

"Really? Why not?"

"He's a lovely man, but–I've read enough cozies to know that something is going on around here, even if he doesn't think so."

"In Happy Rock?"

The faded baroque interior of the lobby. Soft golds and faded velvet. Brass railings and stained glass lamps. "Do you believe in ghosts?" Susan asked.

"Of course not," said Miranda, with more conviction than she actually felt.

"Neither do I," said Susan. "Every mystery has a logical, explicable cause. And yet... a few weeks ago..."

Miranda swallowed, expecting the worst. The sound of chains below the stage's trap room? The sob of a lost soul in the dressing rooms? A chill in the balcony unrelated to air conditioning?

"My pocketbook," said Susan.

"Your what?"

"My pocketbook. A few weeks ago, it was stolen. Or I should say, went missing, because it reappeared later."

"That was you?" said Miranda. "The Case of the Missing Pocketbook?"

"It was. And I can tell you, Ned Buckley did not take it seriously. Not at all. He said I must have misplaced it. I ask you, Miranda. Do I seem like the type of person who would misplace a pocketbook? Do I look like the sort of person who would misplace anything?"

"So, if not Ned, who did solve the Case of the Missing Pocketbook?"

Miranda was teasing, but Susan took the question seriously.

"It was Edgar. He solved it." Then, brightly. "Which reminds me. He left you a note."

A folded piece of paper.

When Miranda opened it, all it read was: *Meet me at the tiger*.

CHAPTER ELEVEN

The Tiger Roars

In the far reaches of the Duchess Hotel, past the dining halls with their vaulted ceilings and beyond the sunroom with its leafy ferns and African violets, past vibrant splashes of hibiscus and the shy elegance of the orchids–beyond all that lay the wood-paneled Bengal Lounge, steeped in generations of pipe smoke and pomp.

Parquet floors and wainscot walls. Frescoes of maharajas and Indian sepoys. One didn't enter the Bengal Lounge so much as wade into it, passing between a pair of teak elephants to do so.

A sign from another era welcomed you: *Women and ladies must be accompanied by and vouchsafed for by reputable companions of male persuasion.*

How exactly one was "vouchsafed for," Miranda wasn't sure. As for the distinction between a lady and a woman, well, who knows? Miranda liked to think she was both.

Leather sofas, so soft as to be almost deflated, lined the lounge. Guests sank into them, had trouble getting out. A billiard table, reading lamps, defunct marble ashtrays.

And above the jade veneer of the fireplace was the lounge's namesake: the giant pelt of a Bengali tiger, stretched taut, the focal point of the entire room. Like the teak elephants that stood guard at the entrance, it had been a gift from the King of Siam when he'd stayed at the Duchess a hundred years before. Time had a way of standing very still in the Duchess, and though the tiger skin was looking a tad threadbare of late, it was a tiger still.

A natural redhead herself, Miranda had an affinity for tigers. Edgar had called her "my tiger," but only, ahem, in bed. *Meet me at the tiger*. A remembrance of a honeymoon spent here at the Duchess, the sated mornings, the high teas and clotted cream.

A red-vested waiter pulled out a chair for her at a table below the tiger. "Madam."

The cocktail menu featured drinks with names like Bombay Zinger, the Gunga Gin, and the We ARE Amused Margarita.

Fuzzy navel. That's what she'd ordered on their honeymoon. And he'd kissed her navel that very night . . .

And here was Edgar now. A corduroy jacket and jeans. Trim and graying. But still the man she'd married. He smiled as he saw her. A bigger one when he joined her.

"So. How did it go?" he asked.

"I sprained my thumb splendidly, thank you."

"Good! I knew you'd nail it."

And now it was Miranda's turn to smile. "And I know that you were in the audience. Susan told me."

Embarrassed, he coughed and said, "I couldn't pass up the chance to see you perform, Miranda. You always commanded the stage. It was beautiful."

"Those were *your* words I was reciting, Edgar. You wrote them."

"No, Miranda. Those were yours. You made them your own; you always did. I could throw anything down on the page and you would bring it to life. Though I do think you probably could've cut the reference to Buster Jones at the end."

She looked around them. "The Bengal Lounge."

"I wanted you to see it one last time, before it's over."

She stiffened. "Over?"

"They're taking it down. Renovating the entire room. It's just as well, I suppose. It's become a sort of dusty diorama of a distant past. But then, the past is always dusty, isn't it?"

The look he gave her, propped up against the pillows, beckoning her back to bed . . .

"Oh, I don't know, Edgar. I don't think all of it is dusty." Then, leaning forward with a small conspiratorial smile, she said, "Thank you, by the way. For paying my dues."

A puzzled look crossed his face, but before he could speak, the waiter reappeared.

"Are the gentleman and the lady ready to order?"

Edgar asked for chamomile tea.

"Fuzzy navel," said Miranda, closing the cocktail menu.

Edgar missed the reference.

"You don't remember?" she said after their drinks arrived. "That's what I ordered, our first night. And then *later* . . . The fuzzy navel? You honestly don't remember?"

"I think I was too beguiled by your eyes at that time," he said with a laugh. "We could have been drinking pickle juice for all I knew."

He was reaching inside his jacket pocket—he was one of the few men who could really pull off corduroy, she thought—when she saw someone heading their way. That green-haired goblin. That sullen little news reporter. And Miranda thought, Oh great. Here we go. Finally, the penny has dropped.

But it wasn't Miranda she was coming to see.

"Hey, Edgar."

"Oh, hey, Finkel." He slid whatever he was retrieving back into his jacket pocket. "What brings you to this corner of the Duchess?"

"We're doing an insert on Annette Baillie for the Saturday paper." It was a weekly. Every issue was the Saturday paper. "Thought the tiger skin might make for a nice backdrop. Sort of suits her, if you know what I mean."

"Oh, I do indeed. Have you met Miranda? Miranda this is–"

"We've met," said Miranda. "On the bus."

Finkel said nothing. Exited with a parting glare in Miranda's direction.

"Who peed in her cornflakes?" said Edgar.

"Is she always so..." Miranda almost said *miserable*. "... taciturn?"

"Nah. She's a good kid. She's looking for a ticket out of here, that's all. Wants to be a real journalist. Doesn't realize how lucky she is to have grown up here, even if nothing much exciting happens in this neck of the woods. I think she's looking for the 'big story.'" He chuckled. "Even if she has to concoct one herself. A story that'll break her career wide open, allow her to escape from Happy Rock to the bright lights of Portland or Eugene. Or maybe even the national press. She's a regular at my bookstore."

"The murder store."

"Sorry?"

"That's what they call it, don't they? The murder store."

He laughed. "Maybe that's why Officer Hinton is one of our regular customers. Though Holly doesn't read murder so much as she reads nostalgia. Pokes around the youth section mainly, the Nancy Drews and the Famous Fives. She's having a child soon, says she's 'bringing another reader into this world.'"

The word *nostalgia* opened up between them. The past is always present in what we do.

Edgar's hand was resting on the tablecloth and Miranda was about to reach across and take it in hers, was deciding what to say, the inflection, the degree of eye contact, the amount of pressure to apply . . . when who showed up but Annette Herself.

She was indeed there for a photo shoot, and she came up behind them, panther-like, her loosely coiled hair shimmering as she trailed her hand across the back of Edgar's chair.

"Hello, Edgar," she purred.

He turned. "Annette. Finkel mentioned you were coming."

Annette cast a feline gaze Miranda's way.

"I look forward to working with you," she said. And was that the hint of a smile?

She departed for the other end of the grand fireplace, where Finkel Erdely was setting up a reflector light.

"Someone seems very interested in you," Miranda said dryly.

"Well," he joked, "I am considered the most eligible bachelor in the Tri-Rock Area." And as soon as he said it, he realized what he'd done. "I didn't mean it that way."

Green eyes blazing. Fire rising. "What other way could you possibly have meant it?" She was trying not to raise her voice.

"C'mon. It's just something they say around here, as a joke. They don't know about . . . us."

That only made it worse.

"Oh, I am very aware of that, Edgar!" And now her voice was rising. Annette and Finkel had both stopped to watch. "I know that you like to go around pretending that I don't exist!"

"That's not true. You know that's not true."

"Bea told me all about it!"

"Well, Bea Maracle is a damn busybody," he snapped. "And she should stay the hell out of other people's affairs." Then, taking a breath to calm himself down, he retrieved the envelope from his jacket and placed it on the table in front of her. "I didn't want it to be this way, Miranda."

She stared at the envelope. She had an inkling of what it contained.

"If you have something to give me," she said, standing up from the table, gathering her bag, staring down at him like a wraith. "You can give it to me at rehearsal. Otherwise, I have nothing to say to you. Nothing!"

She rummaged around in her bag and threw the fold of twenty-dollar bills onto the table in front of him.

"I found that in my bag this morning. You can keep your charity! I don't need any handouts. I am doing *just fine*."

"What are you talking about?"

"The money you so slyly slipped in."

He pushed the bills back across the table toward her. "I don't know who gave you this, but it wasn't me. I offered, but you were too proud to take my help. Remember?"

She snatched the money back up, shouted "Fine!" and then stormed out of the Bengal Lounge, down the carpeted halls, past the sunroom, and out onto that expansive lawn with its panorama of the harbor.

Damn you, Edgar Abbott!

With her bag jouncing and bouncing about on her shoulder, she strode along the harbor road toward Bea's cottage. She could see the B&B on the far side.

Miranda passed a pair of benches with Annette's big fat face plastered over them. The first bench read: *Selling your home? You bet, Annette can get you the highest price possible!* And next to it–right next to it!–the second bench said: *Buying a home? You bet, Annette can get you the lowest price possible!*

How? thought Miranda. How? Nothing in this town made sense.

She saw a patrol car coming toward her. Ah! Ned Buckley! He will run me back to Bea's. Miranda stepped out, hailing him like a taxi.

But it wasn't Ned. It was Officer Carl.

He rolled to a stop. Didn't speak. Stared at her.

Fifty years old and still lives with his mother. Wasn't that what Burt had said? *He's an odd duck, all right.*

Miranda veered away, picking up her pace. She could hear, or rather sense, the patrol car slowly following her. Walking faster now, she cut across to get away from him. The officer hit his brakes—almost bumping her down, in fact—and she yelped, dodging out of the way and then hurrying even faster, bag bouncing.

To someone of a less fertile imagination, this near-miss might have seemed an unfortunate but unintentional incident. But not in the febrile mind of Miranda Abbott. Carl's vehicular lunge in her direction would take on a darker and—it must be said—more ominous significance in the days to come.

By the time she reached Bea's cottage, she was flustered and out of breath. "Water, please, no ice. I was almost hit by a car just now."

Bea was at the kitchen counter washing up. She turned, befuddled. "Water?"

"Yes. No ice."

"Um, okay." She dried her hands, filled a glass from the faucet, took the two steps across to Miranda, and handed the glass to her. Miranda hesitated—this wasn't Aquafina—took a single sip. "I thank you," she said. And she handed the glass back to Bea.

Bea cleared her throat. "About your wet towels, the ones you left on the floor, and the unmade bed, and your laundry and, um, the dirty dishes and tea bags you left on the kitchen table . . . ?" She reminded Miranda about the recycling, as well. "The blue box by the door."

Miranda stopped Bea with a kindly look. "I know what this is about, and please, you shouldn't worry about any of it."

"I shouldn't?" Bea said, feeling relieved.

"Yes, I know how busy you've been, and I don't expect four-star housekeeping. Not right at the start, anyway." She dropped her voice to a stage whisper. "But do you have any *non*-GMO skin care products? The ones in the en suite are a little, how shall I say, *cheap* for my liking. But I don't mean that in a bad way."

Heavens, no.

"Um, okay, I'll see what I can find next time I'm at TB's," said Bea.

"Lovely! See? That's the sort of personal care that I appreciate. I shall be recommending your establishment to all of my friends in Hollywood."

Which reminded her . . .

"I need to call Andrew, give him the good news."

Miranda called long distance, from the sitting room. Bea's face blanched as Miranda dialed and dialed . . . and dialed . . .

It went to voicemail.

"Andrew, darling! It is I. Big news, I am starring in a local theatrical production. Very quaint, very cute. Anyway, thought you might leak it to the press. Give TMZ a call. Maybe YouTube. All is good in Miranda's world!"

Elated, she hung up. "You know what I'm going to do? I'm going to make lemonade!"

While she was banging about in the pantry, Ned showed up. He joined them in the kitchen just as Miranda dumped a bag of processed sugar into a pitcher of water, stirred in several cups of lemon juice, and tossed in–"my secret ingredient!"–a fistful of salt at the very end.

"Cuts down the sugary taste," she confided, much like Julia Child sharing a secret.

She poured them each a generous lukewarm glass of her trademark concoction–ice would just melt and dilute it, she explained–and then said, "Wait, before I forget!"

She ran up to her room to retrieve the playbill Ned had given her that morning. The one where she'd written the key names down on the back.

"I met some new people," she said as she came rushing back in. "Oh. You've finished already?"

Ned and Bea were standing at the sink, empty glasses in hand.

"I'm so glad you liked it! My gay assistant always loved my lemonade. Here, take more. There's lots." She topped up their glasses. "Now, where is my pen?"

She darted out to the sitting room, and when she came back, both the glasses and the jug were now empty.

"Oh my! You must have been very thirsty. Don't worry, I'll make more later. But first–" She spread the playbill out on the kitchen table. "I spoke with the doctor."

"Meadows?" said Bea. "He tell you about his fishing trip a few years back?"

"Now, Bea," said Ned. "What did I say about gossiping?"

"It's not gossip if it involves the play," she said. "He missed that year's production, remember?" Then, under her breath, "Maybe ask his wife about it. If you can find her."

"Bea's a little sore at him still," said Ned. "Doc was the only one who voted *against* amalgamating the theaters. He was with the Peninsula Players, with Bea. And he was upset about the whole thing."

"We were planning our annual Fall Soiree," said Bea. "But once we amalgamated, that got moved up to the spring. Our play sort of got folded into it. We had been doing local history vignettes that year, from Salish mythology to the founding of the Duchess all the way up to the murders at the bookstore."

"Murders? At the bookstore?"

"Didn't they tell you? A grisly set of crimes at your husband's shop, back when it was a private home. The maid, the butler, the wife—all murdered. That's what the play is based on. Doc was mad because that was the only historical element of our fall production that they used."

"I wanted to ask you," Miranda said. "Doc introduced me to a fellow with very large sideburns."

"That'll be Owen McCune, the mechanic. A friend of Doc's."

"That's the name I was looking for!" She added it to the list, along with others:

Owen McCune - *mechanic* - *whiskers* - *Graham's cousin*
Annette - *local celebrity* (and here she underlined the word *local* forcibly)
Denise - *music teacher* - *Graham's wife* (underlining *wife* just as forcibly)
Rodney -

But here, she was at a loss. What to put? Stagehand? Strange? Lumpy? Rodney was certainly not the type of performative extrovert that the theater usually attracted.

Nor was Denise.

A memory of Graham and his protégé Teena emerged. When Miranda had approached him at the so-called wrap party, she'd heard him lean in toward his former student and murmur in her ear, "I believe in you."

Oh, I'm sure you do, thought Miranda.

Memories of the Orpheum in Minneapolis. A young Miranda and an older casting director. A lurid proposition and a glass thrown in his face, with Miranda stomping off, then returning, and him grinning, teeth yellowed, arms open, not realizing she had come back for a follow-up knee to the groin. Wine to the face wasn't enough for the likes of him. "Stay down!" she'd snarled as he crumpled. And he had. After that, he'd cowered whenever Miranda came near him.

As for Graham Penty and his young protégé? When the chance arose, Miranda would take Teena aside and share with her an important lesson: Sometimes, when life comes at you, you just have to kick it in the balls and move on.

Ned cleared his throat. "Okay, so, the reason I'm here is, I just came from the theater. And they've posted the list of actors that were chosen for the play."

"So soon!" said Miranda. She remembered the excitement, the anxious nervous energy of waiting for the casting on any production to be announced. "I suppose when most of the roles are by acclamation, it doesn't take as long."

"Yep. Very punctual," said Ned. "Judy's always been very dependable that way. And, well, there's good news and there's some bad news. The good news is, you've been cast!"

"Excellent! I shall make more lemonade!" And then: "What's the bad news?"

CHAPTER TWELVE

A Downward Spiral

It was after the sixth consecutive episode of *Pastor Fran Investigates* that Ned and Bea started to get worried.

"Maybe we should, I don't know, stage an intervention or something?" he whispered.

"Throw in 'nuther video!" Miranda yelled, slurring her words, wineglass swishing in mid-air. She'd already drained two boxes of Happy Rock's finest and was calling for more *Pastor Fran*.

It was two in the morning, the caramel popcorn was long gone, and Bea was becoming concerned.

"Maybe you're right," she whispered back to Ned, though neither of them really knew what an "intervention" was exactly or how you would go about staging one.

Even worse, Bea had other guests staying there that night. *Paying* guests. A pair of righteous ladies from the school board, in town to throw a wet blanket on something or other. They had driven in from Gladstone and would be meeting with the very woman who had been cast in Miranda's part.

"Annette Baillie is a fine school trustee," said one, all bosom and hair spray.

"Keeps the teachers in line!" said the other, all hair spray and bosom.

They were interchangeable, these two, and Miranda hadn't bothered remembering their names, thought of them simply as Tweedledee and Tweedledumber.

Every mention of You Bet, Annette was a nail in Miranda's heart.

"The maid!" she'd cried when Ned had broken the news. "They cast me as the *maid*? The one who says 'Alas, I have been poisoned! *Gawwck!*'"

"See?" said Bea, trying to look on the bright side. "You've already got your lines memorized."

"Line. Singular. *Gawwck* doesn't count. And no–I am not doing it!"

The two ladies from the school board had shown up soon after, and they had been thrilled–at first–to realize they were sharing a roof with the immortal Pastor Fran. They even settled in that evening to watch what they thought would be a single episode with Bea's guest of honor in attendance.

"Imagine! Watching *Pastor Fran* WITH Pastor Fran!"

But Miranda was already halfway to tipsy town and her running commentary tended to detract from the narrative.

"Ha! We shot that one in Culver City. What a shithole. One of our ADs got knifed in the alley . . . That kid that plays the tear-stained orphan? Little asshole he was. Got arrested for shoplifting later, I think. Or maybe public urination. Saw his mug shot in the paper and thought, Ha! Serves him right . . . Now *that* actress, the one playing Sister Mary, she slept with everyone on the set, from craft services right up to Second AD . . . And that guy? The leading man? The one playing Father McKenzie? Had a fetish for women's underwear. I caught him in my trailer once trying on my corset . . ."

Not even the pets were spared. "That li'l dachshund? The one Pastor Fran is always carrying around? Completely incontinent by the end. My entire wardrobe reeked of pee..."

As the night went on, the strained smiles of the school board ladies gave way first to annoyance, then to anger, and then to real concern.

"But dear, think how fortunate you have been."

"Yes!" said the other. "Think of how your hard work and effort has paid off. You should take pride in your past success."

"And you have such amazing cheekbones!"

"It wasn't the cheekbones, honey. I wore the wrong bra, that's all." She tried to laugh but couldn't. "My entire career. Built on an error in wardrobe. I'd been cast to play a young pastor on *Parrot P.I.!*, and I figured, I'm playing a pastor in a loose tunic, how much support do I really need? I showed up wearing the wrong bra for it, didn't realize they'd added a dramatic scene of me running across the tracks to save that teenager from the clutches of a marijuana gang."

"That's right!" said Ned. "Bea and me watched that episode of *Parrot P.I.!* It was the first-ever appearance of the character Pastor Fran."

"Well, I ran across those train tracks, again and again, take after take, really gave it my all. Didn't realize how... bouncy it would be when they aired it. In slow motion, no less. My character quickly developed a following, and the producers of *Parrot P.I.!* brought me back. More running, more jumping. Even put me on a trampoline at one point, I think. I was wearing the right bra that time, but by then, I'd already become a *very popular* recurring character and, next thing you know, I had my own spin-off. A star was born. Ha! All because I was naive and dumb and wore the wrong bra that day."

It was around then that the two school board members excused themselves for bed.

The next morning, Miranda staggered down, hungover and feeling clammy and cold, with memories of her infamous appearance at the Golden Globes sixteen years earlier lying heavy on her mind. (Miranda had gotten into a drunken red-carpet dustup with Bea Arthur.) Nothing worse than a downward spiral. The ghosts and regrets emerge.

Ned had popped by, ostensibly to help with breakfast, but more to check in on Miranda.

She slid in next to the other two guests as Bea ladled out fruit salad and muesli. The infernal sound of Ned chewing muesli gave Miranda a splitting headache.

"Mornin'," she mumbled.

"Morning!" they replied, and then, "Since we have a woman of the cloth in attendance, we thought it best to wait." They cast a disapproving gaze Ned's way. He was already at the bottom of the muesli bowl.

Wait? For what?

"For grace. Perhaps Pastor Fran would like to do the honors?"

Miranda looked to Bea. They do know I'm not a *real* pastor, right? Even Bea understands that. Right?

Fine.

Miranda cleared her throat. "Okay. But it's been a while." How did it go again? They bowed their heads and Miranda Abbott–aka Pastor Fran–recited, "Our Father Who Arts in Heaven with One Nation Under God, forever and ever, *e pluribus unum*. The end."

It was after the ladies from the school board had left for the day, as Ned cleaned up and Miranda sat slouched over her coffee at the kitchen table, that Bea broached the subject.

"When you said last night that you would never in a million years ever lower yourself to play the maid, never never absolutely never . . . did you really mean that?"

"What part of 'absolutely never' wasn't clear?"

"Well, it's just—Ned and I were talking, weren't we, Ned?"

"We were, yup."

"And remember how I said that whenever I am in a predicament, I ask myself, What would Pastor Fran do?"

"Uh-huh." Miranda was barely listening.

"And do you remember there was that one episode where Pastor Fran tries out for the choir, and she wants to be lead soprano, but she gets cast as one of the chorus instead, but she doesn't give up and she joins the choir anyway, and her singing is so beautiful that she becomes the lead because Father McKenzie is so impressed by her singing that the real estate agent who unfairly got the lead is forced to acknowledge how much better Pastor Fran is and he gives her the part?"

"That seems oddly specific," said Miranda.

"But you do remember that episode?"

"Um, no . . . But we were shooting thirty-nine hours of network TV a year."

"But don't you see?" said Bea. "That's exactly like you!"

"Yeah, I got that. Right down to the real estate agent."

"Miranda, you may not have been cast as the lead of the play, but you still got cast, and that's something. Whatever the role may be, you will shine onstage. I have faith in you! You're a star! You mustn't hide your light under a bushel."

Miranda was not convinced. But then came the kicker.

"Edgar would have to look at you differently. He wouldn't be able to judge you as harshly as he has been."

"What do you mean?"

"Well, I imagine your husband expects you to walk away if you don't get what you want, yes?"

"Probably," Miranda admitted. "He began to complain about

my–quote–'prima donna tendencies.' Can you imagine anything so ridiculous!"

Bea and Ned exchanged looks.

"Heck, that's all the more reason for you to sign up," said Ned. "Play the maid! That'll show him!"

"He *would* be impressed," Miranda said, "by my modesty. By how humble I am being in accepting such a small part."

"And who knows?" said Bea with a wink. "If something were to happen to the leading lady . . ."

"Now, Bea," Ned admonished. "Doc Meadows didn't say Annette had a *bad* heart. He said he wasn't sure she *had* a heart. Not after what she did to Owen."

"I heard differently. Acute arrhythmia, that's what I heard. The stress might get to her. She may have to step aside, and if she does . . . Well, all I'm saying is"–Bea handed Miranda a copy of the script–"you should learn the lead's lines as well as your own. Just. In. Case."

Prima donna tendencies? Ha! Miranda would show them. She would impress upon Edgar how she could be the most humble person who ever lived! She would be magnificently humble! Extravagantly modest!

Even better, in being forced to see her every day during rehearsals, Edgar would no longer be able to deny her existence.

"I shall do it!" she announced. "I shall! Give me five minutes to put on my face, and I will pop up to the bookstore and tell Edgar in person. Chief Buckley, I'll need a ride."

She pranced off, having taken a handful of aspirins and chugged an entire glass of SunnyD.

Ned turned to Bea. "She does know I'm not a taxi, right? And that episode you were telling her about, with the choir and the auditions. I don't know if I've ever seen that one, and I thought we'd watched almost all of 'em."

"There is no such episode, Ned. I just had to get her out of the house. I can't take another *Pastor Fran* marathon. And the horrible anecdotes she tells! It's ruining the show for me." And then, more to herself than to Ned, "I almost liked her better before I met her."

Forty-six minutes later, Ned dropped Miranda off at the bookstore, with a "Ta! I'll call you when I'm done" from Miranda and a world-weary sigh from Ned.

Susan looked up from her latest cozy when Miranda entered, was pleased to see her.

"Hi!"

"Just going to go up, see Edgar—"

But Susan surprised her by saying, "No! I mean, you can wait here. He will be down soon. I can call him. No reason for you to go upstairs. Just wait. Here. Down here."

Before Miranda could figure out what was going on, she heard the familiar lope of feet on the stairs, that same tuneless whistle, and the galumphing burst of a golden Lab preceding him.

"Oscar!" she cried, crouching down to hug the Lab. Then she caught herself. This wasn't Oscar, this was Emmy, daughter of. "Such a pretty girl. Who's a pretty girl? You are!"

Edgar froze. "Miranda?"

"Yes! It is I!" She stood and smiled, all peaches and sunshine.

Edgar approached warily, the way one might an electric eel. "Everything good?"

"With us?"

"With the play. I heard what happened. I didn't stick around to see Annette's audition, but I can't imagine she topped what you did."

"She didn't even read for it," said Miranda, sweetly. "But that's okay. I'm just happy to have been cast. No small parts, only small actors!"

"Wow. You've, ah . . . changed."

Point for Miranda.

"Will you be attending the rehearsals?" she asked casually. "Along with the cast and crew, I mean?"

"Wouldn't miss it for the world. Always a lot of fun. But it's little theater, Miranda. Amateur actors, local production. Don't go in expecting Broadway-quality dramatics."

"I won't, don't worry," she said. "Not with that script! Oh my goodness."

"Yeah, it's a silly little play. But the actors enjoy it and, more importantly, it's well within everyone's abilities."

"And Mamie Dickens? The Victorian sleuth?"

"Oh, that was Charles Dickens's niece. She's a real person. She really did come to Happy Rock. Stayed at this house, actually. That part's historical."

Miranda laughed. "Maybe. But honestly, Edgar. This play is so comically bad. Lord Reginald the Third? The groundskeeper with the suspicious limp who just happens to appear right after the Earl of Wussex mentions how he recently shot an intruder in the foot? The oracle who keeps giving away plot points at key moments? I laughed and laughed. Oh, how I laughed. Though I'm not sure if that was the intended reaction. Everyone seems to take this play *soooo* seriously. As though it were art."

"It's a murder mystery," said Edgar, his voice beginning to cool. "Based on real events in the community, played by members of that community, and enjoyed by members of that community."

"But you're a writer, Edgar! Surely you can see how over-the-top it is. I don't know who this Doug Dirks is, but–"

"Mrs. Abbott!" It was Susan, standing up, interrupting but looking lost about what to say next. "Would you like a . . . cup of tea? I have some in my thermos."

"Thank you, no." Then, turning back to Edgar, "And Strongman

Seth? Unable to open a jam jar at a crucial moment, thereby revealing himself as Lord Reginald's sickly younger brother? Honestly, Edgar, who comes up with something like that and thinks, 'This is gold! Gold, I tells ya! We should rent a theater and charge people to see it!' Instead of, I don't know, consigning it to the trash heap, where it belongs. It is a jumble. An absolute, glorious jumble."

"Maybe that's the point," said Edgar through clenched teeth. "Maybe that was the playwright's intent. Maybe that's all he was trying to do. Create something fun, something positive, something that people could enjoy. Ever consider that, Miranda? Ever think of that?"

"To be frank, I don't think much of this Doug Dirks fellow at all, whoever he is."

"Mrs. Abbott! I really think you should *stop*—and have some tea. Edgar has a lot to do, so why don't you and I just sit quietly over here and—"

"No *thank* you, Susan. What was I saying? Oh yes, about this god-awful travesty of an abomination of an atrocity of a play. Do you know him, Edgar, the writer behind this debacle?"

"Miranda," said Edgar, eyes cold, "I am Doug Dirks. I wrote that play. It was me. I wrote it for the three community companies as something they could perform. Together."

"Oh. I see." A long pause and then, "When I said it was a travesty of an abomination, I meant that in the best possible way. There is a sprightly energy to the words, which seem to leap off the page like a—"

"Is there anything else I can do for you?" he said, his voice like chilled steel. "You're in the play. Good. There is a letter you need to sign from my lawyer. I tried to give it to you at the Bengal Lounge, but you stormed off. As usual. I'll have it sent to Bea's. If there's nothing else, I have things I could be doing. Like not standing here talking to you."

"Edgar, please, I am so, so very–"

A thump upstairs caught her attention. Emmy was down here, no?

"You have another dog?" Miranda asked.

Footsteps above. Ghosts? Please let it be ghosts, not a female caller.

"No. Not another dog. I have a guest. They're waiting for me upstairs. You can show yourself out." With that, he turned and disappeared into his book-laden world.

Face burning and unable to even look Susan's way, Miranda hurried out of the bookstore into the warmth of a Tillamook morning.

It was only when she got outside that she noticed the gaudy vehicle parked in front of Edgar's bookstore. A pink Cadillac with the promotional motto *You bet, Annette can do it! Annette Baillie, Realtor at Large* splashed across the side.

CHAPTER THIRTEEN

Strongman Melvin

Miranda walked along the harbor to the Opera House, past sailboats bobbing on the water and the Duchess Hotel glowing gold, past those grinning realtor benches–and every time she passed them, they looked more demonic. *You bet, Annette can ruin your life!*

The meaning of the pink Cadillac parked at Edgar's bookstore gnawed at Miranda. Had Annette spent the night at Edgar's? She remembered the hand tracing its path along the back of Edgar's chair at the Bengal Lounge, the purring voice, the *Hello, Edgar.* And Edgar joking about being the most eligible bachelor in the Tri-Rock Area.

If so, it meant that Edgar had slept with Annette *after* she stole Miranda's part in the play, *after* Miranda had been humiliated. It was a thought too awful to consider, so she pushed it down, tried her best to avoid thinking about it.

She had a rehearsal to attend!

With its creamy exterior and rococo exuberance, the Opera House was in perfectly placed contrast to the more haughty hotel next to it. People were streaming in through the front doors. That would be the audience. "Audience?" Miranda had asked. "For our rehearsals?"

"Our *opening* rehearsal," Bea had explained. "It's a big deal. Until the big night arrives, that is."

"The actual opening?"

"Dress rehearsal. We always sell out on that night."

Bea manned the box office. She would know.

But until Miranda actually saw the audience flowing in firsthand, she would never have believed it. She avoided entering through the lobby, but only out of habit. She knew there would be little hubbub or hullabaloo upon her arrival. If they were waiting for anyone, it was Annette. *You bet, Annette can cause a stir!*

"Hell-*oh*, everyone! I am so very happy to have you see me!" Annette said as she sailed past to meet her adoring public.

Miranda followed the walkway around the theater to the side entrance. But even there, she couldn't escape the shadow of Annette. That familiar pink Cadillac was now parked in the RESERVED FOR STAFF lot, nuzzled up next to a mud-spattered Jeep. Edgar always drove a Jeep, even when they were in LA. Miranda used to kid him about it. *Not a lot of rugged trails to ascend in Burbank, are there?* Even back then, he was dreaming of escape, she realized.

The Jeep and the Cadillac. Had Annette and Edgar come to the theater in tandem? Had they parked next to each other, exchanged intimacies before slipping in separately?

Next to the Jeep was Ned's patrol car. (Or was it Carl's? A small shudder.) And beside the patrol car was a Ford pickup filled with rusted barrels, loose lumber, caked paint cans, a dented tool kit. Burt's vehicle, she assumed.

Rather than pound on the stage door, Miranda buzzed, and a few minutes later, Susan appeared.

She stood in the doorway and looked at Miranda with heartfelt concern. "Are you okay?"

"With Edgar? Or the casting?"

Susan thought about this. "Both, I guess."

"I've been better."

"Come, come. I'll make you some tea."

Miranda declined the offer, though she would have taken a shot of hard liquor had Susan offered it.

They sat across from each other at the small desk where Susan worked: the mauve receipt book, the metal cashbox, a stack of bound pages.

"Oh. I have a script for you, Miranda. I've gone through and highlighted each character by color. You're blue."

Am I ever.

Susan handed her one from the top of the stack. "The colors help when actors are trying to memorize their lines."

Miranda had exactly one. "I think I'm good."

"Well, when rehearsals start, I'll be in the wings to prompt you if need be. Owen McCune tends to have trouble remembering little things like his cues or his blocking or his lines or hitting his mark or which direction the audience is facing."

Susan caught Miranda staring at the receipt book and instinctively laid her hand over it. They exchanged looks.

"Who paid for my membership, Susan?"

Susan hesitated. "I– I can't tell you that. I'm sorry. Receipts are private. I wish I could, but I can't."

"But you could tell me who *didn't* pay for it, right?"

"I suppose so."

"Was it Edgar?"

Quietly, she said, "No. It wasn't Edgar." But then quickly added, "That doesn't mean he doesn't care about you, though."

"Susan, does he really talk about me all the time? Did he really say he misses me?"

On this, she did not waver. "He does. He truly does."

"Yes, but Bea Maracle said . . ." Miranda's voice trailed off. What was Bea up to? she wondered. "Do you think Bea's trying to drive Edgar and I apart?"

"Honestly?" said Susan. "I have no idea why on earth Bea is saying that. Maybe you should just ask her."

"I did and she stubbornly insisted that Edgar has no interest in me."

Susan gathered up the remaining scripts, gave Miranda a sympathetic nod. "I'll take you through to the stage. The rest of the cast will be arriving soon."

Miranda followed Susan through the backstage maze, past three dressing rooms, one for male actors, one for female, and a third just for the star. Annette's name was already posted on the door. One of the many perks of playing the lead.

Past pulleys and ropes and various backdrops suspended above them, they came out onto the stage itself. The curtain was up and there were indeed spectators in the seats, waiting for the opening rehearsal to begin.

A semicircle of folding chairs once again faced the audience. A table, set off to one side, was lined with plastic water bottles and a fanned arrangement of ballpoint pens.

"Donated by TB Foods," said Susan proudly. She was clearly the one who had swung the deal.

And sure enough, *Enjoy TB in Happy Rock!* was printed on each and every pen and water bottle.

Ah. Corporate sponsorship, thought Miranda.

"As long as you haven't sold out," she said.

But Susan missed the joke.

"Oh my, no. We would never do that. We have complete creative independence from TB Foods. We do thank them in the program, though. Do you think that's wrong?" She looked worried.

No wonder Annette had her own bedazzled water bottle. Miranda reassured Susan that, no, the branding wasn't a problem, and that the integrity of the Happy Rock Amalgamated & Consolidated Little Theater Society remained intact.

Susan stacked the scripts carefully on the table next to the water bottles and disappeared, as was her habit, into the wings.

Burt was onstage with his back to the audience, tool belt hanging low as he directed Rodney with the scaffolding. "Right... *right* ... stage right... the other stage right."

Ned Buckley and Tanvir Singh lugged a stack of painted beams onto the stage. They dropped them with a thump. Like Burt, they were wearing tool belts, though Ned's looked decidedly newer.

Tanvir was sporting a jaunty orange turban today, his beard flowing and his eyes shining.

"Love it!" he said.

He may have been a business owner by day, but banging about with plank and hammer seemed to be his true passion.

Ned's, too.

Meanwhile, in the audience, the entire front row—all older men—were on the edge of their seats watching as Burt Linder reached for his tool belt. He casually laid his hand on a socket wrench, not unlike a gunslinger, and the front row leaned forward in anticipation... But at the last moment, he chose a No. 7 Petersen vise-grip instead—bold choice!—to a murmur of *ooh*s from the stands.

Burt then ambled over to the scaffolding and slowly, deliberately, tightened exactly one flange nut, once, and came back. He stood, arms crossed, surveyed his work, nodded. It was all the front row could do not to burst into applause.

Meanwhile, Tanvir and Ned were ferrying heavy plyboard flats onto the stage, stacking them behind the semicircle of waiting chairs.

"You're building the set?" Miranda asked Burt. "Today?"

"Nope," said Burt.

Ah. Good. The actors' first read-through would be starting soon. You wouldn't want the crew slamming material around onstage at the same time.

"Not building it," Burt clarified. "Assembling. Once I realized it was pretty much the same every time, I just took apart the old one and stored it till next season. We put it back up every year."

Ned, meanwhile, had stopped to catch his breath. He slapped the tool belt that was cinched around his belly.

"What do you think of my belt?" he said to Burt. "Check it out. Brand new. Pretty nifty, huh?"

Burt looked it over. "Not bad. It'll do."

Ned whispered to Miranda, immensely pleased, "You hear that? *Not bad.*"

"It'll be good to start hammering stuff again," Tanvir said, then turned to Burt. "Though I imagine you'll be using a No. 16 stainless steel flathead wood screw with those metal brackets?"

"Yup. Same as last year," said Burt.

"My dad was a carpenter," Tanvir explained. "Old school. He could plum a level with one eye and a frayed piece of string. I'm from Portland, and my mom is from Seattle, but my dad was from Peshawar."

"Khyber Pass," said Burt.

"That's right. Have you been?"

Burt gave a noncommittal shrug. But Ned grinned at Miranda with a "See? He's a spy, what did I tell you?" look.

So he knows where the Khyber Pass is, thought Miranda. Big deal. She remembered something Susan had mentioned about Burt. *He comes into the store now and then, reads a lot of le Carré.*

Those aren't really mysteries. We shouldn't stock them, but Edgar is so kind-hearted he added a small ESPIONAGE *section in one corner just for Burt. He reads through them obsessively.*

Like he was studying for a role, thought Miranda.

Ned and Tanvir went for more sections of the set.

"So, Burt," she said. "Travel a lot, do you?"

"Was up at Jolly Pebble last March. Was jigging for herring. Pacific herring. Me and Doc and Owen McCune. We took Doc's boat up. Salmon weren't running, was too early for that, but a good haul nonetheless."

"I meant perhaps a little farther afield. Like, say, Portland?"

"Never been."

"It's only an hour and a half away. You've never been?"

"Never had call to."

"You're not even a little bit curious?"

"City folk, putting on airs. Didn't see the point."

The Spy Who Never Left Happy Rock. Not exactly le Carré.

Meanwhile, on the other side of the stage, Tanvir's wife, Harpreet, with a mouth full of pins, was taking in the costume for Strongman Seth: leotard with a faux-leopard print and padded foam muscles.

They had apparently found the skinniest kid in high school to play the part. Miranda figured they wouldn't need a prop for the jar in the big climactic scene, could just hand him a regular jam jar to open and then watch him struggle.

"Don't squirm," Harpreet said, scolding him through the pins. "You'll get poked."

Sure enough, "Ow!"

Harpreet had brought in a tray of homemade jalebi sweets for the crew, crispy spirals soaked in sticky goodness, which Melvin had all but inhaled, leaving very few for anyone else. (Skinny though he was, the kid had a gargantuan appetite.) This may have been why

Harpreet kept "accidentally" poking him. The fact that she was humming the song "Jalebi Bai" as she worked only reinforced this theory.

With a sigh, Miranda went over to meet her love interest. This was Strongman Seth? A walleyed stick insect with acne? As the maid, Miranda was supposed to throw "flirtatious looks" the strongman's way, thus motivating him to his showdown with the Jam Jar of Doom. Those flirtatious looks were going to require all of her acting prowess.

Given that Harpreet was having to make major alterations to the strongman costume, pulling it in drastically on the chest and shoulders, Miranda deduced that this was either the kid's first year in the role or he had gone on a crash diet worthy of Atkins.

The former supposition was correct.

"The previous Seth?" said Melvin of the foam muscles. "You mean Seth."

"The one who *played* Seth," said Miranda.

"Hold still," said Harpreet.

"That *was* Seth. That was his name. The part was written for him, that's why it's Strongman Seth. He played it from the very first. I asked if they could make it Strongman Melvin now that I'm wearing the suit, but they said they preferred the alliteration, so I said, why not Muscleman Melvin, and they said Melvin isn't a manly enough name, and I said, well, what about Seth, how is that manly, and they said the original Seth was plenty manly. Ow! Anyway. He retired. He's living in a seniors home in Gladstone. He's, like, eighty-four now. They tried to talk him into staying, said they'd send a handi-bus to get him, but he said he didn't want to keep lifting the papier-mâché dumbbells with a 'Tally-ho!' anymore. Though I gotta say, his Tally-hos were really good. Always got a round of applause. But ol' Seth, he said he was tired of striking poses and pretending to struggle with a jar."

Harpreet tugged one of the biceps closer to the kid's broomstick arms. Marked it with chalk.

The wives of the first row were watching this unfold as intently as their husbands had watched Burt. "What do you think she's going to go with? A cross-stich?" "At least! Won't hold otherwise."

"I don't mean to be boastful or anything," said Melvin, as Harpreet hummed and poked, hummed and poked. Melvin's caveat aside, he was clearly trying to impress Miranda. "But I *am* Junior Vice President of the Happy Rock High School Drama Club. Judy says I represent 'the next generation of thespian.'" There was an awkward pause. "That means actor," he said.

"Yes, I know."

"Plus, no one else signed up. So good thing I got the part! Judy checked with Doug Dirks first. I mean, she checked with *Mr. Abbott.*" Melvin whispered, "Doug Dirks is his pseudo name."

And where was Edgar?

Melvin gestured to the back of the auditorium. Last row. In the darkness. The red of the exit sign gave Edgar a distinctly fiery tone. A backlit silhouette. He was staring at her, she was sure of it. Could practically see his eyes burning from down here. So much for spending carefree nights in rehearsal beside her husband. She had insulted his writing, and writers always take that sort of thing so personally. She'd called his script a travesty of an abomination, but she had also said it was funny. And it was–albeit not intentionally so. But did he focus on the positives in what she said? He did not. Typical Edgar.

Just then Rodney shuffled past, struggling with a heavy Fresnel lantern. He mumbled a greeting to Melvin.

"Hey, Rodney," said Melvin. "How's it going?"

"Good, good." Then, with a sulky look thrown Miranda's way, "Gotta go."

"We go to school together," said Melvin of the Muscles, as Harpreet started in on the other foam bicep. "Rodney's in the drama club, too. Never in the cast, always in the crew. Helps out with every production, every year. Teena did, as well, before she graduated. Mr. Penty–I mean, *Graham*–always gave her a lead role. Teena was a year ahead of me in high school."

"And Rodney?"

Melvin chose his words carefully, trying not to be cruel. "Rodney's a coupla years older than me, actually. He's in his third year. Of twelfth grade. He's had it rough."

"Bullied?"

"Worse. Ignored."

"Done!" said Harpreet, standing up with a creak of the knees. "Take it off very carefully, young man, so you don't–"

"Ouch!"

"See? What did I tell you?"

As Melvin gingerly removed the rest of his muscles, a whiff of teen odor washed over Miranda. More than the usual hormonal funk, it had a hint of... was that horse manure? This was the person that her character was supposed to be madly in love with?

Harpreet turned her attention to Miranda, eyeing her up and down slowly. She was clearly measuring Miranda's size and shape for the maid costume compared to that of the beloved Holly Hinton.

"I will have to let the hips out," Harpreet said.

Ouch.

"And the bust."

Heh heh.

"But you will make a beautiful maid," Harpreet assured her. "You've been practicing your death scene? Because Officer Holly was very good. Very, *very* good."

The way she said it, it sounded more like a threat than encouragement.

CHAPTER FOURTEEN

Broken Glass and Near Misses

Miranda had already added Harpreet and her husband to her playbill cheat sheet:

Tanvir Singh – *hardware & bait store – helps Burt and Ned with the sets*
Harpreet Singh – *Tanvir's wife – handles wardrobe and costumes – owns a fabric store*

To Harpreet's entry she added: *BIG fan of Holly's death scene, apparently.*

She wasn't done with Team Miranda, not yet. Who knew what curveballs the next few weeks would throw her way? She now added Strongman Seth to the list:

Melvin – *in HS with Teena and Rodney – one of Graham's drama students – possible ally? – a bit malodorous*

She didn't know then that what she was really compiling was a list of potential suspects. Murder was the farthest thing from Miranda's mind. The tech work had begun on the play, and that was all-consuming. But murder would come knocking anyway.

Graham's wife, Denise Penty, stayed in the sound booth, watching from behind tinted glass, cueing the sound effects: the creaky winds and *dah-dah-DAH* zings that inevitably accompany the discovery of a corpse in plays like this. She would also be responsible for the lighting cues, which surprised Miranda.

"You're not handling those?" she asked Burt.

"Nope. I set 'em up and I take 'em down. After that, it's see you next year."

"You aren't going to watch the play itself?"

"That depends. Same murderer as last time?"

"Well, yes."

"And same as the time before that, right? And for the last ten years?" A shrug. "Why would I attend? It's a whodunit, and I already know whodunit. It's Graham." He looked out at the audience that had formed for tonight's opening rehearsal. "There's folks come every year and still gasp when it's revealed. Never understood that."

Fair enough, thought Miranda. After ten years, you'd think they would have worked it out.

The rest of the cast was slowly making their way onstage: Graham (Lord Reginald Buckingham the Third) was in his usual cardigan and khakis, Owen (the bewhiskered Lord Wussex) was in cargo shorts and an untucked T, with Doc (Doc) in faded jeans, looking handsome as always.

An older fellow with a prosthetic limb appeared, surpassingly agile but grumpy of face. He picked up his complimentary pen and water bottle and grumbled about the lack of cookies.

"Usually there's cookies," he complained.

Susan, who was onstage making sure everyone got a script, overheard this and apologized. "The budget is tight this year."

"Call me Pete," he told Miranda. "As in, Peg-Leg Pete."

She couldn't tell if he was joking. He would be playing the groundskeeper, and she never once saw him smile, which was just as well because the groundskeeper was a cantankerous character. She wondered if Edgar hadn't written that part specifically for the actor.

Melvin as the strongman. Creepy Carl as the butler. Annette as Mamie Dickens. So that was every role accounted for except that of the Great Oracle Olivia.

Their fireplug director, Judy, burst onto the stage. "Hello, my fellow actors!"

Fellow?

Miranda turned to Doc. "Tell me she isn't..."

"Yup. She's gonna play the oracle this year."

"She cast *herself* in the play?"

"Only as the oracle. Couldn't pass up the chance to act alongside her idol, I guess."

For a moment, Miranda thought he might be referring to her. But no. He was referring to Annette Baillie.

And now a fresh round of applause rippled through the auditorium. Enter Annette.

"Why, hello, everyone!" She was addressing not the cast, but the audience. That tractor beam smile. Annette Baillie! Star of dinner theater and bus-stop benches across the Greater Tri-Rock Area. She curtsied, center stage, and then turned with a swirl of her lemon chiffon skirt to face the other actors.

The tone of what was to come was set almost immediately. As Annette moved catlike across the stage, Rodney, hauling a heavy light kit, got tangled up in her path and she snapped at him, under her breath but loud enough for everyone onstage to catch it, "Out of my way, you fat lump!"

She sat down with a swing of her legs and a flash of toned calf, to a cold stare from Graham.

"Annette, I won't have you talking to my students that way."

"Oh yes, we know all about you and your students, don't we, Graham?" Eyes of ice. "*Under the Yum Yum Tree*, is it?"

Burt was hammering up one of the flats. Heavy hardwood sheets with actual doors and actual windows in actual oak frames. Not a stage window. A window. Heavy-glazed, with segmented panes and a decorative valance grid above–exactly like the ones in the bookstore.

Miranda was agog at how sturdy the set was. No flimsy canvas with lightweight pine crossbeams behind it. No "walls" that shook when an actor slammed the door too hard–something you saw even on Broadway. No, this could have stood for generations. They weren't merely "putting up" a set; this was full-on carpentry.

Ned and Tanvir were helping Burt Linder out, and none of them stopped banging about even when Judy announced, "My fellow actors! Shall we take our seats?" Then, to the audience, "Ladies and gentlemen! The first read-through of the tenth anniversary production of *Death Is the Dickens* is about to begin!"

A voice behind Miranda whispered, "I know who you are."

She turned, startled to find herself facing Officer Carl. Creepier out of uniform somehow.

"You're Pastor Fran," he said.

Congratulations. You figured it out. Well done. Everyone knows who I am, at this point. They just don't care. I've been outshone by a real celebrity. A *local* celebrity–the worst kind. Ms. Annette Herself.

That's what she wanted to say. What she actually said was "Charmed."

"Abbott," Carl said with a sly look. "Miranda Abbott, that's you."

And in that moment, she was sure that he was the one who had gone through her valise. Fondling her undergarments? Searching for souvenirs? She shuddered, tried to move away, but he kept close to her.

"Abbott, with *two* t's. Right?" He gave her a small flutter of a smile. "If you know what I mean."

She didn't.

Instead, she sat as far away from him as possible for the read-through. She could feel his stare burning into her but refused to look over.

The trouble started almost immediately. With Graham's first section of dialogue, in fact. "Why, it's Miss Mamie Dickens, or my name's not Lord Reginald Buckingham the Third! What brings you to the Greater Tri-Rock Area at such a time as this, with the Sherman Anti-Trust Act having just been signed and Mr. Harrison in the White House for his first and only term as President?"

"Graham, darling," said Annette, cutting in, not even letting him finish. "Here, let me show you. Hit the line like this." And she read it emphasizing an entirely different set of words.

Teeth clenched, Graham said, "My dear Annette, are you giving me a line reading?"

"Heavens, no. I wouldn't dream of such a thing. I'm just showing you how you should deliver it, beat by beat, and with what inflection, that's all. If you read your lines as I did, I will be able to do what I need to do to fulfill *my* part. That's all I'm asking."

Graham turned to Judy. "I'm not taking a line reading from another actor. Are you directing this, or is she?"

But as would soon become apparent, in any clash, Judy would

be taking Annette's side. "Try it that way, Graham. She has a point."

On it went, with tension sizzling and Burt and his crew hammering and sawing and hollering the entire way. By the time the first read-through was done, Miranda was exhausted. And this was just Day One.

As the audience filed out, she thought, Those aren't spectators. Those are witnesses. Witnesses to Crimes Against Theater.

Denise had come down from her sound-booth perch, was gathering up her stuff, and Miranda asked her, "Is it always so tense?"

"No," she said. "It's usually much more fun. The problem is obvious, isn't it? It's Annette. Everything she touches turns toxic. Just ask my husband."

Doc Meadows was in high spirits, though. As were Burt and the building crew.

Their director–and now fellow actor–Judy called out to them as they left. "Tomorrow, same time, same place!"

And that was when the awful truth was revealed.

Rehearsals were set for every night of the week, three hours, with two rehearsals back-to-back on Saturday.

"But not on Sunday," said Ned, seeing Miranda's look of alarm. "That's the Lord's day, so no worries."

"Plus football!" said Owen. "The Eugene Gladiators vs. the Gladstone Eugonians."

Ned shot him a glance. "But mainly church and stuff."

"Oh. Right," said Owen.

And Miranda thought: They do know I'm not a real pastor, yes?

"Two rehearsals on Saturday? Two?"

"The full dress rehearsal is coming up, and we still have a lot to get through. But lunch is provided on Saturday," said Ned helpfully. "Word is, Myrtle snagged us a full barrel of pea soup, enough for the entire run. Or was it Mabel?"

Owen gave a wink and a nod. "Cafeteria connections, you see. It's all who you know."

"At least they do feed us," said Doc. "When I was with the Peninsula Players, it was always potluck."

Miranda wasn't sure she'd heard correctly. "They made you bring your own food? To rehearsals?"

"Yup. Not after we merged companies, though." And then, with a tinge of bitterness unusual for him, he added, "Not having to bring our own food was just about the only good thing to come out of the amalgamation."

"And consolidation," Ned reminded him.

"If you want to know the truth," said Owen of the Magnificent Whiskers. "I kinda liked the potlucks."

"That's because I always brought salmon," said Doc. "Some other people only ever brought pasta." He was looking at Owen pointedly.

With a hurt expression, Owen said, "I thought you liked my Spaghetti McCune."

"That's spaghetti with hot dogs cut into it," Doc explained to Miranda.

And so it was that the evening wound down, enlivened only by the fact that Miranda was nearly killed.

Near the end of the night, Miranda was standing center stage, unawares, not realizing how close she was to death, looking out across the empty seats to see if Edgar was still there. But Edgar had slipped away, was nowhere to be seen. Miranda heard someone whistling backstage–bad luck, that!–and she turned to shush the person, only to see Burt sprinting toward her, full tilt, fire in his eyes.

He tackled her, turning to stop her from hitting the floor as they fell, taking the weight of it himself, then rolling over to protect her as a light crashed onto the stage, just feet away from them. Precisely where Miranda had been standing.

The night had ended not with a whimper, but a crash-bang rush of adrenaline.

Burt pulled Miranda up, dusted her off, and in that moment, she had a blurred view of something on his arm . . . a symbol of some sort . . .

"Watch out, there's glass," he said, and then, so angry he was almost calm, he yelled to his crew, "The safety chain! When you hang a light, you put a safety chain on *immediately*. You don't wait. And you do not allow anyone–*anyone*, you understand?–to walk under an unsecure light. If we don't do our job, someone will get killed."

An accident, but still . . . Miranda was unnerved. Her heart was pounding, and the only comfort was in the thought that it was just that: an accident. It had to have been an accident.

Still shaken, she tried to laugh it off. "Who could possibly have wanted me out of the way?" she said. "I'm only the maid. I have exactly one line–and then I die."

Annette was watching from the wings.

And then I die. Miranda had no way of knowing that someone else was taking that quite literally.

CHAPTER FIFTEEN

A Whistle in the Dark

Six days to the murder…

Rehearsals for *Death Is the Dickens* had ground on, hour after endless hour, with the Saturday in particular stretching out like a gaping abyss: pea soup and more pea soup, Annette versus Graham, Carl lurking in the background, Rodney getting in the way—and Owen McCune merrily tripping over the most basic of lines.

He had a touch of Mrs. Malaprop about him, often rendering his dialogue in a more mechanic-friendly phraseology, as in "Well, I'll be, Lord Reginald! You could have knocked me over with a fender!"

Thoroughly annoyed by this, Annette Baillie had made a point of taking jabs at Owen, as well. "Apparently there was no IQ test for the role," she said. (Owen had just rendered "I suspect they are collaborators" as "carburetors.")

"Give it a rest, will ya?" said Owen. "It's just a play. Jeez."

To which she fired back, "Kill anyone lately?"

Owen, wild with rage, started to come at her, and Doc was forced to intercede, taking his friend to a neutral corner so he could calm down.

"What is wrong with her?" Owen demanded, almost hyperventilating.

"My medical diagnosis? Acute cardiovascular agenesis." He grinned at Owen. "Lack of a heart."

"*Kill anyone?*" Owen glared across the stage in Annette's direction with a distinct "If I ever did, I would start with you" look.

Miranda knew that look. Knew it well. She had seen it in the eyes of several of her co-stars when they stared at her, back when the stardom had gone to her head, with her showing up late on set and stepping on everyone's lines and refusing to come out of her trailer. It was a Miranda she hardly recognized now, one that filled her with regret. Perhaps Edgar was being generous when he only said *prima donna tendencies.* There were other words he could have used. That's the problem with epiphanies, she thought. They always come too late.

Melvin sauntered past, whistling a jolly tune.

"Melvin, darling. That's bad luck," she explained for the hundredth time, her smile set in a rictus grin, trying not to be the prima donna that Edgar knew her to be. "Darling, sweetie, one mustn't whistle backstage. Brings an ill wind."

Then, recalling Burt's onstage tackle, the falling light, the crash of metal, the splintering glass, she said, "Were you whistling the day the spotlight fell? Was that you I heard?"

"Um. Maybe?" Who remembers when they were whistling or why?

Not that Miranda believed in such things. A whistle could hardly take down a light, but still. There were traditions involved, things one simply didn't do. Like build a set around the actors while they were onstage.

Burt's crew worked right through the rehearsals with much winching and torquing and mulling things over. Fortunately for the cast, the hammering had stopped of late. Unfortunately, it had been replaced by the dulcet sound of power drills, which were somehow worse.

As for Graham and Annette, things were rapidly going from bad to worse. Annette was now actively changing his lines–with Judy's approval, of course.

"Graham seems to have trouble with his sibilance," she said sweetly. "Perhaps, instead of saying 'Summer seems to surround us in its silence,' he could say 'Goody, I like summer!'"

"Unbelievable." Graham looked to the back of the theater. "Edgar? Really?"

But the silhouette in the last row said nothing.

Annette Baillie leaned in to Graham and said, under her breath, "Looking to Edgar for help? I wouldn't bother. He won't say a thing. He can't. I have him wrapped around my little finger. Just as I have you around the same."

"I think you've got the wrong finger."

"*Yum Yum Tree* going well?"

He bared his teeth. "Always."

Miranda was amazed. Was Judy Traynor really going to allow Annette to rewrite Edgar's play? And was Edgar really not going to say anything about it?

She thought again of that pink Cadillac parked outside Edgar's bookstore, the footfalls Miranda had heard upstairs, Annette's loosely coiled hair, her panther's gait...

"Thick as thieves, the two of them," Doc said, and for a moment, Miranda wasn't sure who he was referring to. "Judy and Annette. Best of buds. Judy even waves her through at the DMV up in Garibaldi. Lets Annette cut to the front of the line every time. I've seen it happen."

Judy works at the DMV? If there wasn't enough reason to hate her.

As dysfunctional as the cast was rapidly becoming, the team of

Burt, Tanvir, and Ned was going great guns. Almost literally. At one point, Ned wielded a nail gun to great enthusiasm, if less effect.

"Good job, except there's no stud there," Burt pointed out after Ned tried to nail-gun one of the paintings to a set wall.

The set itself looked exactly like the inside of Edgar's bookstore, the original murders having taken place there. It was uncanny. Burt had re-created the main room of the store, inch by inch–without the books, of course; it had been a private home, not a bookstore back then–right down to the large wooden desk with the rolltop and the Victorian-era wallpaper behind.

"But wouldn't the wallpaper have changed in the ensuing, oh, hundred years or so?" Miranda asked.

"Yup," said Burt. "But when Edgar took over the store, he went through historical photos from the town archives and matched it. So it's pretty much how it was at the time of the murders."

It certainly gave a bookstore a certain *frisson* of danger, Miranda thought. Especially one specializing in bloodshed and mystery.

More mysteries: Later that evening, a concerned-looking man in a rumpled jacket appeared. He was searching for Teena, and he found her in a corner backstage, deep in conversation with Graham Penty. When he came upon the two of them speaking in hushed tones together, the concern in the man's eyes turned to anger.

"What is this?" he demanded.

Startled, Teena looked up. "Oh, um, hi Dad."

"Christina, get in the car." He glared at Graham, who returned his gaze. And as Teena collected her belongings, her dad, still glaring at Graham, said, with a terse nod of the head, "Mr. Penty."

Graham stared back at him, said nothing.

CHAPTER SIXTEEN

The Maid Dies

Three days to the murder…

There were Broadway plays that opened more quickly than it took the Happy Rock troupe to get to an actual run-through of the play. As the rehearsals dragged on, tensions had only increased. When Lord Reginald the Third (aka Graham) had gone in for his staged kiss with Mamie Dickens (aka Annette), his co-star had stopped him abruptly with a hand to his chest.

"Let's save that for opening night, shall we?" she said.

Later, however, when Graham was required to wrest the poison out of Annette's hand in Act Five, they both applied themselves with great energy and had to be physically separated by Judy to avoid any lasting injury to–or by–either party.

Eyes raging, Annette had growled at Graham, "You think you can wrestle a concession out of me? I'm still a school trustee. And you are never getting out from under the yum yum tree. You will be producing that play forever and ever and ever."

The character Miranda was playing died at the end of Act One. It was a dramatic moment. As Reginald and the others celebrate the arrival of Mamie Dickens, the butler (Carl) pours champagne (unsweetened apple juice) from a crystal magnum (plastic jug). Maid Miranda then sneaks one of the champagne glasses (tumblers) from the tray. This is to bolster her courage in the alluring presence of her lover (skinny teen with a particularly ripe pimple on the end of his Ichabod nose). The maid kicks back the apple juice champagne–and then dies, to the shock and horror, though hardly the surprise, of the audience. Many would have come solely for that moment.

As soon as this scene ends, the lights go down, Act One is over, and Rodney scurries across the darkened stage to gather up the glasses and the pitcher. Teena–who wanted to play the maid, but was now on crew–just as quickly runs in behind Rodney to replace the glasses with a plump roast pheasant (a plastic turkey that had seen better days) and a tray of ice cream sundaes (instant mashed potatoes with coagulated molasses) for the luxurious dinner party at the top of Act Two.

Poor Rodney.

During the first run-through, while hurrying to clear the glasses and the jug, he again got tangled up in Annette Almighty's path.

"You oaf!" she yelled. "If you had an ounce of sense, you would wait until after I exit before you come bumbling in."

A rehearsal didn't go by where Annette didn't snap or hector or humiliate Rodney, and Graham didn't bristle at her treatment of said student. This wasn't a play, Miranda realized; this was a Cold War.

"Places, everyone!" shouted Judy. "Once more. No stopping. Susan?"

"Ready!"

Even holding an open script in front of him, Owen often lost where they were on the page, so Susan had to stand by, ready to prompt him from the wings.

It wasn't just Owen. Most of the actors carried their color-coded scripts during the run-through. Miranda didn't bother, though. She hadn't consulted it even during the initial read-through.

"And where is your script?" Judy demanded.

"I have it right here," said Miranda with a tap to her temple.

"Even your cues?"

Miranda sighed. "Even my cues."

"Wow," said Owen. "Somebody's off book early."

Once again Mamie Dickens arrives in Happy Rock and once again Lord Reginald is delighted to see her and once again the butler pours the apple juice and once again Miranda gets the chipped glass. Every damn time. Was Officer Carl doing that intentionally, just to get her goat? Or was he such a creature of habit that, having given Miranda the chipped glass the first time, he had now locked that in?

"A toast! A toast to Miss Mamie Dickens!"

Finally! Miranda's moment was at hand. She stole a glance in Edgar's direction—his playwright silhouette watching as the scene unfolded—lifted the bitter chalice, and . . . she . . . acted.

A furtive look, as fleeting as it is daring, is thrown, unrequited, to her would-be paramour. A drink! A drink in lieu of courage. A sudden spasm, a slight waver, her voice whispery and raw. "Alas, I have been poisoned," she says, followed by a low, almost subliminal moan. A look of fear, then an awareness of her own mortality, the slow realization of what's to come, the dignified exit, her left knee buckling ever so slightly as she leaves to face the darkness. Alone.

The audience was clearly too overwhelmed to clap, and she exited to a stunned silence. Of approval, she was sure. No slapstick arm-waving antics here!

As director, Judy Traynor had Miranda exit stage left. Stage right was crowded. Ned was there, keeping an eye on the scaffolding, Teena was watching the actors, and next to her was Susan, her prompt book open, tracking Owen's every misspoken line, while Rodney went in and out throughout. It was like Grand Central over there. Not over in this wing, though. Not out here on stage left. Miranda would die without witnesses.

She could now hear the rest of the scene play out, after her character departs from both the play and life itself (below, with Miranda's asides):

EARL OF WUSSEX

This champagne is to die for!

(Not one for subtlety, our Doug Dirks.)

LORD REGINALD THE THIRD

I fear she may have been poisoned.

(What was your first clue? The fact that I just said, "I have been poisoned"?)

THE GOOD DOCTOR

Poisoned? Why, that's absurd! It's the vapors and nothing more, women being of a more fragile constitution.

(Wow. Shitty doctor.)

LORD REGINALD THE THIRD

Nonetheless, I must take my leave to check on her. Good help is so hard to find.

(At least you got your priorities right, huh, Reggie? I die on you,

you'll have to go through that whole "interviewing for a new maid" rigmarole. Tragic.)

At which point, Graham Penty ran out, offstage, and quickly whispered to Miranda, "That was fantastic. Loved what you did with your death scene."

He then bolted back onstage, yelling, "She's dead! She is! She's really dead! Or my name's not Reginald Buckingham the Third!"

End of Act One.

One down, six to go.

As soon as the lights went out—and after Annette Baillie had safely left the stage—Rodney sprinted across to gather up the glasses and jug, with Teena and the dinner settings close behind.

Miranda was now done. She'd died and the play would roll on without her.

She meandered about backstage for a bit, keeping an eye on the lights overhead. She wondered about Teena, who always stayed late at the theater, well after everyone else had gone home. Graham often stayed late, as well.

She passed Annette's dressing room door, next to props. A tattoo, Miranda realized, seeing the star on the door and remembering Burt and the falling light. That's what she'd seen on his forearm. A naval tattoo of some sort. A nautical star.

Tattoos. Teena's dad keeping a close watch on our Mr. Penty. Rehearsals that went on too long. A husband who sat in the shadows. Miranda's thoughts were full of bits and pieces, none of which seemed to fit together. She was aware, vaguely, that there were dark currents running beneath the surface of the Happy Rock Little Theater, but she couldn't see how they interconnected.

Bored, she made her way back to the wings in time to watch the climactic end of Act Seven, could hear cheers from the audience.

Fewer people than before, but still an audience.

The actors took their bows, and when Miranda walked out onstage, she was greeted by a deafening silence. Not a single half-hearted clap from the audience, let alone cheers or roses thrown. The other actors exchanged looks as Judy stepped forward, cleared her throat.

"Miranda. Can we talk about the *choices* you made in *your* reinterpretation of the *role* of the maid."

From long experience, Miranda knew that when a director starts talking in italics, it doesn't bode well.

"Sure. What about my choices would you like to discuss?"

"The lamp, for example," said Judy, referring to a standing lamp next to the butler's table.

"What about the lamp?"

"You didn't knock it over. Holly always knocked over the lamp during her death throes. It was a real crowd-pleaser. Sometimes people chanted 'The lamp! The lamp!' to encourage her."

"Um, I guess I could tip it over."

"Not tip, darling. *Fling*. You are dying! You must *gesticulate* so the audience understands what is happening."

"Saying 'Alas, I have been poisoned! *Gawwck!*' is not enough?"

"This is theater. Not television. One must emote."

Hackles rising, Miranda was on the brink of lashing out when Annette intervened.

"Judy, I think it's fine. It's a different interpretation, that's all. There's nothing wrong with that." But just when Miranda was about to say thank you, Annette added, "It's really not worth spending any time or energy on. It's an insignificant moment with an insignificant character. It simply doesn't matter."

"Excellent point," said Judy. Then, to the cast as a whole: "That's a wrap for tonight. We still have our work to do on Act One! It should come in at one hour fourteen minutes. Not one hour *sixteen* minutes, not one hour *ten* minutes. One hour fourteen. No more and no less. So, Miranda, dear, darling, please... try to stay on track, hmm?"

Miranda looked around for a salad fork to stab Judy in the eye with, then stopped herself. TMZ would love that! *TV's Pastor Fran throws hissy fit at local venue.*

As the cast drifted out, Rodney appeared onstage, dragging a different standing lamp with a single exposed bulb, trailing an extension cord.

"Ghost light," he said.

No theater is ever left entirely in the dark. With an open orchestra pit and the sudden dangerous drop of the stage itself, a single light bulb, often low-wattage and just bright enough to illuminate these possible perils, is set up at the end of every day. Miranda knew full well how the effect of that single pale glow inside an empty theater could be both eerie and wistful at the same time.

As Rodney did his final sweep of the stage and the props table, Miranda wandered around backstage again, where the lights were low but still on, feeling not unlike a ghost herself. She was about to call Chief Buckley for a ride when she heard something. A voice in a back stairwell.

Ghosts on the prowl?

With visions of apparitions in mind, Miranda followed the sound to the top of the stairwell. And when she peeked around the corner, she saw Teena at the bottom of the stairs. Being embraced by Graham.

Miranda stopped. Cold.

Teena was an adult. Was no longer his student. But still. Time for a ball kicking!

Miranda clattered down the stairs as loudly as possible, anger in every step. When Teena looked up, she was crying. In tears, she hurried up the stairs past Miranda, with Graham following, head down, squeezing past Miranda as he went.

Miranda turned, saw a large, ill-defined shadow at the top of the stairs.

"Rodney?"

She came up the stairwell and asked, "Do you know why Teena was crying?"

He stared at her sullenly. "I don't know, but I can guess." Then, all but sneering, he said, "Can't you?"

"I have no idea."

"Maybe because you took her part? She practiced and practiced dying. I helped her, every night. And she was good! She was real good. Then you showed up, and you took the part away from her—and you didn't even audition for it! Just like Annette. She got the lead without reading for it. You're no better than she is. Teena and me, we were in school together. We always had each other's back. We always watched out for each other, protected each other. And you've ruined everything for her."

It set Miranda back on her heels. My god. He's right.

She hurried to catch Teena before the girl left.

"I know why you were crying."

Tear-streaked, Teena turned. "You do?"

"Yes, and I want to help. I am so sorry."

Memories of the Orpheum Theater in Minnesota. The ache and longing just to be cast, just to be included, just to play a part in it, however small . . .

"You can have the role, Teena. You can play the maid. I want you to."

"But Judy—"

"Judy can suck eggs. You can have your death scene, Teena. You can be onstage for the ovation, can take a bow with the rest of the cast."

But Teena refused. And not in a polite "I really want to but I have to at least pretend to say no" sort of way. She was adamant.

"It wouldn't be right. I wasn't cast. I didn't earn it," she said. "You did. Thank you. That's really kind, but I can't. Mr. Penty–I mean Graham–he says that an actor has to 'respect the process.' Graham says you have to trust your director. Graham says that no actor is greater than the sum of the cast. Graham says it is only the play that counts."

"He says a lot of things, doesn't he?"

"He sure does!" said Teena, missing the edge in Miranda's voice. "I don't know what I'd do without him."

"Teena, take the part. Be the maid."

"I can't. I won't."

"Well, at least be . . ." Inspiration! "My understudy."

"Your understudy?"

For one line. Why not?

"Yes!" said Miranda. "You can be my understudy. I want you to."

The sadness in Teena receded. A smile returned. "You would do that for me?"

"Absolutely."

"But why would you need an understudy? Wait. Are you just feeling sorry for me?"

"Not in the least!" And then, remembering what Bea had said, Miranda smiled. "If anything happens to Annette, I would take over as the lead. I would step into her part. And who would be the maid? We need an understudy."

These were words that would come back to haunt Miranda Abbott. *If anything happens to Annette…*

Because before opening night arrived, Annette Baillie, Pride of Happy Rock, scourge of school boards, realtor nonpareil, star of local stage, and former cohost of the KGW morning show, would be dead.

CHAPTER SEVENTEEN

Condemned to Love

Two days to the murder…

The play staggered on like a wounded water buffalo looking for a place to die. Usually a play's opening night rushes toward you. But not here. Not in Happy Rock. Time slowed down in these parts.

Day in and day out, and the exact same performance at the end of it! Miranda was amazed at so much effort exerted to so little effect. Onstage, the power drills had ceased, only to be replaced by the overpowering smell of paint, slapped on while the cast performed to a dwindling but die-hard audience. The paint had since dried. A second coat had been applied. It had dried. Then the sanding started… the power sanding.

Burt had decided to "vamp up" the set in honor of the tenth anniversary, and these "touch-ups" had taken longer than it would have to build an entirely new set from scratch. Would have been easier just to stage it in Edgar's bookstore, she figured, rather than re-create it onstage.

Meanwhile, back at Bea's B&B, with its peeling front porch and purportedly "English" garden, the housekeeping still hadn't improved. Miranda tried to help Bea along, considerately heaping her laundry in one large pile on the floor rather than spreading it around the room, but still. She had mentioned it to Bea over breakfast.

Bea evaded the issue, however, choosing to focus on the blue box. Again.

"It's right near the door, dear. It's where the recycling goes."

Ned cheerfully shoveled another pancake onto Miranda's plate. "Fresh off the griddle."

"These are gluten-free, correct?"

"Um. Sure." Ned had absolutely no idea what gluten was.

"I was thinking," said Miranda, delicately dabbing a wad of pancake into a puddle of organic syrup (or so Bea said). "After rehearsals tonight, why not treat ourselves to a good ol' Pastor Fran Friday! It's been ages."

Ned and Bea exchanged looks. "It's Tuesday."

"But Pastor Fran Friday can be any day of the week! That's the beauty of it. You said so yourself! Ned can bring the popcorn. I'll make a big jug of–"

"No!" It was Bea. "We can't because . . ." She looked to Ned for help.

"Because . . . ," he said. "Because . . ."

He threw it back to Bea.

"The VCR is broken!" she said.

"Yes!" said Ned, beaming. "It's broken. The, ah, flange. It needs a new flange."

A shrug from Miranda. "So ask Tanvir. He owns a hardware store."

"It's, ah, it's an *electronic* flange," said Ned. "Would need a whole new software update for it to work."

"VCRs have software? Who knew? That's a shame. I could use a break."

"Rehearsals not going well?" asked Bea with a kindly look.

"Let me put it this way. Hours and hours of work, and we are right where we started. Owen McCune is still not off book. And opening night is rapidly approaching." Under her breath, she added, "Though not rapidly enough."

"But Susan is," said Bea.

"Susan?"

"She's off book, so she can help. She keeps an eye on everything from the wings, sees what's happening, knows when to jump in. And she has Owen's lines memorized, so it'll be okay."

"That's just it," said Miranda, thoroughly exasperated by these conversations she kept having in this town where nothing made sense and everyone continued on blithely as though it did. "The *prompter* is off book, but the actor isn't. Do you see how ludicrous that is?"

"But that's why you have a prompter in the first place."

"I need a glass of wine. Forget it. Give me a whole box."

"It's morning," Bea reminded her.

"Exactly."

The one thing that cheered Miranda up during her walks along the harbor—after she learned to accept with a tolerant gracefulness that Ned couldn't ferry her over to rehearsals when "police business" got in the way—was when she passed Annette Baillie's realtor benches and saw that someone had drawn fangs on one with a marker. And under that, the words: *lies & damned lies.* The first time she saw it, Miranda walked by, chuckling to herself, then stopped. Came back. Looked again. She recognized that awkward ampersand, that long fluid *S.*

So Edgar was not quite as enamored with Ms. Baillie as it might have appeared. Trouble in paradise?

This buoyed Miranda's spirits, especially whenever she saw

Edgar in the distance, walking along the seawall with Emmy or throwing a stick on the shore for the flowing golden Lab to chase. Or when she saw him making his way up Beacon Hill. Or coming out from Tanvir's Hardwares & Bait Shop.

Happy Rock was small enough that it was impossible for her not to spot him constantly, but big enough for him to avoid her if he wanted to. Miranda would have preferred either a one-road village or downtown Manhattan to this. Let him deal with her face-to-face, or let him vanish from sight. But to have him always in her peripheral vison, yet not be able to approach? That only made it worse.

Once, when Chief Buckley was able to find the time to drive her along the harbor to the Opera House, Edgar had appeared unexpectedly from a residential street, looking sweaty and wild and smudged with dirt. Ned had slowed down and lowered his window. "All good?"

Face pink, Edgar had replied–tersely on seeing Miranda in the car with Ned–"All good."

At the Opera House, meanwhile, things had gone from sour to toxic, just as Denise had predicted. Even ensconced in her sound booth manning the cues, Denise was aware of what was going on. Her husband and Annette were daggers drawn, and their director, Judy, seemed unwilling–or unable–to intervene.

After one especially dramatic blowup, Annette had stormed off the stage, calling Graham a "deviant" and a "degenerate" as she left. She always had the most florid insults. Annette trafficked in hyperbole, as prima donnas often do.

And standing in the wings through all of this, who did Miranda see but Finkel Erdely, notepad in hand, watching everything with a cynical look on her face.

Graham spotted her, and he glared at Finkel, who lobbed it back just as decisively. Miranda knew that look. She'd been on the receiving end of Finkel's withering glower when she'd innocently mentioned the bus ride they'd shared when Miranda had first arrived– When was it? A lifetime ago? An eternity? An eternity plus one?

"She's a former student of mine," Graham grumbled. "Finkel Erdely loves to stir up scandals. That's kind of her thing. I wasn't surprised in the least that she went on to become a muckraking journalist."

Muckraking? *Journalist?*

"We are talking about *The Happy Rock Weekly Picayune*, correct?" said Miranda. "Bake sales and 4-H, yes?"

"Oh, there's muck aplenty for her to rake in this town," he assured her. "Even if she has to manufacture it herself."

How one would manufacture muck was, perhaps, best left for another day.

"But how'd she get backstage?" Miranda asked.

"Press pass," he said. "Full access." Then, as an aside, "I'd stay away from her if I were you. She writes things that aren't, shall I say, entirely true. Always on the lookout for dirt. Wants to land a big sensational story. There's one in the Saturday paper, is what I hear. An exposé of some sort."

"The Saturday paper?"

"That's right."

"*The Picayune* is a weekly, yes? Every paper is the Saturday paper."

"Exactly," he said. "And she's on the trail of something."

What was it Edgar had said about this young reporter? *She's a regular at my bookstore.* The Victorian building with the widow's walk and the transom windows had been the site of a triple homicide in the late 1800s. Morbid curiosity on Finkel's part, perhaps?

She sought out Susan in her office afterwards to ask.

"Miss Erdely?" said Susan. "What does she read? Mainly DIY. How-to books."

"How-to? I thought Edgar only sold murder mysteries."

"How to get away with murder. How to plan the perfect crime. That sort of thing. How to poison someone slowly, how to poison someone quickly, how to frame a patsy. You know. Nonfiction."

"Why would she need DIY books about murder? She's a reporter. At a local paper. In Happy Rock."

"One never knows!" said Ned, who had come into the theater office and heard the last of their conversation. "The keys?" he asked Susan.

"Doesn't Burt have them?"

"Nope. He's done. The set has been put up, the lighting has been rigged, and Burt said he'll see us all at the wrap party at the end of the run."

Miranda had refined her performance over the course of the rehearsals, adding a touch of sadness, a layer of pathos. But the other actors remained stubbornly, painfully, the same. Beat by beat. Line by line. The only one who was asked to alter his delivery was Graham. Every run-through brought fresh suggestions–from Annette.

Annette even gave direction *to the director*, suggesting that, in her role as the Great Oracle Olivia, Judy might step back, behind Annette, when delivering the oracle's immortal "visions," which always conveniently helped the investigation: "I am seeing . . . a . . . size nine man's footprint in the garden outside the back window." Or "I am seeing a . . . vision of a notarized will for the Buckingham inheritance that was recently challenged by an unnamed plaintiff known only by the initials S and S." Gosh, I wonder who it could be? Strongman Seth, maybe?

In spite of his heft and ungainly movements, Rodney had proven good at his job. Running here for props, there for last-minute wardrobe fixes. He'd learned to sidestep Annette, and he worked well with Teena, Miranda's understudy, who also helped set tables and shift furniture between scenes. The two of them were a team.

Teena and me, we were in school together. We always had each other's back. We always watched out for each other.

It was true what Edgar said. It wasn't really about theater, it was about community.

The surprise of the show was Doc Meadows.

He hit it out of the ballpark every single time with his monologue about the disappearance of his character's wife: "Even if my beloved is not with me physically, she remains with me in spirit. She is in my thoughts every day. I hear her footsteps in the hallway, I hear her laughter in the corridors. I can see her in an empty chair, in the setting sun, in the morning light through an open window. I feel her next to me when I go to sleep and in the morning when I wake. She fades . . . only to return. My greatest failing is that I was never able to tell her how I feel. Because I was afraid. Afraid of the depths of my feelings, the ache in my chest . . . I am a man condemned. Condemned to love the woman I married. To love her always, dearly, deeply."

It was the only moment of raw honesty in the entire play. And Doc's delivery was pitch-perfect. Heartfelt and unflinching every time.

Miranda dug out the creased playbill and, sure enough, beside Doc's name she had earlier written: *Marriage problems?*

And then it hit her. Those weren't Doc's words. Those were Edgar's. He had written them. About *her*.

All was not lost!

She intercepted him after rehearsal, as he was trying to slip out the back.

"Edgar! Wait!"

He knew the Opera House well, was hard to catch, but she managed to follow him through to the rear exit.

"Doc's monologue! It's beautiful."

Edgar stopped, hand on the door. He turned his head. "I wrote that a long time ago, Miranda."

Those were feelings from a decade ago. "And now?"

"This play we're doing. It's like a beetle trapped in amber. A time capsule. That's all. Goodbye, Miranda."

Before he could leave, she blurted out, "I know about Annette!"

She was bluffing, but it made him turn around. And at this point, that was all she wanted. For him to Not Leave, to stay, even if it was just for a moment longer.

His eyes narrowed. "What do you mean, you 'know about Annette'? In what way?"

"It's okay. I forgive you, Edgar. I understand. You were lonely. So was I."

Anger in those eyes. "Forgive me? *Forgive me?* My affairs are none of your damned concern."

Affairs? Plural!

Miranda fought her outrage down. She'd had dalliances of her own over the years, a stuntman here, a younger co-star there. Film sets were a hothouse of infidelity, and theater was no better.

Again, Edgar turned to go, and again, Miranda stopped him with another wild accusation.

"I know what you've been doing!" she said.

Again, he turned, and again, he asked, "What do you mean? Exactly?"

"Telling Bea one thing and Susan another, pretending to miss me one moment and then dismissing me in the next breath. Pretending like I don't exist when it suits you. Well, I do exist, Edgar! And I am here, whether you like it or not."

He stomped over, towered above her. She'd forgotten how tall he was.

"You. Never. Came. Back," he said, his voice punching every word. "The note you left when you slipped out of bed? On our honeymoon, no less. *I will send for you.* Well, you never did, did you? You left me on that bed, and in many ways, I am still on that bed, waiting for you to return."

Her voice faltered. "I have returned, Edgar. Don't you see? I have."

"You're fifteen years too late." And with that, he was gone, straight-arming the door and disappearing into the alley.

Back at Bea's, Miranda drained another box of wine, moaned about flanges and lost husbands and insects caught in amber, until Ned and Bea had to put her to bed.

"Bea?" she mumbled as they were tucking her in.

"Yes, dear?"

"Can I have a wake-up call?"

"I think you just received one."

"Bea?"

"Yes, dear?"

"My laundry is really starting to pile up. Can you do something about that? Thanks."

THE BIG DAY finally arrived.

Dress rehearsal! (Also: the night of the murder.)

"Full house," Susan whispered, peeking from the wings.

It was mostly empty, so their definition of "full house" differed from Miranda's. It was a large theater, 450 seats, and it was nowhere near full, even with everyone packed into the center of it.

"We cordoned off a hundred seats for the audience, but we had to move the rope! We've already sold one hundred and sixty tickets, and we're expecting two hundred. That's much more than usual, now that we have a big-name draw."

Miranda no longer took the bait. "Yup. You bet, Annette can sell tickets."

"I meant you," said Susan. "Even back when Annette was ruling the roost, we never sold this many seats. She knows that. It's why she's so cold. Word got out that you'd be doing a cameo, and people have come in from as far as Eugene."

A cameo! Yes, thought Miranda. That's what this is! Not a minor role, not a public humiliation, a cameo. I am gracing them with my presence. Suddenly, she perked up.

One of the posters had been put up backstage, and Miranda noted her name in bold at the bottom.

"I did that," said Susan with a proud smile. *"Featuring a cameo by Golden Globe–nominated actress Miranda Abbott!"*

Miranda felt her eyes mist over. "Thank you, Susan. You've been a good friend."

The moment was ruined, however, by a voice from behind that made Miranda jump.

"Two t's."

She turned and there was Officer Carl in his butler's jacket, grinning at her. He pointed to Miranda's name on the poster. "Abbott, with *two* t's. Glad they got that right, huh?"

"If you'll excuse me, I must check my wardrobe."

Miranda was already in her Victorian maid's outfit—which was decidedly frumpier than the frilly skirt and fishnet French maid getups they kept trying to put her in during her Pastor Fran days—*"Undercover at a manor! Owned by a Frenchman!" "Undercover at a school for maids! Owned by a Frenchman!"*—but any excuse to get away from Carl. She went to check her wardrobe.

The murmur of the crowd.

An announcement over the PA: "Ladies and gentlemen, tonight's dress rehearsal begins in five minutes. Please take your seats."

That old excitement returning. God, how she missed this. Even if it was only a cameo.

The actors had assembled in the wings behind Strongman Seth, whose luminescent pimple would lead them onstage when the moment came.

And as they waited for the curtains to rise and for Denise's overture to begin, Annette turned to her fellow cast members and said, "It has been an honor. I invite you all to join me at the Bengal Lounge for a drink after tonight's performance." And with a glance Miranda's way, she added, "Major cast members only, of course."

Of course.

And now the overture has begun, and now the lights have dimmed, and now Ned is saying cheerfully from the sidelines, "Good luck, one and all! Good luck, good luck, good luck."

Damn you, Officer Buckley!

The music swells, the curtains rise, and the applause follows.

Miranda came up with several cutting retorts to Annette's last-minute dig, but decided to save them for after the performance, when Annette would be leading the "major" cast members Pied Piper–style toward the Duchess Hotel.

Miranda Abbott never got a chance to deliver her cleverly crafted ripostes, however, because exactly one hour and fourteen minutes later, Annette Baillie was gone. For good.

CHAPTER EIGHTEEN

"She's (finally) dead!"

Harpreet Singh had done a splendid job on wardrobe this year. When the cast walked out onstage at the start of the dress rehearsal, the applause rose in a wave as much for what the actors were wearing as for who they were playing.

And the costumes were very good. Certainly, Miranda had performed in shoddier garb in professional productions. Officer Carl in his long-tailed butler's jacket, looking very much like a dour penguin. Lord Wussex in whiskers and herringbone tweed, cap pulled tight. Lord Reginald Buckingham the Third in top hat and scarlet cape. Melvin in his muscles, with that faint scent of something that always surrounded him like his own personal pungent brand of cologne. The groundskeeper with his hand-knitted sweater and not-so-suspicious limp. (He did have a prosthetic limb, after all.) Here was Judy as the oracle, in peasant skirt and shawl, with bangles and bracelets rattling. Here was Miranda, looking frumpy in her shapeless maid's outfit. Maids of that era were apparently outfitted in mop caps, white aprons, and black gunny sacks.

And here, of course, was Annette Herself, resplendent in shimmering taffeta. She had demanded a new costume, from scratch, and she'd gotten it: a tight bodice with a hoop skirt, layered in fabric. She seemed to float onto the stage rather than walk, an hourglass figure with bounteous cleavage and a demure to-the-floor hem, laid out in purple like the royalty she was. Was there really a time when ankles were considered more risqué than someone's pale pillowy breasts pushed into your face?

In spite of the drab getup she was wearing, Miranda's entrance also caused a stir as people whispered and gestured in her direction. Susan's framing her appearance as a "cameo" had worked, something Annette Baillie clearly resented, stabbing a look at Miranda every time she moved across the stage in her role as the maid to take a jacket from someone with a curtsy.

Up in her booth, Denise was hitting every mark with creaky winds and thunder, as Owen McCune stepped forward to deliver his very first line of the play.

"Good..."

He drew a blank.

From the wings, Susan whispered, "*...afternoon.*"

"...afternoon!"

After that, he mostly got through it, though he did refer to Mamie Dickens's beautiful "shade of dipstick," as opposed to lipstick.

Finally, the moment was on hand: Miranda was about to deliver her one and only line of the play.

"I say, a toast is in order, or my name isn't Reginald Buckingham the Third! A toast! A toast to Miss Mamie Dickens!"

The butler (aka Carl) carefully poured out each glass one by one.

Carl had–once again–given Miranda the chipped glass. Hell with this, she thought. When Carl turned to hand a drink to the

Earl of Wussex, Miranda switched the glasses out, swapping hers with Annette's.

The others then raised their glasses. "A toast! A hearty toast!" cried Lord Buckingham the Third.

While the others chortled and drank, Miranda, as the maid, furtively snatched up a glass of her own and, throwing one final look of longing the strongman's way, downed her champagne apple juice.

Here, then, was Miranda's moment!

Trust Annette to upstage her.

Miranda paused, quietly drew her energy inward. Closed her eyes with a flutter, stumbled one way, then the other, and allowed the growing awareness of her impending doom to swell and expand within her soul... But when Miranda opened her eyes, the audience wasn't looking at her; they were staring past her to Mamie Dickens instead.

Miranda turned just in time to see Annette knock over the lamp.

True, Miranda hadn't been paying much attention during the last rounds of rehearsals, but her first thought was, Has Judy changed things up? When did this happen?

"*Gawwck!*" said Annette, and Miranda thought, Hey that's my line.

It was seven seconds to the murder...

Mamie Dickens staggered offstage, and Graham followed, rushing out of sight. He came back looking pale and distraught.

"She's dead! She is! She's really dead!"

He'd delivered these lines with much more passion than he'd shown during rehearsals. Talk about taking it up a notch! Talk about living the moment! This was his Yale training in action, she was sure.

When no one moved, Graham repeated his lines. "She's dead! She is! She's really dead!"

An awkward moment followed, and then Susan whispered from the wings, *"Or my name's not Reginald Buckingham the Third."* At which point, not knowing what to do, Denise played the *dah-dah-DAH* zing.

Graham then vomited behind the sofa (upstage; he was a professional). Wow. They teach that at Yale? Miranda was impressed.

She looked to Judy for direction–*Do I say my line? Do I follow Annette stage left? Do I wait for her to return?*–but Judy was as baffled as she was.

Rodney came out onto the stage, only to freeze when he realized the lights were still up. Had Act One ended or not? He stood, not knowing what to do or where to turn.

Doc Meadows was the first to realize what Graham was really saying, and he ran off to check on Annette. Miranda followed, not sure of her cues, saying quickly as she left, "Alas, I have been poisoned, too."

Backstage, Annette was laid out on the floor, with Doc working her chest.

"Call the ambulance," he shouted to Miranda. This was Happy Rock. Not *an* ambulance, *the* ambulance.

She fumbled with her phone, thankful that Andrew had indeed topped up her plan. Doc stayed with Annette, never giving up, doing chest compressions, again and again, then breathing through her mouth, her head back, nostrils held shut, then again to the chest. He was still working it when the town's EMS arrived and took over. They wheeled her out the back on a gurney, still compressing her chest, as Doc slumped to the ground, exhausted and out of breath.

Ned appeared. "Doc?"

But Doc just shook his head. "Bad heart," he said, and Ned nodded.

Miranda returned with Ned onto the stage, where Rodney and

the rest of the cast, Judy included, were standing frozen in place like a *tableau vivant*, though perhaps *tableau mort* would have been more accurate.

Was Annette Baillie really dead? Surely they would be able to revive her? Surely she would sweep back in again tomorrow with her usual disdain for her co-stars? Surely not this.

Ned frowned. He circled around the table and the butler's serving tray, looking at the jug of apple juice and the various glasses the actors had placed there. It was a frown . . . not of accusation or even suspicion, but unease.

In the shadowy auditorium, the audience was buzzing in equal parts confusion and speculation. Ned walked out, center stage, and held up his hands for silence.

"Ladies and gentleman! Chief Buckley here."

From various members of the audience: "Hey, Ned! Look guys, it's Ned! They finally gave you a part, eh? Ha ha." No one joined in on the laughter.

Ned squinted out at them, then, cupping his hands around his mouth, called to the sound booth. "Denise? Can you bring up the houselights?"

The lights slowly came on.

Half the town was here, it seemed.

"I'm afraid there has been a mishap," said Ned with admirable understatement. "Tonight's performance has been canceled."

A murmur of protest. No one had realized just how serious it truly was. What was going on backstage? They craned their necks to see. The sense of dread was palpable. Death had appeared onstage.

"I'm shutting this down. Show's over, folks!"

Ned could see Bea standing at the back of the auditorium with a *What the heck is going on?* expression.

"You can talk to Bea Maracle on the way out about a refund," said Ned. "She handles the box office."

No one did, though. It would go down as the most exciting night of theater in Happy Rock history. Those who missed it would rue the day.

As the audience slowly emptied, Ned turned to address the cast. There was a steely resolve in his voice, one Miranda had never heard before.

"Nobody move. Everyone stay exactly where you are."

He looked from one person to the next, memorizing who was there and where they were standing.

"Where's Teena? Get her out here, too. And Susan from the wings. And where did Rodney disappear to? Everyone! Front and center. Now!"

Denise had already come down from her booth, and Doc was back onstage, sitting slouched on the sofa, resting his forehand on his fist, wondering if there was more he could have done. The cast chose to ignore the faint scent of vomit that now pervaded the stage like fear.

"Listen up. Annette's been taken to the ER," said Ned. "Doc tried his best, but it doesn't look good. So fingers crossed, okay?"

"We should send flowers," said Judy, and the others agreed.

"There'll be time enough for flowers," said Doc quietly, though he didn't elaborate on whether he thought they would be of the "Get Well Soon!" type or bouquets of a different ilk.

Carl, the butler, was staring at Miranda, the maid. Had he seen her switch the glasses? And so what if he had? Annette's heart had given out. Having to drink from Miranda's chipped glass would hardly have triggered a full-on cardiac arrest. But even then, at the back of her mind, Miranda was aware that, as well as being the butler, Carl was also an officer of the law.

"And where the hell is Rodney?" said Ned, getting impatient. "He was here a moment ago. Where'd he go?" And added under his breath, "It's like herding cats."

It was only then that Chief Buckley noticed the glasses. Or lack thereof. And the jug. They had disappeared.

"Who cleared this table?" he demanded.

"That would be Rodney," said the strongman. "He's supposed to clear the set for Act Two."

"Well, go get him and tell him not to touch anything else."

Owen McCune piped up. "You figure this is a crime scene, Ned?"

"I don't know what it is. But I don't want anyone moving anything around, onstage or in the wings. Got that?"

When they returned, Rodney was looking sheepish.

"He was washing out the jug and glasses," said the strongman.

"What! Why?"

Rodney mumbled, "Play was over. At the end of the show, I wash up. It's my job to wash up."

Teena appeared, and she concurred. "That's one of his assignments," she said. "If you give Rodney something to do, he does it. Right, Rodney?"

He stared at his feet, smiling shyly, but Ned was having none of it.

"It *wasn't* the end of the play, though, was it? It was only the end of Act One. So why the big rush, Rodney? Why were you in such a hurry to wash out the glasses and jug?"

He looked hurt. "But it *was* the end of the play, Mr. Buckley. You said so yourself. You said, 'Show's over, folks.'"

"You did say that," said Owen.

"He's got you there," said the strongman.

At that point, Doc's phone trilled and everyone stopped speaking.

"Hmm . . . hmm . . . I see." Doc hung up, took a deep breath, and looked at the rest of the cast and crew. "She didn't make it."

Judy's knees went weak. She sat down next to Doc, gutted.

Graham said quietly, "I could have been kinder."

"I'm locking this theater down," said Ned. "We will be padlocking the doors as soon as we get everyone out. Don't worry about the mess Graham made. That'll dry with time. Everyone, just go back to your dressing rooms. Gather your personal belongings. Officer Carl will accompany you. I don't want anyone moving anything that doesn't belong to them. Got it?"

They filed out, numb.

Miranda hung back, considered mentioning the chipped glass, but decided against it. She could see Ned staring up to the back of the empty auditorium, where Edgar was still sitting, watching. He hadn't moved this entire time.

She remembered what Ned had said to her that first day when he dropped her off at the bookstore. *You know the owner? Tread carefully, okay? Surrounded by murder all day? Gets my police instincts up. Who knows what someone like that is capable of.*

Ned called up to Edgar. "Mr. Abbott! Can you come down here? I'd like to speak with you for a moment."

What happened after that, Miranda never knew, because she had to hurry to catch up with the rest of the group as they went backstage, collecting paperwork, scripts, jackets, receipt books (in Susan's case), and zit cream (in Melvin's). They hesitated when they reached Annette's dressing room, wanting to show their respects but not sure how.

"Don't go in there," growled Carl. "That's off-limits. Go and change outta your costumes. You can leave 'em on the hangers provided in the dressing rooms. And then meet me back here. As a group."

Softly, Judy was sobbing.

"A bad heart." This was what they whispered as they hung up

their costumes. "A bad heart, no one's fault." This was what was spoken in hushed tones as they were led outside by Officer Carl, into the parking lot behind the Opera House. "A bad heart."

"Her face," said Graham. "It was all twisted around. It was horrible."

She had managed to upstage the other actors one last time; had, in effect, stolen Miranda's line.

They stood under streetlamps that cast overlapping spotlights on the cast and crew.

A bad heart, no one is to blame.

And yet, visions of that chipped glass stayed with Miranda . . .

Judy addressed them, eyes shining, trying to be strong. "The show must go on," she said, pain in her voice. "It's what Annette would have wanted. The show must go on. *We* must go on. The tenth anniversary of *Death Is the Dickens* will be dedicated to her memory."

Go on? How? thought Miranda.

Bea said, "C'mon, Miranda. I'll give you a ride."

Teena was huddled in conversation with Rodney. Graham looked sickly.

"Never saw someone die before," he said. "It was worse than I expected."

But what exactly he'd been expecting wasn't clear. Was it just his repulsion around dead bodies, or something more?

Officer Carl was manning the rear exit, making sure no one tried to sneak back in. But why would they? What exactly did Chief Buckley suspect? And where was Ned, anyway? Where was Edgar?

Under a pall, the cast and crew drifted away. Bea led Miranda across the parking lot to her boxy Volvo, past Edgar's mud-spattered Jeep and the pink Cadillac with *Annette Baillie, Realtor at Large!* splashed across the side.

"Excuse me! Ms. Abbott?"

She turned, and who was scurrying toward her but Finkel Erdely, camera on her shoulder, notebook in hand.

"Can I talk to you for a second?"

Miranda pirouetted away from her. "I have nothing to say to you!"

Damn paparazzi.

But the goblin wedged herself in between Miranda and the passenger door of Bea's Volvo.

Bea called across the roof of her car, sweetly. "It's late, dear. And there has been a terrible tragedy. We just want to get to bed."

But Finkel Erdely was nothing if not dogged, and she would not be dissuaded. "It'll only take a moment. It's for the Saturday paper."

Of course it is! Every paper is the Saturday paper. You're a weekly, for god's sake!

Finkel clicked her pen with great authority.

"Now then, Ms. Abbott, is it true that you and Annette Baillie weren't getting along?"

Miranda, instantly outraged. "What! Who told you that? Where are your sources?"

"Sources? My own two eyes. I saw the looks she gave you. Now that she's deceased, will you be taking over the lead?"

Miranda hesitated. "Perhaps. But that's not–"

"Awfully convenient, her death, yeah?"

Temper, flaring. "Considering the upheaval this has caused the entire production, I would say it is most *in*convenient."

"But you did audition for her role, yeah?"

The warnings that Graham had given her came back to Miranda. *Loves to stir up scandals... I wasn't surprised she became a muckraking journalist.*

With that, the proverbial penny dropped.

"You were on the student paper, weren't you?" said Miranda.

"You've been causing trouble since you were in high school, isn't that right?"

With a slight sneer, and hitting the "Mr." harder than necessary, Finkel said, "I see. Did *Mr.* Penty tell you about all that?"

Miranda leaned in closer. "Let me guess. You were in the drama club, too?"

From the flare in Finkel's eyes, Miranda knew she had hit the mark.

"But you were never cast in the school play, were you?" said Miranda. "No. That always went to Teena. Am I right? So you wrote for the school paper instead, found your true calling, exacted your revenge somehow. And you're still exacting your revenge against the world even now, aren't you, Ms. Erdely? I've met reporters like you. I've met them many, many times. Bitter and petty and resentful of other people's success."

And now it was Finkel's turn to lean in. She said, voice calm, "Didn't you used to be somebody?"

Miranda pushed past her into Bea's car.

"Better a has-been than a never-was!" she cried–though she didn't really believe that. As much as she wanted to think otherwise, Miranda knew that Ms. Erdely had won this round.

CHAPTER NINETEEN

A Mysterious Note

"Today's soup de jour is split pea," said Mabel—or was it Myrtle? Same soup as was served every day during rehearsals. The soup that came in barrels labeled, rather suspiciously, Miranda thought, PROPERTY HRHS. Forget the Case of the Missing Pocketbook. Maybe Ned should be investigating this.

The cast had gathered for lunch the next day at the Cozy Café to decide what, if anything, to do about Annette's demise.

They were crowded around a table, one draped in plastic with equally plastic flowers alongside the ketchup bottles, saltshakers, and sugar packets. The entire town was teeming with real flowers. Why on earth would you need plastic ones? So thought Miranda—forgetting that she was in Happy Rock, the Town That Logic Forgot.

The menu at the Cozy Café had clearly been culled from school lunchrooms across the Greater Tri-Rock Area.

"I think I recognize this lasagna from our school cafeteria," said Graham with a frown. "That was two weeks ago."

"You do realize," said Miranda to the lovely Myrtle—or was it

Mabel?—"that 'du jour' already means 'of the day.'"

"Correct. And *today's* soup du jour is pea. Same as yesterday's soup du jour and same as tomorrow's soup du jour."

Judy had called this meeting, and she was adamant through her tears that the show would go on.

It was cast only. No crew. Just the actors. Teena was in attendance, though, in her role as Miranda's "understudy." Of the actors, only Doc Meadows was absent.

"Heard he was at the hospital, talking to the staff about last night," said Melvin, looking decidedly less of a strongman now that he was out of costume. Though still pungent.

"Heck, I saw Doc comin' out of the police station," said Owen, whose whiskers remained Wussex-worthy.

"I imagine Doc's wife will be thrilled," said Pete sourly.

Several people nodded at this.

"Why is that?" Miranda asked.

"If there's no show this year, frees him up, don't it? Will make *her* happy, anyway."

"But there will be a show," Judy insisted.

"They ordered an autopsy, is what I heard," said Pete.

"An autopsy? But why?" said Graham. "What's the point? Everyone knew she had a bad heart. Let it go."

He was being squeamish, Miranda thought. Or was there a reason he dreaded an autopsy, what it might uncover?

"Bad heart? No heart, more likely," Owen muttered.

Only Judy seemed genuinely upset at Annette's passing.

"As your director, as a fellow actor, as a friend"—and here her voice broke—"we owe it to Annette to soldier through this. I know it's what she would have wanted. She was always a team player, always put the needs of the ensemble above those of her own."

"This is Annette we're talking about, right?" said Graham.

But Judy wouldn't budge. She repeated her mantra: "The show must go on."

"But our lead is dead," Miranda said.

With a meaningful look, Judy turned her eyes to Miranda. "Which is what I wished to speak with you about. I know they are terribly big shoes to fill, and you won't do nearly as good a job, but could you possibly take over the lead?"

Gosh, when you put it like that...

Miranda had spent every rehearsal listening to Annette butcher her lines with a hammy over-the-top delivery, aided and abetted by Judy. Miranda could memorize lines easily enough, something that had come in handy when shooting hours of network television every week. So, sure, she could take over the role. Whether she *should*... ? That was a different question entirely.

"Would I be able to play Mamie Dickens?" she asked. "I suppose. But are we really going to go through with this?" She looked to the rest of the table but received no help.

Judy laid a hand on Miranda's arm. "This is the biggest event of the year. We can't let the community down."

Nods of agreement around the table. And in accordance with the rules and regulations of the Happy Rock Amalgamated & Consolidated Little Theater Society, a motion quickly moved, followed by a show of hands. Unanimous. It was settled. *Death Is the Dickens* would go on. But the last to raise her hand had been Miranda Abbott. Did the show really have to go on?

Before they could leave, Chief Buckley showed up.

"Hey, Ned!" said Owen McWhiskers. "Cast only, buddy."

But Ned didn't banter back. "I've already spoken with the crew. I will need statements from the actors next about what happened last night."

"We know what happened," said Graham. "Her heart finally gave out."

Ned looked at him. Didn't smile. "I'll start with you, Graham." A nod to Teena. "You don't have to stay for this. Officer Carl, I'll need your help."

"Sure thing, Chief."

Carl had already submitted his report, being both an officer and an eyewitness. And Teena had been interviewed by Ned earlier as part of the crew, even if she was also an understudy. She stayed anyway, in no hurry to go home, waiting for the others to finish.

He spoke with them each in turn, one-on-one, in a corner booth. He had a diagram of the theater, including backstage, and asked them to mark with an X where they had been standing. He asked about the events of that night, the chronology of it, how it unfolded, step-by-step, and their relationship with the deceased; although, this being a small enough town, he knew most of their relationships with Ms. Baillie already, however fraught.

"Do you really think there's more to it than just a heart attack?" Miranda asked when it was her turn.

He looked at her, not with the warmth of a Pastor Fran Friday, but the poker face of an investigating officer. "Just crossing our t's, ma'am."

The actors left the café, weighted down with pea soup and the ballast that was the lasagna. It had been a heavy day, in every sense. Teena seemed chirpy enough, though. She sidled up to Miranda.

"It's just like you predicted!" she gushed.

Miranda was momentarily confused. "What do you mean?"

Did Teena think Miranda had *predicted* Annette's death?

"It's happening exactly as you said it would. You will be stepping into the lead, and I'll be taking over the role of the maid. I get to be onstage!"

"Not just onstage," said Graham, falling in beside them as they walked out into the parking lot. "You get to be First Victim. That's really big! That death scene is a highlight." He caught himself in time to add, "I mean, may she rest in peace."

Miranda's unease was starting to bubble to the surface. She asked them about Rodney.

"Why would he wash the jug and glasses so thoroughly with everything that was going on? Didn't he notice the commotion that was happening around him?"

"Oh, that's just Rodney being Rodney," said Teena. "Give him a task and he will do it, no matter what."

Teena's father was waiting for her in the café parking lot, leaning against his vehicle, arms crossed, watching them approach. The two men exchanged looks the way some might cross swords.

"Gotta go!" said Teena, bounding away. "Bye!"

Graham watched her leave.

It was a beautiful day in Happy Rock. It was always a beautiful day in Happy Rock. Sunlight on the water, sailboats bobbing, the seaplanes landing, and the seagulls lifting off. Miranda followed the harbor around to Bea's cottage, thinking about her upcoming role and what it meant to step into a dead woman's shoes.

She arrived at Bea's cottage, noting that the front veranda *still* hadn't been painted, even though Miranda had alluded to this in the most devastating way. (She'd described it as "rustic," but Bea had taken this as a compliment.)

A patrol car was pulling away from Bea's as she arrived. Must be Ned, Miranda figured.

The front door was unlocked, as per usual. You could have marched Napoleon's entire Grand Army through Bea's place without anyone noticing.

Bea was in the kitchen, from which the aroma of peach cobbler wafted, and for a moment Miranda considered taking cocktails on the veranda, but decided against it. (Bea's cocktails all seemed to involve an inordinate amount of SunnyD. But did Miranda complain? She did not. Again: compassionate.)

Instead, she schlepped her carry-all up the stairs to her room, entering with a deep breath. Her laundry was folded on the bedstead–*finally!*–with a fresh basket of soaps and creams and–

What was this? A letter had been slipped under her door. Fans. They can find you anywhere.

Miranda emptied her bag on the bed, as was her habit, just in case more magic money had turned up. Picking up the folded letter, she retired to the lounge area (i.e., Bea's loveseat beside the dresser). She put up her feet and unfolded the sheet of paper. It took her a moment to realize what she was looking at: a crazy assortment of fonts, all different sizes, cut from magazines in a classic ransom-note style, looking like something out of *Pastor Fran*. Stranger still was the message. Just five words, but what a wallop they packed:

It shOuLd HuVE BEen YoU.

Who spells *should* correctly, but not *have*? And what did it even mean? That *she* should have been cast as Mamie Dickens instead of Annette? Well of course. That went without saying.

Or did it mean . . . ?

But that was ridiculous. Annette's heart had simply given out. It was tragic, but hardly nefarious. Or was it? More dark thoughts were beginning to bubble up.

"Did anyone stop in while I was away?" Miranda asked, heading into the kitchen. "Maybe to drop something off?" The note was so ridiculous it had to be a prank.

Bea took off her oven mittens, considered the question. "Well, we had some guests check in and some other guests check out, and there were a coupla workmen who were putting in a new drainpipe, and a delivery boy, but he was picking up, not dropping off, plus the lady next door who got the wrong mail, happens sometimes because our numbers are only one off, and Denise, who was selling raffle tickets for the school band..."

Entire Grand Army, thought Miranda.

"I was thinking more of someone who might have gone up to my room," said Miranda. "Slipped something under my door."

Bea wiped her hands on her apron. "What would they have slipped under your door?"

"This," said Miranda, and she handed Bea the letter.

Bea read it out loud. "'It should huve been you.' Huh. What do you think it means?"

They sat down at the kitchen table to puzzle it out.

"They spelled *have* wrong," said Miranda. "Rodney has repeated twelfth grade several times, yes?"

Bea wasn't sure what Miranda was getting at.

"Perhaps his spelling is weak."

Bea considered this. "I suppose Graham would be able to tell you if that was true. Far as I know, Rodney is not–what is the word?– dyspeptic."

"Dyslexic."

"That's what I meant. You know, I always thought it was cruel, giving that condition a name that is so hard to spell. As for Rodney, I can't imagine him ever threatening anyone, if that's even what this is."

"It's either that or a warning."

"But Rodney wouldn't hurt a fly!"

Miranda snorted. On *Pastor Fran Investigates*, any time a character was described as someone who "wouldn't hurt a fly," it was almost a guarantee that they were the killer. It got to be a drinking game at one point.

"Not a fly, maybe," said Miranda. "But he was putting up the stage lights the day I was almost killed by one. It crashed down just inches away from me. Burt was the only one who noticed. If he hadn't tackled me when he did..."

Miranda began going over the events of the last few weeks in her head. The falling Fresnel spotlight, the apple juice and the chipped glass, that time she was almost run over by Officer Carl in his patrol car. It had certainly felt like he'd been trying to mow her down. Between Rodney's "accident" and Carl's reckless–murderous?– driving habits, something didn't add up.

Speaking of patrol cars...

"How is Ned doing?" Miranda asked, hoping for some inside information on Annette's death.

It was impossible for Bea to keep a secret under wraps. If anyone was going to spill the beans, it would be Bea. She was a born bean spiller.

But no. She had nothing to share.

"I haven't seen or spoken with Ned."

"But when I was walking up here just now, I saw his patrol car leaving."

"*Ned's* patrol car? I'm afraid you're mistaken."

"Did Officer Carl stop by this morning?"

"He may have. I was in the kitchen all morning. If he did, I didn't notice."

And now that Miranda thought about it, Carl hadn't just hit the brakes; he had swerved right at her.

Bea was studying the ransom-style note, getting her fingerprints all over it, Miranda thought with a groan. For someone who watched a lot of TV mysteries, she wasn't a very astute investigator.

If that's what this was. An investigation.

Bea finally put the letter down and declared, "I think it's a prank. But..." And here her thoughts trailed off into uncharted territory. "Even if it is a prank, who did this is still a mystery."

"It is indeed," said Miranda.

A mischievous smile surfaced in Bea's eyes. "And everyone loves a mystery! This could be good publicity. You should go to the media!" she said. "Show them the letter. I bet they'll expect you to help solve the Case of the Mysterious Note. *Pastor Fran returns!* That sort of thing."

Leak a story to the press? Create a media frenzy? Artfully raise Miranda's profile? There was only one person for her to call.

"To the sitting room!" cried Miranda.

Bea got a queasy look on her face. "Long distance?"

"LA!"

Andrew Nguyen had once convinced the tabloids that Miranda was next in line to be named to the Supreme Court should Ruth Bader Ginsburg retire. The article ran alongside a Bat Boy exposé and a story about UFOs buried in the White House Rose Garden.

He was at the golf club folding towels.

"There has been a death!" she cried as soon as he picked up. "And a mysterious note. Very mysterious. The letters were cut out of magazines, ransom-style, and it was slipped under my door when I was out."

In spite of himself, he had to ask. "What did the message say?"

"'It should huve been you.' Ominous, no?"

There was a long pause. "That seems like a police matter."

"Nonsense! Let's call TMZ!"

"Let's not and say we did."

"Thank you, Andrew! I knew I could count on you."

"Look, I've got a lot of towels that need folding."

"Oh, and one last thing, darling. I've been meaning to ask. Can you check with your Yale contacts, see if any of them have ever heard of a Mr. Graham Penty?"

"My Yale contacts? What Yale contacts? I'm not a private eye, Miranda."

"Thank you!"

"Miranda, I'm not calling up Yale University to ask about–"

"Oh, and Andrew?"

Sigh. "Yes, Miranda?"

"I miss you."

And damn it anyway, he said, "I miss you, too." And he did. That was the damnedest thing about all of this.

CHAPTER TWENTY

The Book of Secrets

What if the cryptic message slipped under her door wasn't merely a prank? What if it wasn't just some surly jab?

It should huve been you.

That's what the message said: I wish it had been you that died. And what if that's exactly what it meant? Literally. It should have been *you. You* were the one who was supposed to die, not Annette.

Miranda remembered Ned circling the glasses and the jug onstage, and how annoyed he was when he discovered that Rodney had washed them. She remembered Pete at the Cozy Café, gleefully announcing that an autopsy had been ordered. Miranda knew from her years as Pastor Fran that autopsies were only ever ordered when something was fishy. When a possible crime had been committed.

Annette Baillie had raised a toast of apple juice champagne onstage, and moments later she was dead. But the other actors had imbibed from that same jug, and they were fine. Maybe someone had slipped something into Annette's glass just before she drank from it?

Miranda shook her head and told herself that this wasn't an episode of *Pastor Fran*, that she was letting her imaginative powers run wild, and yet…

Rodney may have cleared away the jug and glasses, and he may have washed them out afterwards. But it was the butler who had poured the actual drinks, and it was the butler who knew which glass everyone was supposed to have drunk from.

It should huve been you.

Thoughts of the falling spotlight came back to her, and of Officer Carl in his patrol car, accelerating wildly across lanes of traffic, crazed look in his eyes, spittle flying, trying to cut her down with his vehicle, laughing manically all the while. *Two t's! Two t's!* (Miranda may have been embellishing what happened slightly.)

I can't go to the police, thought Miranda. Because Carl *is* the police. I can't tell Chief Buckley about this either, because Carl is his right-hand man. I would need solid evidence before I go accusing anyone of murder, especially an officer of the law.

But Miranda had no evidence; Rodney had seen to that. Washing out those glasses had removed that line of inquiry. No wonder Ned had been so irked. Was Rodney working in tandem with Carl? Or had Carl known that Rodney would simply do it anyway, would dutifully remove the evidence and wash away any traces of poison without being asked, that he would become an unwitting accomplice?

What was it Teena had said? *That's Rodney being Rodney. Give him a task and he will do it.*

Everyone knew that. Including Officer Carl. And hadn't Carl been fondling her underwear, before she came to pick up her valise that first day?

After her call to Andrew, she went back into Bea's kitchen, pulled up a chair, and said, as breezily as she could manage, "Tell me about Carl."

This surprised Bea, who turned from the sink and said, "What would you like to know?"

"Is he single?"

"Oh my, yes. His mother, you know." Bea's voice dropped. "Not really an option with him. He used to be so active when he was young. Very sporty. Now, well, not so much. On a brighter note, though, he is still very much a boy at heart. He collects... things."

"Trophies?"

"Not exactly. He used to come to our Pastor Fran Fridays religiously until– Well, until he couldn't anymore."

"Let me guess. His mom?"

Bea nodded.

"Bit of a mamma's boy, then?" said Miranda.

Bea beamed. "Yes! He really is!" And then, out of left field, added, "You two would make a nice couple."

"What? Who? Me? No!"

Bea's eyes twinkled. "Oh, I see what you're doing. Asking if he's single, what his hobbies are."

"No no no," said Miranda. "I'm not interested in him–I mean, I am interested in him." As a suspect. "But not in that way."

Bea made a locking-my-lips-and-throwing-away-the-key gesture. "Don't worry," said the biggest gossip in Happy Rock. "Your secret is safe with me!"

Terrific, thought Miranda. Not only is Carl trying to kill me, but Bea thinks I have crush on him!

Miranda didn't need any of this. Not now. What she needed was an ally. Someone she could trust. And she knew exactly where to go.

She just needed to confirm one thing first. "Bea, when I first arrived, you didn't anonymously pay my membership fee so that I could audition, did you?"

"I'm afraid not, dear. Why do you ask?"

"And it wasn't Ned who paid for me either, right?"

"Chief Buckley? Heavens, no. He would have mentioned it."

"Great!" Miranda headed for the door. "Gotta run!"

"Where to?"

"The murder store."

THE SHADED LANE behind the Duchess Hotel wound its way to the top of Beacon Hill. Miranda kept her hand inside the carry-all bag slung on her shoulder, gripping her mace lest Carl should suddenly appear. She stayed to the grassy verge, ready to spring, cat-like, in case Carl decided to chase her down in his car—again. How one would mace a car was not clear, but with every crunch of tires behind her, Miranda tensed up, ready to run.

She was almost at the top, was leaning into her walk, when who came bounding down the other way but a beautiful blond Labrador retriever.

"Emmy!"

The golden Lab galloped over to Miranda, tail flailing, just happy to be a dog and happy to be petted.

Coming around the corner in Emmy's wake was not Edgar, but Susan, looking as ethereal and petite as ever.

"Heading to the bookstore?"

"I am," said Miranda.

"Edgar's out, I'm afraid. He has some . . . meetings."

"With Chief Buckley?"

Susan called Emmy back. "I have to make sure she doesn't get too far ahead. And no, not with Ned. It's with some real estate lawyers. Not sure what it's about, but Edgar seems concerned."

In fact, it was Susan that Miranda had come to see.

"Is there anyone up at the store?" She could wait for Susan to finish walking the dog.

Susan laughed. "I hung a *Back in Five Minutes* sign on the door. But the key is under the mat. Let yourself in."

Which is exactly what Miranda did.

The honeyed light, the musty smell, the shelves lined with mysteries. Maybe she should have stayed in Happy Rock all those years ago. Maybe she should have stayed to help run the bookstore with Edgar instead of gallivanting off to Hollywood one last time.

The large desk with the rolltop was very familiar to Miranda now, after spending endless rehearsals sharing space with the desk's replica onstage.

I wonder if it's here, thought Miranda as she came near. I really should check before I speak with Susan.

Having made the decision, reckless though it may have been, Miranda moved quickly, yanking open the desk drawer and—Yes! There was the ledger and the mauve receipt book that Susan had taken with her when the theater was evacuated the day before. Susan would hardly have left those behind.

It was a shallow drawer—the ledger and receipt book barely fit—so Miranda had to pull them out to lay them open atop the desk. She flipped through, looking for her name.

Susan's ledger was meticulous, if eccentric, handwritten in cursive ink, with numerous categories for expenses paid and income received. Under MEMBERSHIP FEES there were no fewer than three categories: *Annual*, *Lifetime*, and *Auditions*.

Annual memberships included hundreds of names, all dutifully entered and paid in full. This was a town that supported its Little Theater. Far fewer lifetime memberships were listed: Edgar, Burt, Susan, plus Myrtle and/or Mabel, along with various other board members and the original Strongman Seth, now in a nursing home in Gladstone, and several who must have passed on, as Susan had added "in memorial" beside their names.

What Miranda was checking for was the entry on this year's audition fees. She found it, with her name right at the bottom, of course: Lucky number thirteen, she thought with a sigh. (Between Ned's repeated wishes of "good luck" anytime the actors went on and Melvin's constant whistling backstage, is it any wonder this production was cursed?) Not that Miranda believed in such things.

At the top of the page, Susan had written a note: *Judy Traynor's annual membership fee also applies to the cost of auditioning.* Oh right, thought Miranda. Although Judy was directing the play (which was covered under her annual membership), she was also in the cast. No double-billing on Susan's part. No sir. Susan had undoubtedly gone through the entire *Rules & Regulations* very carefully to make sure that Judy Traynor wasn't required to pay any additional fees for auditioning. Hence the note.

But Miranda wasn't interested in the director. She was, as actors always are, interested in her own name. Beside hers was written: *Paid in full.*

Only it didn't say by *whom*. Dammit.

I have to be absolutely sure, thought Miranda. My life may depend on it. So she dove into Susan's mauve receipt book next, flipping through the pages wildly, looking for the date of that fateful Wednesday when Miranda had first shown up for the auditions.

The question was this: Was Susan the sort of person to write a receipt to herself? Of course she was. And there it was: a *payment received* stub for Miranda Abbott's membership fee, made out to one *S. Lladdwraig* from one *S. Lladdwraig*. She of the unpronounceable name.

Miranda had found her ally.

Normally, the friendly bark of a golden Lab would fill you with joy. Not so this time. When Miranda heard Emmy barking and the sound of the door handle turning, she had to scramble. She shoved Susan's receipt book and ledger back where she'd retrieved them from inside the desk's shallow drawer, then hurried across to one of the tables, snatching up the first book she could find. A DIY number titled *How to Kill Your Husband*. Dammit. She grabbed another one instead. *How to Kill Your Wife*. Double dammit!

Fortunately, Emmy came thumping in ahead of Susan, and Miranda was able to put the book back before anyone noticed.

"Who's a good girl? You are! Yes, you are!" Miranda pulled Emmy's ears playfully.

The store had several leather chairs throughout, and Susan slid one over for Miranda. They sat and enjoyed Emmy's antics for a while.

"Susan," said Miranda. "Why didn't you vouch for me?"

"Sorry?"

"At the auditions. When I arrived in your office at the last possible minute, just before the cutoff. Burt ended up having to vouch for me so I could get my membership sorted out in the nick of time. But why didn't you vouch for me? You could have."

She stammered. "It–it would have been a conflict."

"How so?"

"I was the one filling in your application and . . ." Her voice trailed off.

Miranda smiled. "*You* paid my membership, didn't you? That's where the conflict would have been. If you paid my membership, you couldn't have vouched for me, too."

"I was hoping you wouldn't find out."

"At first I thought it was Edgar who had paid for me."

"Edgar said you were in tough financial straits. But he also said you had been too proud to accept his help earlier. So I did it in secret."

The kindness almost overwhelmed Miranda. "But why?" she said. "You barely knew me."

"Oh, but that's not true. I've heard about you from Edgar, about how much he cared for you, how the two of you parted, how you broke his heart, and how he always wondered if he shouldn't have followed you back to Los Angeles. He hated the city, but he loved you. I paid your membership fee so that you could join our theater company and, maybe, patch things up with Edgar."

"My notion exactly," said Miranda with a wry smile. "But God had other plans."

"He always does."

"Is Edgar's store in trouble?"

Between Edgar adding fangs to the bench of a now-deceased realtor, the meeting with the lawyers that Susan had alluded to, and the fact that Edgar was the only paid employee at the bookstore, Miranda was starting to wonder if Edgar's dream was running out of steam.

"Well," said Susan. "With the silverfish and the bank loans, it's been tough. But he'll get through. I know Edgar. He's resilient."

"Edgar fishes?" What other skills had he gained during their years apart, she wondered.

"Not fish. *Silverfish*. The bane of any bookstore. Almost as bad as termites. Annette had the bookstore inspected for a possible refinancing. She would have held the mortgage if it had gone through, but even then, she turned it down. Edgar was angry, but I told him, 'She's just doing her job.' It's an old building, Miranda. Lots of history. But lots of creaks and moans, too."

"Don't I know it! Burt included every crack and cranny when he built our set."

"He's very meticulous," Susan said approvingly. "Right down to the windowpanes."

It made Miranda think: Burt had also mentioned a fishing trip. Last March. Too early for salmon, he said, but they went anyway.

"Did Edgar ever go?" Miranda asked. "Fishing with the boys, I mean."

"I don't think so. The prime salmon run is during rehearsals. If he did go, it must have been for sturgeon. There's sea bass and some trout. Lingcod and perch, too. And Pacific herring, of course."

Of course.

Too many fish. Miranda's head was swimming. But this conversation would come back to haunt her, though she didn't know it at the time.

The moment had come.

"I have a confession, Susan. I'm not here to see Edgar. It's you I wanted to speak to. I need your help. It's about Annette."

"I see." Susan shifted in her seat. She wouldn't look Miranda in the eye. Why was that?

"I think it was poison," said Miranda.

"Poison?"

"Yes. I think Annette was poisoned, and I think that I may be next."

Susan was baffled. "You?"

"Opening night could be the death of me, in every sense. And I can't go to Ned because–well, I think Officer Carl may be involved."

"Carl? But he wouldn't–"

"Hurt a fly, I know. But look around you!"

Miranda gestured to the shelves surrounding them. She got up and began pulling out books at random.

"Here is a twelfth-century monk who investigates murder. Here's a mime who solves crimes–with gestures alone. A dental surgeon who vows to get to 'the roots' of every murder. A Celtic nun. An

Egyptologist. A gardening detective. Plus a detective who gardens; not the same thing, apparently. Here is a hummingbird that solves crimes. There is even"–she read the cover–"an actor who solves crimes. Okay. So that one's a little far-fetched. But you see my point."

She didn't.

Miranda began to choke up with emotion. "Pastor Fran never had a female friend. She never had a sidekick, never had a Watson to her Holmes. I always asked the writers for someone to share the burden of the show, another woman, a female comrade-in-arms. Instead, they kept giving me stalwart priests and orphaned altar boys to help me solve the cases. I don't want them, Susan. I want you–at my side–to help me unravel this."

Susan said nothing. She was staring at the floor, and when she looked up, her eyes were sad. "But you're not Pastor Fran. You're Miranda Abbott."

"Yes, true. You're right. And it is Miranda Abbott who is in danger. Something dark is going on, and I don't know what it is. You must help me, Susan."

Softly. "I can't."

"The apple juice was poisoned. I know it was. And Carl is involved–maybe Rodney, too. I'm convinced of that. You must help me. Look at the books you read. You're the only one who can help put the pieces of the puzzle together."

"There is no puzzle. Annette had a bad heart."

Miranda, exasperated. "Why won't you believe me? And why won't you help me?"

"Because I saw you!" There was anger in Susan's eyes. Anger and sadness. "I saw you switch the glasses. I saw it happen. I saw it from the wings. You switched those glasses, and then Annette died. I never told Ned. I never told anyone. But I saw you." Her voice went soft again. "I saw you."

CHAPTER TWENTY-ONE

Into Burt's Lair

Miranda wanted to avoid getting caught out in the open. Wanted to be safely home before dark. And she really did think of Bea's place as home now, certainly more than her dismal apartment at the De-Lux Arms with its Murphy bed and hotplate.

She hadn't expected that: how comfortable Happy Rock would become. She hadn't expected how dangerous it would feel, either. It was a strange combination of cozy and lethal, of sunny and sinister.

Behind McCune's Garage–"our Great Eyesore," as Annette had described it–a gravel lane disappeared into a fold of darkened evergreens. Miranda had spotted a distinct pickup truck turning down that lane on one of her drives with Ned, a pickup loaded with corroded barrels and loose lumber. And when she walked around the corner, her instincts were proven correct.

Burt's truck was parked in front of a log cabin shaded by thick trees. Although still mid-afternoon in town, under the towering shade of pine and spruce, it was already evening.

The lights were off, but Burt was home–to judge by his pickup.

Miranda held her mace tightly in hand as she moved forward, step-by-cautious-step, up to the front porch with its rickety screen door.

"Hello?" she said, and her voice was swallowed by the immensity of the forest around her.

In the moist temperate rainforests of the Pacific Northwest, planks are always slightly damp, slightly soft. And so it was underfoot as Miranda crossed Burt's porch, peered through the screen. Silence inside.

"Hello?"

She rapped on the side of the doorframe. Nothing. Tried the handle, was surprised when it swung open, unlatched.

Now, if there was one thing that Miranda Abbott had learned from her days as Pastor Fran, it was that anytime an unlocked door swings open, a dead body is usually on the other side. How many dead bodies had she stumbled upon as Pastor Fran? A hundred? Maybe more. And in real life? Exactly none.

She took a steadying breath, gripped her mace more tightly than ever, swung her bag back over her shoulder, and momentarily considered tiptoeing away, off the porch, and then fleeing.

But she couldn't turn back. Not now.

Susan had all but accused her of killing Annette, though she also insisted that it was just a faulty aorta that had done Ms. Baillie in and nothing murderous.

But the hesitation was there in Susan's eyes, and Miranda had pressed her on it.

"You don't really think I killed her? To get a part? In a play?" A lead in a network show, maybe . . . but community theater? C'mon. Miranda had certain standards.

"No," Susan had admitted. "I don't, but . . ."

"But what?"

"Others might not be as kind in their assessment."

Miranda had left the bookstore feeling sick, had been having trouble breathing as she hurried down Beacon Hill, expecting the screech of Carl's demonic tires at any moment. She felt she was being hunted by forces she didn't understand.

What to do? What to do?

And in that moment, she'd remembered Burt's tattoo. The old codger/coot had a faded nautical star inked on his forearm.

Once during rehearsals, Pete had mentioned his own time in the military—"merchant marines," he'd said, emphasizing the "marine" rather than the "merchant"—and Miranda had innocently noted, "Burt was in the navy, as well. Right?"

Pete's reaction was not what she'd expected. Instead of hearty camaraderie, he had rankled at the very idea.

"Burt Linder? In the frickin' military? Give me a break. He was no member of the armed services. He didn't protect people. He danced with the darkness. I lost my leg for my country! Burt, he didn't lose a goldarn thing. Except maybe his soul."

With that, he had hobbled away, muttering under his breath.

Stunned by the vehemence of Pete's response, Miranda had stood there, mouth open, till Doc approached and told her not to worry about it.

"Don't let him rile you. Ol' Pete didn't lose his limb in combat. Fell asleep on the dock, dead drunk. Rusty nail. Gangrene. I was the one who took his leg off."

"And Burt?"

On this, Doc was more equivocal. "With Burt, who's to say what's real and what isn't?"

And now, here she was on the threshold of an open door, looking into the very darkness Pete had accused Burt of dancing with.

Maybe the darkness is what she needed.

She couldn't seek Ned for protection, because that would open up access for Carl. She couldn't talk to Bea of the loose lips, Susan had turned her down, and Edgar was nowhere to be seen. That left an old man with a faded tattoo in a secluded log cabin. Desperation personified.

She stepped through, into the other side.

In the half-light, the interior slowly took shape. A Formica dining table circa 1968. A stack of firewood beside a potbellied stove. Duck paintings on the wall. A swaybacked sofa with a loosely crocheted and somewhat tatty afghan thrown over the back. The Saturday paper, lying spread on the well-worn linoleum floor . . . and Burt Linder, slumped back in his leatherette La-Z-Boy recliner.

He wasn't moving.

"Burt?"

Silence.

Miranda stuffed the mace into her bag, panic rising, and rummaged for her phone instead. She pulled it free, tried to dial 911. Nothing. But Andrew had topped up the minutes! Then she realized, Oh, right. I still have to charge it.

Faced with a dead phone and an equally dead Burt, Miranda rushed over to the kitchen counter and grabbed the receiver from the wall-mounted phone, but it was an empty shell and it fell apart in her hands.

Okay. So no landline. He must have a cellphone somewhere, then. She pulled open drawer after drawer—came upon photographs in one, yellowing with age—but nothing she could call 911 with. Then a thought struck her. What if she wasn't alone in here? The interior was murky with shadows. Who was to say Burt had died of natural causes? What if he had been, ahem, helped along on his journey?

She needed to call 911 for Burt—and maybe for herself, as well. There was a tree-trunk end table right next to the La-Z-Boy. Maybe Burt had left his phone way over there. She crept closer . . . and closer, but there was only some licorice and a pair of reading glasses.

Then she noticed the pocket on the front of Burt's shirt. It was sagging from the weight of Burt's phone.

Would she be able to do it? Would she be able to reach inside and retrieve something from a dead man's shirt?

She took a gulp of air, channeled her inner Pastor Fran, and was about to stretch across when–with a sudden strangled gasp–Burt's entire body spasmed.

Miranda yelped and leaped back, only to see him spasm again, then twitch, then mumble something. Not dying. Snoring. His head lolled to the other side, and he drifted back into slumberland.

He was asleep. *Of course* he was asleep. That's what old men do, she thought. They fall asleep in their favorite chair while reading the paper.

She decided not to wake him. Miranda was having second thoughts about her choice of would-be protector. *Stand aside evil-doers or Burt here will take a terrifying nap!*

She wandered back to the drawer with the photographs instead. Inside, she found a picture from his wedding, a beaming bride next to Burt, looking impossibly young and incredibly happy. A military headshot, buzz cut and a determined jaw, looking impossibly young and incredibly forthright. A bleached Polaroid of him in the desert in a lightweight linen suit, hand resting on a gun, pointing at two gentlemen in military uniforms (looking slightly less young and incredibly dangerous).

Beneath this sheaf of snapshot mementos was a stack of expired passports. She flipped through them. Entry stamps from Cairo, Bombay, Peking, Ceylon, Burma, and Leningrad of the former Soviet Union.

So engrossed was she in this cache that she didn't notice a figure slide out from the shadows behind her.

A creak in the floor gave it away.

Miranda spun around, and in an instant, it all came back to her: the training, the endless practice, the muscle memory, the ferocity, even the *Haii-ya!* She finally landed the high pitch required for that cry; turns out all she needed was a dose of adrenaline and fear. Miranda Abbott slashed a karate chop directly down across the shoulder of...

Burt Linder.

He looked at where she'd struck him, then up at her wild eyes.

"What was that?" he asked.

"It was, um, a karate chop?"

"A movie karate chop, maybe, but you have to shift your weight on the follow-through and keep your shoulders straight. What you want to do is come in higher, a side slash just behind the ear. Carotid artery. Or even better, strike upward, into the throat itself. Crush the larynx. Immobilizes them every time. And don't waste energy with that silly cry. A grunt will do."

The side of her hand was sore, and she rubbed it now, feeling abashed.

"You're alive," she said.

"And with karate chops of that quality, I will be for some time."

"When I did it on the show, they crumpled."

"Paid to crumple, I imagine?"

"Yeah."

She looked to the drawer she'd been sifting through before he'd crept up on her.

"Those photos, the passports. I didn't mean to snoop, but what is this, Burt? What's really going on here?"

"I'm a spy. Didn't they tell you? Everyone knows that. I'm surprised you weren't made aware of it."

"A spy?"

"Retired. Did no one mention it? Usually that's the first thing they tell about me. Sure, you can set a record for second-largest coho salmon caught in the Greater Tillamook Bay Area, but all anyone ever wants to talk about is that time you parachuted into Albania to lead an armed rebellion against General Hoxha."

"Pete did mention something about your past work. Said you 'danced with the darkness.'"

"Sounds about right."

"He was with the marines, yes?"

"Merchant marines. Delivery boys, essentially. Following in on our wake."

"CIA?"

"Off by one letter. I was DIA. Defense Intelligence. The CIA topples regimes and sends exploding cigars to Fidel Castro. We sought to minimize casualties on the field, identify ambush points, potential assets, possible allies, difficult terrain. Went in ahead of the action, with assumed identities."

"So . . . a spy?"

"Yup."

"But when I asked, you said you had never left Happy Rock."

"I said I'd never been to *Portland*. Not the same thing."

"You've really never been Portland? It's a bus ride away."

"Never cared to. Didn't see a need. I never was one for city folk, with their arrogant ways. These big cities, they're all pretty much the same. London. Moscow. Paris. Portland. What's the diff, really?"

"Paris and Portland? You're asking me what the difference is?"

A shrug. "I prefer life out here. Fishing's good. People are genuine. What's Paris got that Happy Rock doesn't?"

"You want a list, starting with restaurants that are open past eight p.m.? 'Cause it could take some time."

"Slower pace out this way. Plus, I hardly ever have to assassinate anyone."

When Miranda blanched at this, he added, "Kidding. I'm retired, remember?" Then, having remembered his manners, he asked, "Tea? I have chamomile. That's Edgar's doing. I was a perfectly good java drinker till he came along."

Miranda hid a smile. That's me, she thought. If nothing else, I can claim to have introduced herbal tea to the manly men of Happy Rock, Oregon.

Burt said, "I have to admit, I haven't seen many episodes of your TV show. That one with the lady pastor."

He filled the kettle, and they sat at the table, waiting for the water to boil.

"But I did catch one episode on Cable 9, late one night. Was pretty good. Murder at the magic show."

"Ah, yes. They wanted me in sequins and a high-cut leotard, dressed as a magician's assistant. A teenager's idea of sexy."

"Question I have is, that table where you were cut in half? Couldn't figure out how that worked. I mean, your legs were in one end, toes wriggling, and you were in the other end, smiling and waving away after the two sides of the table had been pulled apart."

"That was a leg model," Miranda said with a laugh. "And she had better gams than I did, I can tell you."

"Hidden compartments, and two actors. I get that. But what I couldn't figure out was how the two sides fit together afterwards. They were way too shallow. The two of you wouldn't have been able to fit in at the same time. How did that work?"

"I have no idea. I didn't build the sets on my show."

"But you did examine it at the end, when you caught the killer."

"My *character* examined it. And anyway, it would have just been a prop, not an actual magician's rig. It would have been a replica of the real thing."

"A replica? Makes sense. Concessions have to be made, I suppose."

"Concessions?"

"For staging purposes. I build sets, so I get it. But still. Always wondered how that worked. I guess the answer is, it didn't. The actors just pretended."

Miranda smiled. "Not pretended. *Acted.*"

"Same thing."

The kettle boiled, a piercing whistle, and Miranda blurted out, "I think the production is cursed."

He lifted the kettle and the whistle died. "Cursed?" he asked, over his shoulder. "Because of Annette?"

Other whistles. Melvin backstage, churning up bad luck. Ned wishing "good luck" before they went on, the light crashing... But when she explained this to Burt, he remained dubious.

"Want to know why people aren't supposed to whistle backstage?" Burt asked. "Because there was a time it could have been the death of you–in a very real sense. Whistling could have gotten you killed in the early days of theater."

"Did the whistling conjure up ghosts?" This was an element she hadn't considered. Not Rodney or Carl, but a phantasm . . . She shook her head free of the notion. There is no such thing as ghosts, she told herself.

"Not ghosts. Scaffolding. In the early days of theater, it was sailors who were hired to do the rigging and ropes backstage. Made sense; they had the skill set for it. And sailors communicated by whistles. Couldn't be shouting instructions during a gale. So coded whistles told them what to raise, what to lower, what to release. Some dumbass actor wandering around whistling a tune could find himself sliced in two by a backdrop. That's why you didn't whistle. Today? Just a tradition, really. What some would call superstition."

And how often those two are entwined.

"Same with the ghost lights," continued Burt. "The ones that are left onstage when the theater is empty. Those aren't to keep ghosts away, as some say. It's so you don't fall off the stage in the dark and *become* a ghost. Everything supernatural has a real-world explanation. So, to answer your question, the production isn't cursed, because curses–like ghosts–don't exist."

Burt poured their chamomile into mismatched cups, and Miranda said, "I think someone killed Annette. And it wasn't a ghost. I think she was murdered–by mistake."

"Murdered? By mistake?"

"I think I was the intended target."

Burt took a seat. Didn't laugh. Didn't scoff or roll his eyes. He just nodded and waited for her to go on.

"I know it sounds crazy!" she said. "You weren't in the theater that night, but I'm convinced that one of the glasses we drank from was laced with something. And I think I know who did it."

He waited.

Another deep breath. "It was Carl."

"The butler?"

"That's right."

"You're saying the butler did it?"

"Yes! I switched our drinking glasses at the last moment, and Annette died, and now Ned has ordered an autopsy."

Burt sipped his tea. Thought a moment. "If it *was* murder, and I'm not saying it was . . . Why?"

"Jealousy?"

Miranda lived in a world where jealousy–especially professional jealousy–was the most insidious of emotions.

"Mrs. Abbott, I inhabit a realm of facts, not conjecture and not flights of fancy. Let's be analytical about this. Means, motive, opportunity. Who benefits, financially or emotionally, from Annette's death—or yours, if you were indeed the assigned target? Ask yourself who has a vested interest in seeing you dead. How does it affect larger geopolitical alignments? Is a foreign power involved? Embassy staff? Could it be a false flag operation?"

"Um, not a lot of foreign embassies in Happy Rock."

"Good point. But the question stands. Even if you know *what* happened. Murder. And you know *how*. A poisoned chalice. You still don't know the *why* of it. When you figure that out, it will lead you to the *who*."

"I know who. It's Carl."

"Do you, though? Way I see it, could have been anyone on that stage. Cast or the crew, am I right?"

"I guess. Unless..." The Case of the Broken Window Latch reared up again. "Ned had investigated a loose latch on one of the theater windows. I suppose someone could have come in through there, undetected."

"The broken latch? That was me."

Miranda wasn't sure she'd heard right. "You?"

"Testing the perimeter. Plus, I figured Ned could stand to lose a few pounds. It's a narrow enough window, would have been hard for him to squeeze through. Might teach him a lesson, girth-wise. A wake-up call, him struggling to enter a possible crime scene. Thought it might motivate him. He's a fine investigator, but not exactly a gazelle in the physicality department. He wouldn't be able to run down an illegal arms dealer across a desert tarmac to save his life."

"When would he need to?"

"Ya never know."

"A lot of arms dealers show up in Happy Rock?"

"Admittedly, no. But if one ever does, Ned will be woefully unprepared. He couldn't even get through that window I left open. And even with the new latch I put on, it would only take a No. 2 Phillips screwdriver and five minutes' effort to bypass it."

"So you loosened the latch. Ned investigated. And then you fixed it."

"Yup. Not my finest clandestine operation, but there you go. Time slows us all down." He finished his tea. Grabbed the keys from a bowl on the table. "You comin'?"

"Where to?"

"If we want to sort this out, it's pretty clear what we gotta do. Talk to Carl."

CHAPTER TWENTY-TWO

Sexy Nurse (comes with stethoscope)

It was on the second day of their honeymoon they that came upon Oscar.

They hadn't been looking for a pet, least of all an exuberant golden Labrador puppy who would melt Miranda's heart from the moment they met. But that was how the afternoon had played out.

In a postcoital glow, Edgar and Miranda had taken a languid breakfast at the Duchess Hotel's sunroom and then strolled, arm in arm, along the outer harbor. From the Opera House, they meandered aimlessly through quieter lanes, past clapboard homes entwined in hydrangea and lilac, dragon wing and scarlet fire.

In one yard, a handwritten sign read PUPPIES TO A GOOD HOME. Puppies, plural. But there was only one left, an energetic ball of golden fur who came running over, nipping and yipping, and bouncing about like–as they say in Minnesota–"a fart in a mitten."

"Last of the litter," said the elderly man who walked out to see them.

Miranda had already plucked the puppy up and was nuzzling its warm tummy.

"Same color as the Oscar statuette," she joked. "Maybe it's an omen, Edgar! Maybe, when we get back to LA, I'll be offered meatier roles."

Edgar watched her holding the puppy. "I suppose we'll have to pick up a pet carrier for the flight home. Some doggy toys. And treats."

"You don't mean . . ."

A smile. An Edgar Abbott smile, the best kind. "I do indeed."

He took out his wallet and turned to the owner of the home. "How much for Oscar?"

Miranda laughed. "You can't buy an Oscar, Edgar! A Golden Globe, maybe."

But the owner's expression turned sour at seeing Edgar's open wallet.

"I'm not *selling* them. This isn't some puppy mill. Lulu had a litter even though we were keeping an eye on her. The puppies are free to a *good home*."

"Oh," said Edgar, missing the emphasis the man had placed on *good home*. "Even better. We'll take . . . her?"

"Him. And what makes you think I'll just hand him over? You could be a pair of ax murderers, for all I know."

Thus began one of the most exacting job interviews that Edgar or Miranda had ever faced. It had been easier auditioning for the role of Pastor Fran.

"Do you have references?"

"Um, sure. I guess. Here's my agent's business card and here is the head of NBC."

"And how much square footage for the dog to run around in?"

"Um, a lot? We have a house on a hill, a big yard."

"Is someone around, generally, so the puppy won't be left alone all day?"

"Well, my husband works at home," said Miranda. "He's a writer, so..."

In the end, they were begrudgingly allowed the honor of adopting Oscar. Edgar had a half smile during the entire process, thoroughly charmed by the steps taken to ensure they were indeed "providing a good environment" in which to raise a puppy. That was the moment, Miranda now recognized, when Edgar first began to fall in love with Happy Rock. It was the beginning of the end of the life they once had, though she didn't know it at the time.

When they came upon a bookstore whose proprietor was about to retire, that just sealed the deal for Edgar. And for her.

Oscar's owner agreed to keep the puppy while Miranda and Edgar were in town, though they came over every day to play with the little guy. They even smuggled him into their hotel room in Miranda's shoulder bag, and–when he had chewed up the toilet paper rolls and peed on the bathmat–smuggled him out again just as stealthily.

When Miranda abandoned Edgar, she'd also abandoned Oscar.

And now the path had taken her full circle. Not to sunshine and happier times, but to the unsettling awareness that someone in this pleasant town wanted her dead.

And that someone, she was sure, was the very man Burt Linder was now taking her to see.

As Burt's pickup juddered down a side road, Miranda was again tossed about like a die in a cup. Dusk was falling and the sky was the color of a deep bruise.

"That's his place up ahead," said Burt, gearing down as they approached.

The saddest house in Happy Rock. A townhome from the 1970s, it was vinyl-sided and painfully narrow.

"Ladies first," Burt said when Carl opened the door for them, bewildered.

Through gritted teeth, Miranda replied, "Age before beauty." There was no way she was going in alone.

"Suit yourself," said Burt, stepping through ahead of her.

Miranda entered with a lump in her throat, feeling not unlike a fly gingerly approaching a web. It was more a hallway than a home, really, crowded on either side with row upon row of action figures lined up in display cases. The air inside was stale, and the light dingy and yellow, as though filtered through wax paper. It felt like a museum—or perhaps an incredibly focused hoarder's lair. A very tidy hoarder. The action figures were arranged by program, character, and year (to go by the labels that had been carefully affixed on each shelf). *Space: 1999, The A-Team, Doctor Whatsit*, even *Hart to Hart*.

Hart to Hart had their own action figures? thought Miranda. Why?

No *Pastor Fran* memorabilia, though. Good. Not an obsessive fan, then. Obsessive, yes—but not a fan. In this, though, she was not entirely correct. He was a fan. Of a different order.

Along the top of the display cases and gathering dust—unlike the action figures, which were immaculately kept—were Officer Carl's high school sports trophies. Softball, basketball, boys relay. Ribbons and medals and various plaques. MVP. Team Player of the Year. Sportsmanship Award. Glory days, long gone. Teams that were no longer around.

Embarrassed, Carl waved them over to the small kitchen area. Not even big enough to be called a nook.

"Sorry about the mess."

It was dingy, true. But tidy. The only "mess" Miranda could spot was a single tea bag on a single saucer. Even Carl's civilian T-shirt was neatly tucked in, with belt cleanly drawn.

He cleared the saucer, sat down across from them.

"I know why you're here," he said, somewhat sheepishly.

"You do?"

"You figured it out, right? Wait here. I'll be right back."

And he disappeared down the narrow length of the townhome. In a panic, Miranda turned to Burt, who sat calmly at the table as though nothing were awry. What if Carl came back guns blazing?

He returned, not with a service revolver, but with something even more disturbing.

"Never took it out of its original packaging!" he said proudly. "I store this one in the vault. That's what I call my bedroom closet. Out of direct sunlight and away from cooking fumes. Have to keep it pristine."

He laid the plastic-fronted box reverently on the table in front of them. It was an action figure, if it could be called that. A sexy nurse in a white miniskirt–and a priest's collar. Pastor Fran, undercover in a hospital. *Healing lives and punching jaws!* read the packaging.

"Comes with a stethoscope, a first-aid kit, and a nurse's cap," said Carl.

And that same damn collar, Miranda noted.

"I thought they pulled all of these out of circulation?"

"They did!" Carl said, eyes shining. "But my dad worked at a shipping company. Brought one of the prototypes home. When we found out they'd been recalled, the last thing he said was 'This one is very rare.'" A pause. "Then he got sick, and then he died. But I kept my Nurse Fran in mint condition, just like he told me to."

Why had they pulled this particular toy from the market? She couldn't recall.

"Your name," said Carl. "See, here in the corner? The company in Taiwan misspelled it. *Watch Pastor Fran on NBC, starring Miranda Abbot!*

Oh, right. They'd spelled her name wrong. She remembered

throwing a fit about it. The toy company pleading. Marty forcing them to back down. They'd had to pull the entire line of sexy Fran nurses. Which was just as well, because her creepiest fans were always the ones who liked "that nurse episode" the most.

Is that what Carl was? A creepy fan?

She shot a glance Burt's way, got nothing in response. Decided that the time had come to assert herself in no uncertain terms.

"Is that what this is?" she demanded sharply. "Some sort of fetish? I know you went into my valise that first day, fondling my underwear."

"What? No. Ned dropped it off at the police station, was very evasive about who it belonged to. No baggage tag, so I had to open it up, look inside. I went through it trying to find ID of some kind. A phone number I could call. Anything. But there was nothing. So I zipped it back up. When you came in, I thought, That's her! That's Nurse Fran! I had you sign for it so I could check your signature. Looked up your autograph online, to be sure, and–yes. It was you, all right."

"I remember you studying my signature," she said.

She also remembered that her clothes had been more neatly folded than before, but she thought it best not to draw attention to the fact that her belongings were tidier *after* having being rifled through.

Speaking of autographs...

Carl held up a permanent marker and asked, shyly, "Would you mind? Do you think you could sign it? The packaging, I mean."

"Sign it? Why?"

"A rare edition? Signed? It would be the only one in existence. Would be incredibly valuable."

Her eyes narrowed. "You want me to sign this, just so you can sell it?"

"That's the idea, yup."

Miranda, anger rising. "You want me to autograph a cardboard box with a toy inside so you can flog it at the eBay store?"

"Or any specialized memorabilia site, really. Maybe Bid-Maxx or Auction-Plus. Or maybe I can sell it via a fan site. There's lots of collectors out there who would pay top dollar for something this rare."

Five... four... three... But before Miranda could explode in full Miranda splendor, Carl added, "For my mom."

"Your mom?"

A voice in a distant room beckoned weakly. "Carl, sweetie? Who's there?"

He looked at Miranda. "Would you? It would mean a lot."

Fifty years old and still living with his mother. Not as a freeloader. As a caretaker. As a son.

Miranda followed Carl to his mother's room. She was bedridden with a degenerative disease that had left her wasted and wan. But she smiled through the pain, more pleased that Carl had a friend over than that it was a celebrity.

"How lovely," she said.

She was tired and couldn't speak for long, but she held Miranda's hand in hers and thanked her for stopping by.

"We get so few visitors."

When Carl closed the bedroom door softly behind them, he said, "It would help me pay for long-term care. A rare edition of Nurse Fran, signed by Miranda Abbott? I could afford to move her to a place in Gladstone. Was working up the courage to ask you."

Miranda signed the box.

"So you didn't try to run me over?" she asked after they were back at the kitchen table.

"I wasn't trying to run you over. You looked scared–"

"I was! Of you."

"You looked like someone running from something. I was following at a safe distance to make sure you were okay, but then you suddenly veered out, stepping in front of my vehicle. I had to hit my brakes."

"So you didn't slip this creepy note under my door?" She flattened it out on the table.

Burt squinted at it, having trouble because he'd forgotten his reading glasses. "Looks like something outta *Pastor Fran*."

"I saw a patrol car leaving Bea's when I arrived, Carl. And she said that Ned hadn't been in. So it must have been you. And I found this note soon after."

"That was me," he admitted. "Not the note. But I did stop by. Ned was shutting down production of the play, and I was worried you'd be leaving town soon. Had to catch you before you did, ask you to sign the Nurse Fran collectible. Didn't want to miss that chance. You weren't there. But now you showed up here, so it worked out in the end."

"But why the chipped glass?" she asked. "In the play. Why did you always give me that glass?"

"Annette told me to. 'This is Miranda's glass. Always.' And, well, as an actor, you want to keep everything the same every night. That's only professional, right? I mean, we're an amateur company, but we have to maintain professional standards."

Of course it was Annette who made sure Miranda got that glass. A passive little twist of the blade. Give the TV star the chipped prop. There is nothing more petty than an actor who resents their co-star.

Except Miranda hadn't been the co-star. She was barely in the cast. She was a cameo.

"It bugged her," Carl said. "How, even with only the one line, you brought in more ticket sales than we ever had before. Maybe that's why she made sure you always had that chipped glass. I saw you switch them, by the way. Or rather, I noticed that Annette had it. I saw the look of rage she threw your way onstage and, well, I didn't want to say anything, but..."

"But what?"

"I thought maybe it was her anger at what you'd done that triggered the heart seizure that killed her. I was standing right beside her. I could tell she was livid."

Two actors, parrying over a glass.

"Except . . . ," he said. "Ned doesn't think it was her heart. Neither does Doc."

"Poison, right?" said Miranda. "Ha! That's why they ordered the autopsy. I knew it! After I switched glasses, I thought, That was meant for me. In fact, and I'm ashamed to admit it now, I suspected you at first. I thought you'd had Rodney wash out the glasses afterwards to cover your tracks."

Carl was aghast. "Why would I want to kill you?"

"That's what I said," Burt noted. "No motive."

"Heck, I wanted you to sign my Nurse Fran action collectible. Would be hard to do that if you were dead."

If not Carl, who then?

Miranda's thoughts were whirling away from her.

"Did Annette tell anyone else about the chipped glass?" Miranda asked. "Did anyone other than you two know that I always got stuck with that glass?"

"Are you kidding?" said Carl. "She was gleeful about it. Practically announced it. Chortled over it when you were backstage."

So any number of people would have known which glass Miranda would be drinking from. The circle of suspects had just gotten bigger.

Remembering that Carl was indeed still a police officer, Miranda presented the problem to him directly. "If it *was* poison, who do you think did it? Your professional opinion."

"That's a big if. We don't know for sure it was poison. We'll have to wait for the coroner's toxicology report."

Toxicology? That word. Where had she seen that?

"But if I had to pick a suspect, I suppose it would be . . . you."

Miranda was gobsmacked. "Me?"

"You were the one who switched the glasses."

Burt nodded at this. "Fair point. And there was bad blood between you two."

"Hardly!"

"You asked," said Carl. "I told you."

"But that's absurd! If I did do it, why would I run around accusing people? Why would I be working so hard to get to the bottom of this?"

"Could be setting up an alibi," Carl said with a shrug. "Misdirection. Exactly like what you're doing now. *Why would I try to find the real killer if I am the real killer?* Deflecting suspicion. Something like that, anyway. Again, we'll have to wait for the toxicology report to know what really happened."

There was that word again.

Miranda was stunned. She had come here to confront her would-be murderer only to be (hypothetically) accused of the same.

"So," she said, face flushed. "I suppose you are going to arrest me now, lock me up in a dungeon, feed me stale bread and tap water?"

"This is Happy Rock. We don't have dungeons. You asked my opinion. I gave it. But no, I'm not arresting you." Unstated was the implication: *yet.*

Burt had been listening carefully throughout, and he now asked a single question.

"You said Rodney cleared out the glasses and the jug at the end of the scene. Did he also set them up at the *start* of the scene?"

"He didn't," said Carl. "Not Rodney."

"If not Rodney, then who?"

Carl hesitated, then answered. "Teena."

CHAPTER TWENTY-THREE

Under the Yum Yum Tree

Rodney and Teena. Teena and Rodney.

After they left Carl's townhouse, Burt drove Miranda back to Bea's.

And all the while, Miranda kept turning it over in her head. Something Rodney had said: *Teena and me. We always had each other's back. We always watched out for each other, protected each other.*

Something Melvin of the foam muscles had said stuck with her. *Rodney? Bullied? No, worse. Ignored.*

Burt dropped her off at the B&B with a polite nod and a "Take care now, you hear?" No judgment in his voice. Miranda had all but accused a respected member of the local police department of murder, but Burt didn't hold it against her.

"Just glad to clear that up," he said, putting his battered pickup into gear.

Bea was onto Miranda with breathless questions as soon as she set foot inside.

"So? Did you call anyone in the media? About the note? The one that was slipped under your door?"

Bea was still convinced that it would be good publicity for Miranda, the town, the play.

"In *Pastor Fran*, she's always threatened by the real killers, who are trying to scare her off the investigation, and," said Bea, with misplaced pride, "it never works!"

But I'm not Pastor Fran, thought Miranda. Though even she wasn't sure at times.

"I'm tired and weary and ready for bed," she said.

"But the night is still young."

The night may be, but I'm not, she thought. A bath and bed was all the excitement she could face right now.

"But first, tea," Bea insisted. "Come to the kitchen. I just made a fresh pot. Denise is here."

Graham's wife, the music teacher and sound booth magician, she of the statuesque presence and awkward demeanor, was at the kitchen table, a gift basket of shortbread and marmalade at hand.

"She was selling raffle tickets earlier," Bea explained. "And I won the consolation prize! Shortbread from the Cozy Café. Have some, dear."

"Rehearsals are starting up again," said Denise. "Tomorrow." She was oddly introverted, yet imposing.

It would be cast and director only, Denise explained. "More an emergency meeting with the actors, is how Graham tells it. To figure out the next move."

"Cancel the production, surely," said Miranda. "That's the next move, yes? I know I voted, very reluctantly, I might add, to go on with it. But it just seems strange."

"Oh no, dear," said Bea. "Couldn't do that. It wouldn't honor Annette's memory. Plus Mabel has already arranged the catering. Or was it Myrtle?"

We always had each other's back.

Miranda asked Denise, "Was Teena bullied in school?"

"Are you kidding? She was the 'it' girl, the popular one. She was the lead in every play. Look at her! She's gorgeous."

Miranda, treading lightly. "Your husband certainly seems . . ." She chose her words carefully. ". . . fond of her."

"Of course he is," said Denise. "Only natural."

"Now Rodney, he had a hard time of it," said Bea.

"Please," said Denise with a roll of the eye. "He could graduate anytime he wants. He's only a credit short. One of his required courses. Avoids taking it so he can stay in school."

"And is he good at spelling?"

"Spelling?" The question was so unexpected it took Denise a moment to process it. "No idea. I taught music. He struggled with the recorder, I can tell you that. But he loved the drama class. Not as an actor, of course. Always on crew. Teena sort of took him under her wing."

"Well," said Miranda, wielding one of her aphorisms, "You don't take drama. Drama takes you." It almost made sense. Until she added, "And together you take *yourself*. To drama class."

"Wonder if Doc will attend the rehearsals," Denise said, musing aloud.

"Busy with the autopsy?" asked Miranda.

"Oh, the Portland Coroner's Office will handle that," said Bea. "She means because of his wife."

Denise nodded gravely. "She will be pleased to have an excuse for Doc to drop out of the play this year. Just in time, too."

"She doesn't sound very supportive," said Miranda.

Bea rushed to her defense. "She's lovely. It's just, well, Doc's wife is of a higher class."

Denise nodded and the table went quiet. Clearly, Doc's higher-shelf wife had not been pleased with his commitment to the local theater.

"It was different when he was with the Peninsula Players," said Denise. "She came to every one of their Fall Soirees, didn't she? But after the amalgamation, well . . ." She stopped herself, not wanting to speak badly of the doctor's wife. Got up, excused herself from the table. "I really must be going."

As Bea was clearing the table, Miranda asked her about the Cold War she had witnessed between Graham Penty and Annette Baillie.

"Why the tension?"

Bea tried to evade the question—"Oh, they're both great actors, and you know how it is, how actors will clash"—but couldn't. She sat down, and even though they were alone now, she whispered, with a furtive look, "Yum yum."

Was Miranda having a stroke? Had she heard right?

"Yum yum?"

Bea nodded sagely, as though an unstated understanding had passed between them.

"Could you elaborate?"

"Well, Denise was telling me just now how relieved they were after Annette's passing. Sad, naturally! Tragic, of course. But still . . ." She leaned in. "Annette has been hounding Graham for years, ever since she was voted out of the Happy Rock Amalgamated & Consolidated Little Theater Society on an anonymous complaint. Naturally, Annette suspected Graham of spearheading the campaign against her."

"Did he?"

Bea's voice dropped. "I think he may have. They weren't getting along, even then. After that, it got worse. She ran for school trustee and used the power of her celebrity to get elected, and ever since, well, it's yum yum all the way."

"Could someone please explain what 'yum yum' means before my head explodes?" She knew it was a reference to the school play they performed every year, but beyond that, they might as well have been speaking in some strange local argot.

"Graham wrote a play for his students, *with* his students, one that tackled real issues. The pressures young people face both at school and in their home life. The pain and stress. All of that. The students loved it but, well, Annette shut it down. Every year. Every time. Too 'suggestive,' she said. 'Inappropriate,' she said. Really, it was a way to stick it to Graham, to force him to keep staging the same play, year after year, *Under the Yum Yum Tree*, forever. He was trapped in a Circle of Hell, he said. His students supported him, but the school board? Not so much."

"Was that the scandal the reporter"—she almost said *goblin*—"broke, back when she was at the school paper?"

"Finkel Erdely? That's what got her a job in journalism right out of high school."

If *The Weekly Picayune* could be considered journalism, thought Miranda.

"And she's already angling for a bigger prize. Portland or Eugene, or even national press."

"So I heard," said Miranda. An ambitious young woman, our Miss Erdely.

"I really shouldn't be telling you this," said Bea. But Bea was a natural-born gossip and Ned was nowhere to be seen, so there was no one to rein her in. "Finkel got her hands on a copy of Graham's play—went undercover as a member of the drama club to get it, is what I heard—and printed the most salacious details in the school paper, out of context, just before the play was to open. Well! That caused a stir. Next thing you know, Annette had it shut it down. Finkel did well by the scandal, but not the students. And certainly not Graham."

"I know this sounds strange, but did Graham and Annette ever have an affair?"

"What?!" Eyes wide, hoping. "What did you hear? Tell me. You have to tell me. I can keep a secret."

No. You can't.

"It's just, the tension between them, it almost had an erotic undertone."

"I wish. No, it started with her getting the boot from the theater company and escalated with his attempt at staging something at Happy Rock High that was stronger, more hard-hitting than *Under the Yum Yum Tree*. He went to Yale, y'know."

Of course I know, thought Miranda. It's practically on the drive into town: *Welcome to Happy Rock. Did We Mention That Our High School Drama Teacher Went to Yale?*

"Graham wanted something that spoke to the real lives of our young people, something that spoke to them and what they were going through. It was, well, sexual in parts. And angry. Too sexual and too angry, Annette said. But here's the good news!"

"Let me guess. His wife, Denise, just told you that Graham is finally going to stage his play now that Annette is–" Out of the picture? "No longer with us."

"How did you know? Oh my, you are a regular sleuth, just like–"

"Pastor Fran." She thought of her failed *Haii-ya!* karate chop against Burt, her erroneous j'accuse of Officer Carl. "Pastor Fran is a lot smarter than me, though."

"Oh, don't say that!"

Miranda rose. Cricked her neck. It had been another long day. She was about to take her leave, soak in the en suite bath a while, when a thought struck her.

"The theater is locked down. Where are we supposed to rehearse?"

"Judy found the perfect space. The right size, acoustics. Worst case, we can even stage the play there. The show must go on!"

•••

"THE GARAGE?!" SAID MIRANDA the next day. "Owen McCune's garage?"

Bea had dropped Miranda off at the "perfect space," even though she could easily have walked it. Everything was pretty much within walking distance in Happy Rock.

Behind the police station, a small row of shops were lined up like tchotchkes, quaint and charming with bay-window displays and the ubiquitous gingerbread trim. Harpreet's fabric store, the Old Timey Toffee Shoppe, the flower shop, the Realtor's Law Office, Tanvir's Hardwares & Bait Shop, and, at the end of the street, the oily junkyard that was McCune's Garage: a Quonset hut with a derelict gas pump beside it. Vehicles in various stages of dismemberment were parked–abandoned?–out front.

Owen, in coveralls that were more grease than cloth, was sitting on an oil drum, having what looked to be a very serious conversation with Tanvir, who had been given the Super VIP seat of honor: a low-slung lawn chair that looked ready to spring apart at any moment.

"Wouldn't worry about it," Owen was saying. "It's his job. He's gotta check up on everything, however minor."

Tanvir, in a turquoise-blue turban today, looked down at the littered ground in front of Owen's garage. "I know, but still. It's worrisome."

"Problem, gentlemen?" Miranda asked as she approached, putting on a brave smile. She assumed it had to do with the play, or perhaps the choice of, ahem, "venue." But it was closer to home than that.

"Ned was in the store today," said Tanvir. "Asking questions. But not of the friendly kind."

"Questions?"

"About Edgar."

Owen got up, wiped his palms on a rag, extended a handshake to

Tanvir. "Wouldn't worry about it, buddy. That's just Ned being Ned. I gotta go. Rehearsal's about to start." Then, with a grin, "Actors only."

Doc was again AWOL. So was Carl.

Inside the cavernous interior of McCune's Garage, Judy had assembled a sad assortment of mismatched chairs, stools, barrels, and wooden crates for the actors to sit upon. The very air inside was oily. And Miranda wondered, Is there a murderer among us?

"Tragic, tragic news," said Judy. "Our dear beloved Officer Carl has . . ." She held back a sob. ". . . decided to put the needs of his 'job' ahead of those of the theater. He has informed me that he won't be able to attend and may not be able to take part in our opening night at all due to his 'investigation.'"

Miranda could hear the air quotes in Judy's voice.

"But we must not be angry!" cried Judy, as though the cast were about to boil over in uproar. "I absolutely forbid any of you to hold it against him! True, he has selfishly put us in a very perilous position–Who will be our butler? Who, I ask you? Who?–but we must soldier through for the sake of the community, for the sake of the show, for the sake of Art Itself!"

A smattering of applause from Melvin turned awkward when no one else joined in.

Teena was giddy at finally joining the cast. "With a line and everything! When I die, should I clutch my throat and *then* knock over the lamp? Or should I knock over the lamp and then clutch my throat?" she asked, hand raised like the diligent student she must have once been.

"Darling," said Judy. "Make it your own! Live in the moment!" Then, in passing, "But Holly always went lamp and then throat, so maybe stick with that."

"Can't wait!" she said.

The real issue was Doc's presence–or the lack thereof. Was he ditching them, as well? That would be a harder role to fill, especially given the power of his monologue in Act Five.

"Wife is probably using this as a pretext," said Owen. "Puttin' the pressure on him to quit while the quittin's good."

Miranda leaned close to Owen, while still keeping tactfully away from the grease of his coveralls. "His wife?"

"Yup. A bit snooty, you know. Understandable, I guess, her being from royalty and all."

"Royalty?" That got Miranda's attention!

"Royal family, yup."

"British?"

He looked at her. "In Happy Rock? No, not British, *Salish*. The Tillamook Nation, stretches all the way up the coast. A daughter of the chief. She married beneath her, you see."

"All women do," said Miranda, quoting Lady Astor.

"Ain't that the truth."

"Wait." *Fourteen generations of doctors*. That's what Doc had said. "Is he Salish, as well?"

"Of course he's Salish. Comes from the nobility, too, though not as high-ranked as his wife." He laughed. "She reminds him of that fact now and then. Jokingly, I think."

"A line of medicine men?"

"Healers. His dad was GP and obstetrics. Delivered half the town, and Doc delivered the other half. And his dad's dad before him, his dad before that, then you get into traditional medicine."

"Is that why his wife resents him taking part in the play? It's beneath his dignity?"

He gave her an "Are you for real?" look.

"Of course not. She loves a good show. But when they switched from a Fall Soiree to a Spring Jamboree, well, that's prime salmon season. Chinook salmon. Up the Nestucca and Three Rivers tributary. Smack dab in the middle of June. Right when our show opens. A huge encampment, smoking salmon along the shore. Half the Salish Nation is there, Doc's wife and her family prominently among them. Because of the play, Doc isn't able to go—though truth be told, I think he enjoys eatin' the salmon more than he enjoys catching 'em. I've gone jigging for herring with him. Likes to sit and relax more than jig a line. He misses it, though. The spring salmon run. I can tell. Misses his wife something fierce when she's gone."

"That's why he opposed the amalgamation," said Miranda.

"Yup. But he respected the consensus of the theater community. The two larger ones already had a long history of holding a spring show, so it only made sense. Still kinda sad. His wife has never seen him act. Not in a lead, not like this."

Just when you think you know everything about Happy Rock...

Miranda now had the lead but was oddly muted in her enthusiasm. This was not how any actor wanted to get a role. Miranda wanted to earn it. But now, the director, Judy, was calling for quiet during the read-through—yes, they were right back to read-throughs again—saying she would take Doc's lines for the time being.

Doc's lines.

And that's when it hit Miranda.

Even if my beloved is not with me physically, she remains with me in spirit... I feel her next to me when I go to sleep and in the morning when I wake.

She turned to Owen. "This is your first time playing the Earl of Wussex, right?"

"Yup. Usually, I play the butler. No lines, so it was a little bit easier to memorize."

"And Doc Meadows? He's been with this show from the start?"

"Every season without fail. Edgar wrote the parts for us, for our abilities. Or who we were at the time, back ten years ago. Some have come and some have gone, but Doc? Yeah, he was there from the start."

Not Edgar's words, she realized. Edgar's words written *for Doc.* It wasn't Edgar's wife that the monologue was alluding to. It was Doc's.

"Why are you crying?" asked Owen.

She wiped her eyes. "Oh. It's nothing," she said. "Nothing at all."

Nothing whatsoever.

The next day, Miranda phoned Edgar at the bookstore. "I'm ready to sign those papers."

CHAPTER TWENTY-FOUR

A Killer Is Caught!

"Pastor Fran, Pastor Fran, Pastor Fran," Atticus Lawson chirped, reciting the name in a smiling singsong. "Can't believe Pastor Fran is in my office."

This would be the local attorney, above the flower shop. The same Atticus who'd passed out while speaking at the Loyal Order of Joyous, Igneous & Cretaceous Bricklayers, a service group that had about as much to do with bricklaying as the Masons did with masonry.

"It's not Pastor Fran," she said tersely. "It's Miranda Abbott. And we're here to sign divorce papers, not autographs."

Edgar was sitting next to her and a million miles away.

The atmosphere in Atticus's cramped office, lined with Tillamook Community College Law Certificates and faux-wood paneling, was stifling. She just wanted to sign and get out.

"Won't take but a moment, Pastor Fran." Atticus caught himself. "Pastor *Miranda*, I mean to say."

A shuffling of papers, stamped and counter-stamped, notarized and sealed with an embosser. Nothing is official until it's been embossed. And all the while, Atticus was burbling away about "Pastor Fran, Pastor Fran, Pastor Fran."

It became a refrain in Miranda's head as she signed the papers. She slid them over to her husband–now former husband–who signed his scrawl as quickly as she had, barely looking, avoiding eye contact all the while.

As Miranda hurried down the stairs afterwards, with *Pastor Fran, Pastor Fran* still echoing in her ears, Edgar called to her from the top. "Miranda, wait!"

But she was gone.

Gone from his life. From the play. From Happy Rock.

She would go back to Bea's, phone Andrew, pack her valise, and arrange a ride to Portland. She would give up the lead and fly back to LA, even if she had to max out Andrew's credit card to do so. That was the type of sacrifice she was willing to make! Anything to get her out of this sleepy sun-drenched purgatory.

That was the plan, anyway.

None of it went quite according to script, however, because not long after he left the lawyer's office, Edgar Abbott was arrested for the murder of Annette Baillie.

MIRANDA RETURNED TO BEA'S cottage, feeling wistful, unaware of what was happening.

The tangled garden and the peeling paint. The Adirondack chairs and the view of the bay. It had almost felt like home. She would miss those Pastor Fran Fridays. Would miss the crisp air that reminded her of her childhood... It was time to move on. When she returned to LA, she would beg Marty to take her back. She would play the grandmother in that commercial and any others he wanted her to, even though she was nowhere near old enough for those parts. (It was always easier to age an actress than make her young again.) Miranda Abbott would take the Metamucil—figuratively and otherwise.

But Bea was waiting for her, distraught. She pulled Miranda in, hugged her like a squeezebox.

"I'm so sorry. It's awful. Awful."

What was? The divorce?

"Don't feel bad," said Miranda. "I could see it coming. In truth, it was long overdue. And, well, Edgar did warn me."

Eyes like saucers. "He warned you? About *the murder*?"

"What? No."

And that was when Miranda learned what had happened to her (ex)husband.

"It was poison!" gasped Bea. "Annette's heart gave out on her. That part is true. But they found toxins in her system. That's what induced the heart attack. If she hadn't had such a weak constitution, the poison would have acted more slowly, maybe after the curtain call. Either way, it was murder. You were right. She was killed, Miranda!"

Suddenly the message—*It should huve been you*—took on a more immediate and ominous meaning. Someone was out to get her. Not Carl, perhaps, but someone on that stage. Her initial suspicions had come roaring back, based on a single ineluctable fact: if Annette had been poisoned, it was only that last-minute switch of the glasses that had saved Miranda.

Miranda Abbott had been the intended target all along. Someone in Happy Rock wanted her dead.

But who?

"Edgar," said Bea. "They've arrested him."

Miranda's head was swimming.

"I need to sit down."

She fell into the floral sofa in Bea's sunroom. It couldn't be Edgar. It couldn't, because Annette was not the real target.

Miranda knew that if she could prove this, they would have to refocus their investigation. Look for another suspect. But Officer Carl had not been swayed when she'd run this same theory past him. If anything, it had only made him suspect *her*.

Bea fetched some SunnyD, which Miranda threw back like a shot of tequila. Have to get the blood sugar up, Miranda thought, for what's to come. She would need her wits—and her glucose levels—properly attuned.

Bea sat beside her, looking frazzled. "Don't worry, dear. I'm sure it's a mix-up. I mean, he may run the murder store, but he's not a murderer. He's your husband."

"Was," she said. "Was my husband."

"Autopsy results don't say *who* killed someone," Bea noted. "Just that they were killed. So there's hope yet for Edgar. A toxicology report is only a tool, not a verdict. You said so yourself on *Pastor Fran*."

And there it was again, that word.

Miranda turned to Bea. "Do you remember that episode of *Pastor Fran* with the poison?"

"Which one?"

"The poison that was in the cocktail that the wife served to her husband."

"Hmm. Have to narrow it down."

"The one with the poison that was in the husband's cocktail that the wife served to her husband *after* they went to the ballet."

"Again . . ."

"The one with the poison that was in the husband's cocktail *after* they went to the ballet *with* the foreign businessman who had stolen the *diamonds* from a shady drug lord."

"Russian? Or Moldavian?"

"I don't know!"

"Is that the one where the murderer turned out to be the chief medical examiner, who was having an affair with the lead ballerina, who was the sister of the Moldavian drug lord?"

"Yes!" said Miranda. "That one."

"I know the very episode! Season Four: 'Toxic Toxicology.'"

That was what Finkel had been reading! A toxicology report from the Portland Coroner's Office. The memory of it came back to Miranda like a thunderclap, the bus to Happy Rock winding its way along twisting roads, bouncing Miranda around–so much so that this was what Miranda mainly remembered: the bouncing and jouncing and juddering. But she hadn't been alone on the bus that day. Finkel Erdely had snuck up to the city that same day and was returning, asleep and snoring through every hairpin turn.

Why would Finkel have been reading a report on toxins *before* anyone was poisoned?

And what was it Graham had warned Miranda about? Finkel was on the prowl, looking for the Big Story, one to break her out of local news. That she'd find it, even if she has to manufacture it herself.

What could be a bigger story than a famed actress of murder mysteries being murdered *in the middle of a murder mystery*? It was Miranda who had been the intended target. Bad luck for Annette that the glasses had been switched, but good luck for Miranda.

"I need to see Ned," she said. "Right away."

Bea fretted. "Are you sure, dear? I mean, he is the one who arrested Edgar."

"Then he's the one I need to talk to."

The Happy Rock jail was a single cell at the back of the station. Bea drove Miranda over, and Ned came out from his office to meet her at the front desk. Emmy followed Ned out, the galumphing oversized dog, happily being a dog, as per usual.

Only in Happy Rock would the arresting officer offer to take care of your golden Lab for you when he locked you up.

"Chief Buckley, I wish to speak with my husband. I need to see that's he's okay."

"He's fine, Miranda. We're waiting on bail. Edgar owns property in town, is a longtime resident. I don't see him as a flight risk. But Judge Dower will still need to sign off on it. He's out of town right now. Nothing was on the docket, so the judge is up the Three Rivers tributary, fishing. We'll have to track him down. Prime salmon season, y'see." He looked her in the eye. "Miranda, I'm sorry about what is happening. I really am."

"I thought you were his friend, Ned!"

"I am his friend. But I'm also an officer of the law. And the evidence points very clearly in his direction."

"Ha! What evidence?"

"The fangs. That was the first thing that made me go 'Hmm . . .'"

"Fangs?"

"On Annette's real estate bench. She filed a complaint. Blamed Graham Penty, naturally. I went over to check. Recognized Edgar's handwriting straight off. *Lies & damned lies*. Anyone who's been to his bookstore knows the man can't write a decent ampersand for love nor money."

Fair enough, thought Miranda. Edgar did seem to have a very specific form of dyslexia when it came to ampersands.

"But how is that evidence of murder?"

"It isn't. But it does get my instincts up. You ask yourself, What is a respected business owner like Edgar doing scribbling such things on a park bench? It makes you wonder. Remember that day we saw him coming out from a back lane, all sweaty and smudged with dirt?"

"I do."

"Well, after I dropped you off, I circled back in my patrol car. Sure enough, several of Annette's real estate signs had been yanked out of people's lawns and curb-stomped to the ground. Many of 'em had footprints on her face. Edgar's footprints. I snapped a photo of them on my phone. Checked his boots next time I was in his store. That was him, all right. He destroyed those signs. Tore 'em out in a fit of rage, as I see it."

"So??"

"Escalating violence."

"What! Drawing fangs on a bench and then later pulling up real estate signs is not an escalation."

"It is in Happy Rock."

Miranda was about to object when Ned said, "*Lies & damned lies.* That's an odd thing to write, don't you think? Not 'Darn you, Annette!' or even the b-word. I looked up that phrase. It's a reference to statistics. To the misuse of data. Something Annette was particularly good at. He tell you about his bookstore? About what's been going on?"

"Not in so many words."

"I suppose a man doesn't share everything with his wife. Bottom line is, Annette's been trying to pull Edgar's bookstore out from under him. She offered to act as a guarantor on a bank loan. To help cover the cost of a new roof, a boiler, other renos, long overdue. This allowed her to commission a complete and *very* thorough home inspection. She then walked away from the deal and used the details in that report—*misused* them, Edgar would say—to launch legal proceedings with the town to get his business license pulled. She wants the lot rezoned as purely residential, rather than mixed business-residential as it is now. And who would have been waiting in the wings on the foreclosure? You bet. Annette. That's prime real estate he's sitting on. Have you seen the view? Of course you have. You're his wife."

Was, she thought.

"Edgar had been badgering the lawyers who handle Annette's real estate closings, trying to get them to release privileged information to him. Annette complained. He began leaving angry messages on her phone. And just before dress rehearsal, she received a note backstage: *Break a leg! Hope you die out there!* We found it in her dressing room."

"But how could you know it was from Edgar? I can think of half a dozen people who wanted her dead, people she bullied and demeaned. Not just him, but Rodney, Owen, Graham, me. On it goes. So how would you ever know that the letter was actually from Edgar?"

"He signed it."

Oh.

"Sent it along with some dead flowers."

She could feel her confidence deflate. "Maybe someone forged the signature?"

"Nope. I asked him. I said, 'Edgar, you write that?' And he said, 'Yup.' I tried to give him a way out, said, 'Did you mean *die* like the way actors use it? To have a bad performance?' And he said, 'Nope. I meant die as in die. As in cease to exist. As in *Exit stage left, pursued by a bear.*'"

"So he confessed..."

"Um, yeah, see, here's the thing." Ned rubbed the back of his neck, confounded by what he was about to say. "He confessed, all right. Confessed to everything. The angry letter, the dead flowers, the vandalism and destruction of private property, harassing the lawyers. Everything except the actual murder."

"None of what you cite necessarily points to murder," she said.

"Maybe not, but the boric acid does. It's sold as a pesticide, a fine dust, easily concealed. In humans, it can trigger a slow and fatal poisoning. Or in Annette's case, cardiac arrest. Among its many uses . . ." She knew what he was going to say: a pesticide. ". . . is for the control of silverfish."

She felt her heart go weak. Light-headed and feeling queasy, she realized what Tanvir Singh had been speaking with Owen about, why he was so concerned. *Ned came in, asking questions. But not of the friendly kind.*

Ned cleared his throat. "When I looked through the papers that Annette had submitted to have Edgar's bookstore rezoned, I noted silverfish among the many complaints she cited. So I went to Tanvir's hardware store, and yeah, Edgar picked up two extra doses of the stuff just a few weeks ago. Ordered it in special. Highly concentrated. Odorless. From the coroner's report, I'd say one entire dose was used on Annette."

"And the second dose?"

"Who knows? It's still out there somewhere. Or maybe Edgar used it the way it was intended. He does have a silverfish problem. It's an old house. Stuffed with books. Hard not to in these climes."

"I have to see him, Ned."

"I don't know if that's such a good idea."

"I'm his wife."

"Okay. I'll get Holly to give you a pat down, check you aren't smuggling in a file for Edgar."

Why would I do his nails? she thought. Then realized he meant the tool for cutting through prison bars.

"I remember that one episode of *Pastor Fran*," he said, "when you filed your way out of a submarine . . ."

But she was no longer listening. She was trying to remain calm, trying to make sense of what was happening.

One flicker of hope remained. If she could demonstrate that Annette was not the true target, but that Miranda was, then it followed that Edgar was not guilty of murder–no matter how much he loathed or resented Annette.

Unless . . .

But again, she pushed the fears down. Why would Edgar want to kill me? she thought.

The enormously pregnant Holly Hinton struggled out from behind the desk–she was *huge* now–and came over, walking not unlike an enormous duck.

She gave Miranda a tired but warm smile.

"I hear you really nailed my death scene during rehearsals. Good on you. I'm no Meryl Streep. And I'm certainly no Sarah Bernhardt. I only ever knocked that lamp over by accident the first time. But after that, well, you know how demanding a crowd can get. Sorry I couldn't make it to the theater to see the dress rehearsal. Other than the murder, I hear it went well."

She gave Miranda a cursory pat down, and then looked through the large bag Miranda had brought with her and ran her hands up and down the sides of Miranda's skirt as best she could, given her prenatal girth.

She missed it, thought Miranda.

Officer Holly was looking for something obvious: a weapon or a bomb or escape gear. She missed the real item that was being smuggled in. Not a file, not a weapon, but a single sheet of paper, folded over. But one as potentially explosive as any bomb. It looked like a ransom note but made no demands, save to remind Miranda: *It should huve been you.*

Edgar was alone in his cell, sitting on a cot, and he looked up when Miranda entered.

Holly hung back outside the cell to give them privacy, and as soon as she did, Miranda slipped the note to Edgar.

"Do you know what this is?" she whispered.

She was going to tell him, *This is your ticket outta here! It proves I was the target, not Annette,* when Edgar replied, "Of course I do. I wrote it."

CHAPTER TWENTY-FIVE

Marijuana Gangs & Miniskirts

They'd been happy once. Even during the worst of the NBC maelstrom, with the rewrites and long nights, even with the grind of network television, even amid the stress and storm, they'd always found time to curl up into each other, just the two of them.

"It's you and me against the world," Edgar would whisper.

"So when do we attack?" she would whisper back.

That laughter now seemed a long way from here. From this cell. This moment.

How well do we really know anyone? She'd told herself that he was the same Edgar she'd left sleeping in the Duchess Hotel fifteen years ago. But was he?

"Why did you lie?" she said. Her voice sounded distant, even to herself. It was as though she were watching the scene unfold on a monitor.

"Lie?"

"About me. About us. You tell Susan one thing and Bea another, and I don't know which version is true."

"I've only ever been honest with you," he said.

"Really? Because Susan said you talk about me all the time, always with fondness, with tenderness. Is she lying?"

He stared at the cell floor. Softly, he said, "No."

"And Bea says you practically deny my existence. That you get angry when she even asks about me. Is she lying?"

He looked up. "No. She isn't."

"So why–"

"Because Bea Maracle never asks about *you*. She asks about Pastor Fran. She hangs around the bookstore, constantly bringing up that show and your role in it, trying to talk me into attending those damned Pastor Fran Fridays of hers. Well, I am thoroughly sick of Pastor Fran! I didn't want Pastor Fran in my life. I wanted you. But I couldn't have one without the other, could I? Bea wanted to talk about Pastor Fran. I wanted to talk about my wife."

She could see the hurt in his eyes.

"Susan never did that. She never asked me about Pastor Fran, she asked me about you, about Miranda Abbott, a real person, not some fictional character, not someone *who never existed.* And this?" He threw the ransom-style note back at her in disgust. "This just brings it all back."

Miranda clutched the note in her hand. "Why did you write this?"

"Didn't have a choice, did I?"

Her voice dropped. "Did someone . . . force you to write it?"

"I was paid, so I guess you could say it was my choice."

"Someone *paid you* to write this?" Murky images of conspiracies churned through her mind. Was the entire town in on it?

"Of course I got paid! You think I'd write something that ridiculous for fun? I mean, look at it." He gestured to the note. "Killer was supposedly high on marijuana. The producer said, 'He should misspell it, the way crazed junkies do.' This from a man who had more cocaine in his bloodstream than platelets. All about family values, that guy. I pointed out that if our crazed junkie had had the presence of mind to carefully cut out the letters from several different magazines—while wearing rubber gloves; no fingerprints of course, that would have made it too easy—and then just as carefully glue them onto a piece of paper in the correct order, he would probably have the presence of mind to spell the word *have* correctly."

"It's from the show? That's what you meant! You wrote it *for the show.*"

"It's everything I hated about *Pastor Fran*. The ransom-style clues and the karate chops. The car chases and the homilies. How they kept trying to get you into a bikini or a miniskirt—I know, I know; those miniskirts bought us that house, but still—they never took advantage of the sharp wit, the wry humor, the real emotional heft, the sheer talent you could have brought to that role. My wife became a hackneyed role, and I'm the one who did it. I wrote her into that corner."

Quietly, Miranda folded the note and put it away. Had the same person who'd slipped that note under her door also tried to frame her husband?

"What are we going to do, Edgar?"

"About us?"

"About you, about this." She gestured to the jail cell.

"Atticus is working on my case. We're waiting on word about the bail."

"Atticus Lawson? The one who handled our divorce?"

"Same one."

"The one who has a debilitating fear of public speaking? The one who passed out when he had to address his lodge meeting? That's who will be representing you in court?"

"The very one. It was either him or those real estate shysters who were trying to foreclose my store on Annette's behalf." He gave Miranda a sardonic look. "There may have been a conflict of interest if I had hired them, given that their testimony contributed to the charges now laid against me."

"But Edgar, this is murder. This isn't some minor traffic ticket or a bit of paperwork that needs tending to."

"Atticus'll be fine. I've known him for years. He saved Owen's garage when Annette came circling, smelling blood. He can get me off these bogus charges. And they are bogus, regardless of whether the evidence seems to point squarely in my direction. Ned was reluctant to arrest me."

Officer Holly rapped on the bars. "Sorry guys. Time's up."

With that, Miranda gathered her things, looked at Edgar. "I will do my best to get you out of here."

She thought he would say something gruff, like *I'll be fine, don'tcha worry about ol' Edgar.* Instead, he smiled and said, "You and me against the world, right?"

"Always."

It was time for her to go on the attack, to solve this conundrum and save her husband–*ex*-husband–once and for all.

She stood, then turned and said, "I just want to say, I'm sorry, Edgar. About the play, about mocking it the way I did. I didn't know you were Doug Dirks at the time. What I said upset you, and I apologize. I didn't mean to insult you."

"You didn't," he said.

"But–"

"You didn't insult *me*, Miranda. You insulted the town. Back when I first opened the bookstore, word got out that I was a writer, and eventually each of Happy Rock's three different community theaters approached me, asking me to write a play just for them. One company wanted to do a mystery, one a period piece, one about something local. Three separate companies, each competing for a devoted but small audience. I agreed–on condition that it would be one play for all of them. That's how the different companies first came together. They joined forces to stage *Death Is the Dickens*. That was ten years ago. The audiences have grown, and the play is now a highlight of the town calendar. But"–he leaned forward–"here's the thing. I wrote that play *as a comedy*. I was lampooning the very tropes I'd been forced to write on shows like *Pastor Fran*, stuffed them all into one theatrical extravaganza. I thought they'd laugh. I really did. But when I showed up on opening night, the audience cheered, they clapped, they gasped. They gave it a heartfelt standing ovation. And that was the moment."

"The moment?"

"Of no return. My opening night epiphany. Sitting in that audience, the sincerity of the production, the honesty of the reactions. I realized how cynical, how jaded, I had become. Here was real theater. And more importantly, a real community. After that, I knew: I was not going back to LA. Not then, not ever." He looked into her eyes. "I'm so sorry, Miranda. I know you came all this way hoping I would return with you. But that's never going to happen. This is my home now and has been for some time."

Another rap on the bars, more urgent than before. "C'mon. Time's up and I really gotta pee."

It was Edgar's turn to ask a question.

"Why did you do it, Miranda? Why did you finally agree to sign the divorce papers?"

"Doc's monologue," she said. "In the play. I had thought you'd written those words about me. But then I realized they were written for Doc."

"It never occurred to you that it could be both? That we could both be hurting?"

•••

MIRANDA FLED THE STATION, not in tears, but with determination. A renewed vigor to find out what the heck was really going on in Happy Rock.

There was only one place for her to go, and it wasn't the police.

Past the fabric store and the hardwares, past the toffee shop and the flowers, all the way to Owen McCune's grease-infused garage at the end . . . and then past that, too.

She followed the gravel path leading to the cabin. To a pickup parked out front. And to Burt Linder, answering the screen door.

He was momentarily taken aback.

"Oh. It's you." He looked past Miranda.

"Expecting someone?"

"I am, but come in. I already have the kettle on."

Burt moved his reading glasses and a heavy, ring-bound slab of papers to one side, and then waved her to the kitchen table with a "Sit, sit" gesture.

Before he could ask, she said, "It's Edgar. They've arrested him."

"I know."

"They think he murdered Annette."

"I know."

"Well?" She waited, but he didn't say anything. "Aren't you going to help me track down the real killer? You have the training, and you know this town better than anyone. We have to move quickly. We need to know who killed Annette Baillie!"

"We do know. It was Edgar. The evidence is there."

Miranda was flabbergasted, but Burt was happy to elaborate.

"He fits the checklist. Motive, means, opportunity. Ned Buckley is a gifted investigator. He doesn't need my help, and he certainly wouldn't have arrested Edgar without cause. To quote Theodore

Woodward, 'When you hear hoofbeats, think horses, not zebras.'" A pause. "Unless you're in Africa."

"And what about unicorns!"

"Unicorns?"

"Imaginary footsteps. Footsteps of the mind. What about those? Where do those fit into your snug little theories? What is it they say? A lack of evidence doesn't mean that the wrong evidence is the right evidence."

"No one says that."

"Well, they should! You got me all mixed up with your unicorns and zebras."

"Hey, you're the one who brought up the unicorns. I have no idea what you're talking about."

"It was *me* they were trying to kill. Not Annette! Ned is looking in the wrong direction. The falling light, Burt. Tell me I imagined that."

"Accidents happen, Miranda."

"And who was responsible for securing that light? You were the crew foreman. Tell me that. Who?"

He squirmed a little, then answered, "Rodney."

"And what happens if I die? Teena gets moved up into my role, onto the stage, where she belongs."

"And how would that benefit Rodney?"

"It would repay Teena for the kindness she has shown him. Love makes people do crazy things. Killing me would have been a way to clear a path onto the stage for the girl he secretly adores. The one who always had his back in high school."

Burt's eyes grew cold. Stone cold. It must have been the same look that many an enemy agent saw just before Burt took them out.

"You don't accuse a young man of murder lightly."

"Then you tell me, Burt! If not Rodney acting on his own, who then?"

"Sometimes a falling light is just a falling light. And you are way over the line with these accusations. First it's Officer Carl. Then it's Rodney. Who will be next?"

As if to answer his question: the sound of a car approaching, a crunch of gravel, a whistling kettle, and a lively knock on the door.

"Hey, Burt!" Then, on seeing Miranda at the kitchen table. "Oh. It's you."

It was Finkel Erdely.

Only then did Miranda notice what Burt had shoved to one side on his Formica tabletop. A thick bound report. Even before Miranda flipped the cover over, she knew what it was. *Toxicology Report: Portland Coroner's Office.* It was dated three years earlier, something Miranda hadn't been able to spot when she was on the bus.

Finkel went over to the counter to remove the kettle and fill the teapot. Threw a disdainful look Miranda's way.

"What's *she* doing here?"

Burt stared at Miranda. Hard. "She was just leaving."

Miranda didn't budge. She slapped her hand against the coroner's report. "I saw you," she said to Finkel. "On the bus. With this. Are you still going to deny it?"

Finkel came over, put two–and only two–cups on the table.

"Do I still deny sneaking away from work to go up to Portland on the q.t. to acquire a copy of a restricted medical report, even though my editor explicitly told me not to? Yeah. I still deny that."

"Miranda has some wild theories of her own," said Burt. "Figures it was Rodney who killed Annette–accidently, you see, while actually trying to kill *her*."

"Rodney? But he wouldn't hurt a fly."

"That's what I tried to tell her," said Burt, taking a sip of chamomile.

"And how about you?" Miranda demanded of the goblin. "Would you have the same compunction?"

"Oh god, here we go," said Burt. "She's found her third suspect."

"Well," Miranda said, challenging Finkel with a glare. "Maybe you can tell me why you have a toxicology report from *before* Annette died. Studying up, were you?"

"I was," said Finkel. "Absolutely."

"Ha! I knew it." Only then did the thought occur to Miranda that she was now inside a remote cabin accusing a possible murderer of murder.

"I wasn't studying up on how *I* could commit murder. I'm not even sure it *was* murder. What do you think, Burt?"

Burt put on his reading glasses, flipped through the pages till he got to the summary of chemicals. "If it wasn't suicide, it was still a contributing factor."

Finkel nodded at this. "It's what I figured. Either way, Owen should know."

"Still going to run the story?" asked Burt.

A frown. "Not sure. It's been pulled twice already, and now that Annette's dead..."

"Fair enough," said Burt. "A dead woman can't defend herself."

"What are we talking about?" Miranda was baffled. What did this have to do with Edgar?

"*We* aren't talking about anything," said Burt. "*Finkel and I* are discussing the death of Judy Traynor's husband."

"The one who drove off the road?" Miranda remembered Ned mentioning it. It was written on her playbill somewhere, alongside Judy's name: *director – mean – husband died.*

"That would be the one," said Burt. "After the accident, Annette offered Judy much-needed succor. Provided a sympathetic shoulder on which to cry, and a handy scapegoat on which to focus her anger. Owen McCune. Annette launched a campaign of rumor and innuendo against him and his garage—the Great Eyesore, as she dubbed it—saying that the brake lines had failed due to Owen's sloppy work, that he was really to blame. Damn near ruined him."

"I always figured there was more to it," said Finkel.

Burt peered through his glasses, looking more like a professor emeritus than he did a former spy. "A regular cocktail, isn't it? Antidepressants, painkillers, alcohol. That's a recipe for intracranial bleeding. Coroner doesn't say for certain. They can't, because of the head trauma from the accident, but this one time in the Khyber Pass, we took out a notorious arms dealer in just such a fashion. Lotta hairpin turns in the Khyber Pass. Just like here. Either way, this clears Owen of any mechanical neglect. I mean, he was never charged with anything, but the court of public opinion, especially in a small town like this, well, it can be just as brutal."

A thought occurred to Miranda. First Edgar and the bookstore. Now this.

"If Annette sought to run Owen McCune out of business, to what end?" she asked, though she already had an inkling.

"That's prime real estate," said Burt. "A quaint street with a big ol' garage at the end, taking up space and ruining the property values? Never mind that Owen's granddad built that garage before any of those twee shops showed up. Annette figured, Owen's garage goes under, she can swoop in, reap a windfall. You ever reel in a 52-pound king salmon? No? Well, if you did, you'd know how that feels. The excitement of it. The frenzy. McCune's Garage was her 52-pound salmon."

"And all it took was some well-placed rumors," said Finkel.

Miranda's mind began to whir anew, but before she could say anything, Burt cut her off.

"Don't go getting any ideas about Owen, okay?"

"I know, I know. Wouldn't hurt a fly, right?"

"Somethin' like that," said Burt. "So don't go off on any new tangents, okay? They arrested the right person. Sadly."

But as Miranda Abbott was about to discover, not everyone in Happy Rock agreed with Burt's assessment.

CHAPTER TWENTY-SIX

Cozies to the Rescue!

Miranda was sitting on the front veranda—which Bea still insisted on calling a "porch"—feeling defeated, a glass of SunnyD in hand (she had offered to make lemonade but Bea wouldn't hear of it), wondering where she'd gone wrong. Not just with the investigation, but with everything.

Knights in shining armor don't always arrive on horseback. Nor are they always men. Sometimes they are diminutive clerks driving a small blue hatchback.

Susan Lladdwraig pulled up in front of Bea's cottage and lugged a canvas bag that was almost as big as she was up the steps. She faced Miranda and said those three words that Miranda had been waiting to hear from someone—anyone—in Happy Rock.

"I believe you."

With that, Susan dumped her canvas bag onto the Adirondack chair next to Miranda's. An avalanche of paperback mysteries tumbled out.

"Everything we need is in here. If we're going to exonerate Edgar, if we're going to solve this, the solution will be contained in these."

Cozies to the rescue!

Miranda went through the pile. *Mrs. Petunia*, mainly, but also the *Tic-Tac-Toe Lady*, who fought crimes by solving a particularly demanding game of X's and O's every time. And *The Ghost Detective*, who solved crimes from the Great Beyond via a series of coded knocks during séances, not to be confused with *The Ghostly Detective*, who solved crimes *on behalf* of ghosts, *The Knitting Circle* ladies, who solved crimes while knitting, again not to be confused with *The Crocheting Club*, which was an entirely different concept altogether. Plus *The Number Two Ladies Detectives Agency* "which always seemed a bit of a knockoff to me," Susan admitted. Their motto was: "We try harder."

If Susan and Miranda were going to crack the case, they would have to try harder, as well.

"Edgar is in trouble, and he needs our help," said Susan. "I will be the Watson to your Holmes."

"No!" said Miranda. "Not Watson. Not a sidekick, but a co-star. With a lower billing, of course," she hastened to add. "But a co-star still!"

"Like Jude and Carole!"

"Like Crockett and Tubbs!"

"Who?"

"Who?"

Susan retrieved a notebook and pen from her purse, and got down to business right away.

"Let's start with the message that was slipped under your door."

Miranda spread it out on the wooden table, moving her SunnyD to make space. The paper was now so creased that some of the letters were starting to come unglued, but the message remained, misspelling intact.

"Hmm," said Susan authoritatively. (If anyone could "hmm"

authoritatively, it was Susan.) “That’s odd. Why would someone spell *should* correctly but not *have*?”

“I asked myself the same thing. It was Edgar.”

“Edgar wrote this?”

Miranda could see the alarm on Susan’s face.

“The words. Not the actual message. They’re taken from an episode of–” And that was when she realized. “Susan, how often is recycling collected in Happy Rock?”

“Every two weeks, why?”

But by then Miranda was already gone, storming into the B&B with Susan hurrying to catch up.

And there it was by the back door: that infernal blue box that Bea kept reminding Miranda of. A stack of glossy magazines was piled neatly inside. Celebrity gossip, for the most part, plus some home décor and gardening magazines. Miranda picked up the top one, flipped through it, found a page with letters carefully excised.

Bea couldn’t even bring herself to throw out the evidence once she was done, thought Miranda. She just had to place it in recycling. Always was a conscientious member of the community, our Bea.

Next magazine, same thing. Certain letters had been painstakingly cut out. Miranda recognized the fonts and the missing bits that the note had been assembled from. Of course it was Bea! Who else would know *Pastor Fran Investigates* so well as to re-create a specific message from a specific episode?

They called Bea in, and when she saw the magazines, she blushed, deeply abashed.

“Oh my. I knew you’d figure it out eventually.”

They sat at the kitchen table with Bea wringing her hands.

“Why?” Miranda asked.

Bea couldn’t have been the killer–she was nowhere near the

stage that night, eliminating both means and opportunity–so why the cryptic message?

"I thought you might investigate it, like in the show. And you did! It was so exciting. Like being in my very own episode. Like having Pastor Fran in my home. The real Pastor Fran. The one who tracks down criminals."

"That was just a show," Miranda said, and Bea had tears in her eyes.

"Not to me. It was more than that. *Pastor Fran* was about making sense of tragedy, about thwarting the badness in the world, about making sure that goodness prevailed."

A widow, still grieving. VHS tapes and caramel popcorn and storylines that always featured a happy ending. This was what *Pastor Fran* provided.

"And don't forget," Bea said quickly, "I thought it might be good publicity for you. *Pastor Fran returns!*"

"But I'm not Pastor Fran. I'm Miranda Abbott. And my ex-husband is in jail for a crime he didn't commit."

Susan looked at her. "Ex?"

A nod from Miranda. "We signed the papers this morning."

"Are you mad at me?" Bea asked with pleading eyes. "Please tell me you're not mad at me. Tell me you'll forgive me."

Miranda smiled. "Pastor Fran always forgives."

Reassured, Bea took her leave, feeling blessed.

Susan said, "I notice you referred to Pastor Fran, not Miranda Abbott."

"*Pastor Fran* forgives her. Miranda Abbott is still pissed off as hell."

"It does set us back quite a bit... Or does it?"

"How so?"

Susan mulled it over and said, "The menacing letter under your door wasn't real. So there was no actual attempt at communicating with you after Annette died. No follow-up threats. No ominous warnings. Just days before, someone had wanted you dead. But then you switched the glasses and Annette died instead. And after that... silence. Why? Why did they give up so easily?"

This was making Miranda nervous. "You're saying someone should have kept on trying to kill me?"

"They should have. But they didn't. Lots of opportunity to, I'd say. Another dose of poison at the Cozy Café. Hit and run. Toxic tree-frog blow-dart. Okay, so I may have been reading too much Mrs. Petunia on that one. But the fact remains, they didn't try again. Why?"

"Why am I still alive?" It was a strange question to ask.

"Precisely. They wanted you dead. Why would they settle for Annette?"

"Because Annette's death had already served their purpose?" Miranda suggested.

Susan didn't follow this. "How?"

"Well, for someone involved with the play, the effect was the same. For Teena. Hear me out. When Annette died, I was removed from my original role. Same as if it had actually been me who'd been killed. Teena steps up, takes my place. It would have been the same result if I *had* died." This brought Miranda's train of thought back around to Rodney. "It's funny. I'd assumed that if it was Rodney, he acted alone. But what if he was being used, what if he was maneuvered and manipulated into it?"

The idea percolating in Miranda's mind was this: Have I misread Teena all along? Is she playing Rodney for a fool? The perfect crime would be to have someone else do it for you, dropping hints without directly asking. Was Rodney a lovelorn patsy in all of this? And what exactly was going on with Teena and Graham?

"Susan, did Graham really go to Yale?"

"Absolutely."

"How do you know that?"

"He told us."

Now it was Miranda's turn to go "Hmm."

Susan didn't like the sound of that. "I'm not sure what any of this has to do with Annette's death," she said.

"It casts doubt. We don't know if Graham truly went to Yale. It's just his word, isn't it? And if he lied about that, what else is he lying about?"

"But it's not just *his* word," said Susan. "Yale was where he met Denise. She was in music, he was in theater. You know she's from here, right? This is her hometown, so it was a big deal when she got accepted. The Pride of Happy Rock. Unfortunately, she's struggled with anxiety since she was young, and Yale and the big city overwhelmed her. Graham gave it all up to come back here with her, and he never complained, never resented her for it. Quite the opposite. He tries to include her as much as he can, getting her out of her comfort zone, taking her to public events. And it's working. Slowly, she's getting better, becoming more comfortable with who she is."

"But–"

"Graham Penty is a good man," Susan said firmly, as though closing a door. Clearly, she did not approve of this line of inquiry. "Let's stick to the evidence, rather than conjecture. The poison that Tanvir shipped to the bookstore."

"Do you think Tanvir could have been mistaken or even lying? Or that maybe someone else ordered it under Edgar's name, as a ruse?"

At this, Susan faltered. A worried look came over her. "I'm afraid it's true. We do have silverfish and Edgar did order that pesticide, *but*"–Susan refused to concede even this evidence, damning though it was–"do you really think Tanvir's Hardwares & Bait Shop is the only place in town that sells pesticides?" A look of inspiration came over her. "C'mon! Grab your bag!"

"Where are we going?" Miranda asked.

"To the smelliest place in Happy Rock."

"Owen's garage?"

"Even smellier."

The S.J. Fertilizer Supply Company was located in a handsome brick building at the far end of the harbor, downwind from the genteel clientele of the Duchess Hotel, thankfully. The motto was: *No one spreads manure like we do at S.J.'s!*

A warm waft of odor washed over Miranda as she climbed out of Susan's hatchback.

"Historic building," Susan said, proudly.

Historic smell, too, thought Miranda.

The bakery next door to S.J.'s was going out of business, with ALL ITEMS HALF OFF!! posted in the window.

The odor of the ordure only grew stronger when they went inside. The interior was vast and as dark and dank as a mushroom farm. Mounds of different varieties of manure lined the shop the way a spice merchant or a tea peddler might display their wares. True, the store had a beautiful pressed-tin ceiling, long hardwood counters, and a vintage cash register, but the effect of this was lost to the deeply pervading smell, sickly sweet like sewage, that had been absorbed into the very walls themselves. Susan dinged the brass bell on the counter for help.

Who would work in such a place? Miranda wondered.

"Hey, guys!"

Of course. Melvin of the foam muscles.

There was a tray of sugar cookies next to the cash register. "Want some?" he asked.

Miranda could taste the smell of manure in her mouth. "I thank you, no."

"Are ya sure? They're really good." He scarfed down a couple. "They're from the shop next door. They're shutting down, so everything's on sale." He frowned. "No one ever seems to stay there very long. The potpourri shop, the perfume store, even the fishmongers, they all close down almost as soon as they open, it seems to me. A real shame. Anyways. What can I do for you ladies? In the market for some manure, are ya? Because if you are, you came to the right place! No one spreads manure like we do at S.J.'s!"

Miranda's eyes were beginning to water. Susan took the lead on this, flipping open her notebook like a regular Cagney and/or Lacey.

"S.J. sells all manner of farm and gardening supplies, correct?"

"For sure."

"But it's not just fertilizers, mulch, soil. You also sell weed control. And pesticides, correct?"

"Some. Mainly bulk. Tanvir's has more choice."

"Boric acid?"

"Sure."

Trying not to wheeze, Miranda asked, "Did anyone in the cast or crew purchase chemicals here? Teena, say?"

"Teena? Nope. I would've remembered–she's gorgeous!–and even if I wasn't here when she came by, she would've mentioned it to me later, for sure. 'Hey, Melvin! Wassup! I was in your shop the other day. Good selection of manures! Want to go out sometime?' That sort of thing."

"How about your classmate, Rodney? Or your drama teacher, Mr. Penty?"

"Rodney, I don't think so, and Graham's wife does all their gardening, so I don't see much of him, but Pete stops by now and then, and Burt for sure. Not certain where Doc gets his from, and

Judy used to come in all the time, but I don't see her much now."

"How well do you know Rodney?" Miranda asked.

"Rodney? He's okay. Kinda quiet. A little sad. He's been deliberately flunking out of his final math class because he doesn't want to leave drama club. He's, like, one credit short. But doesn't want to graduate. Drama club is everything to him. So Mr. Penty–I mean Graham–he figured out a way to convince Rodney to finish high school. Deal is, if he does finish, Graham will make sure Rodney's on every crew of every show at the Happy Rock theater. Worked out an arrangement with Burt to include him."

"And you're sure Rodney has never been in here, never purchased boric acid?"

"We don't really keep receipts or records or anything. It's kinda hard to say who bought what, or how much, or when."

The bookkeeper in Susan winced at this. How hard was it to keep track of such things?

Well, thought Miranda, this has been no help. Her eyes were streaming and her throat was raw, and she was about to leave when Melvin said, "Huh."

This would turn out to be a very crucial *huh*.

"I mean, if you're asking about the cast and crew, there is someone else who used to come in here *a lot*, but I don't think it helps you very much now."

"Who?"

"Annette."

"But she had a condo by the water," said Susan. "Plus a penthouse in Portland. Hardly had a reason to buy manure in bulk. Why was she here?"

"Not to buy anything. Just to 'inspect the premises,' as she put it. Always real nice. Liked what she saw, said it had 'structural integrity' and 'true architectural value.'"

"I'm surprised she didn't try to shut it down," muttered Miranda. "The way she tried to with McCune's Garage. Not as an eyesore, perhaps, but certainly as a blight on the community. A nose-sore of sorts."

"Oh no, like I said, she was really happy with it. Said it would go for a good price, once we aired it out a bit and, maybe, hung an air freshener or two. Or three. Maybe a spritz of Febreze. Said she'd cover the cost of a full steam cleaning. Would pull out the wall paneling, replace the floor."

"Aha!" said Miranda. "Annette had designs on this place, as well!"

"She sure did. But heck, we weren't complaining! She wasn't trying to run us out of business or anything. My grandpa, he's planning to sell the building. He's in a seniors home in Gladstone. He's, like, eighty-four now."

"Your parents don't want to maintain the family store?" Susan asked.

"Let me put it this way. My mom said she would take over S.J. Fertilizers when pigs fly, and even then, she'd have to see them doing loop-de-loops first. Nope. Mom works at the Duchess, Dad at the insurance office. Neither of 'em wants to carry on our family tradition. And I'm still in high school, so selling the place makes sense."

"Wait a minute," said Miranda. "Eighty-four. A seniors home in Gladstone. Your grandfather is Strongman Seth?"

"That's what the S in S.J. is." He pointed to an engraved plaque on the wall: *Seth Jacobson, purveyor of the finest manure.* "My grandpa could throw a 90-pound sack of fertilizer onto a flatbed well into his seventies, with a 'Tally-ho!' and a 'How-dee-do!' Mr. Abbott used to watch, amazed. Small but mighty, my grandpa. The original strongman."

"I didn't know that was your grandfather! You never mentioned it," Miranda said, almost scolding him.

A teenage shrug. "Why would I? Everyone knows Seth is my papa. I figured you knew, too. Everybody knows everybody in Happy Rock and how they're related to each other, even if it's through marriage."

"That's right," Miranda realized. "Like how Owen McCune is Graham's cousin."

"Right. Same thing with Teena."

"What about Teena?"

"Y'know. How Graham's her uncle."

CHAPTER TWENTY-SEVEN

Team Miranda, On the Move!

It's strange how knowledge affects perception.

What we *think* we know is directly related to *how much* we know. Ghostly sounds, revealed to be a loose shutter banging in the night, will dissolve on our discovering their true cause. And a cunning young murderess can suddenly become a girl in pain just trying her best, all on a simple turn of phrase. *Graham's her uncle.*

Miranda rewound the events in her mind, saw them for what they were: a surly dad and a crying girl; the "Just Graham" (no Mr. or cousin–and certainly no Uncle Graham); Teena's admonishment to "be kind" when it came to Denise (her aunt) and even Teena's affectionate pat on Graham's back.

"Teena's home life is pretty crappy," Melvin said. "Her dad bullies her constantly. Nothing physical. He puts her down, makes fun of her, tells her she's not going to amount to anything. Never went to a single play she acted in. Her mom ran off. No wonder. Her aunt Denise knows what it's like better than anyone. She was, like, tormented by that brother of hers the whole time she was growing up. Probably why she has so much trouble asserting herself today."

Family matters, even if it's broken. *Especially* if it's broken.

"It's why she always volunteers, always stays late, never complains. Even in high school, Teena hated to go home. Threw herself into the clubs and activities, student council, all of that. Rodney was her ally. They were both, I dunno, loners I guess, even if Teena was one of the popular girls. Being popular doesn't mean you aren't hurting. Sometimes being popular is just a mask to hide behind."

Don't I know it, thought Miranda.

"Graham and Denise always looked out for her. She spent a lot of time with her aunt, I know. Denise was the one who urged Graham to give her a shot at the lead in the school play. And after that, well, she was on fire. Except . . ."

Melvin looked uncertain about how much he should share. Had he already blabbed too much about Teena's private anguish?

Susan gave him a gentle look. "Go on. It's okay."

"After working with her uncle Graham in the drama club, Teena wanted to follow in her aunt's footsteps, study at Yale. Her dream, I guess. And a pretty good dream, as far as dreams go."

Memories of Miranda as a young girl, wanting to escape. And isn't that what we all want? To escape, whether it's *from* something (in Teena's case) or *to* something (in Miranda's case, with a yearning for lights brighter than those of St. Olaf, Minnesota; or in Edgar's case, to a quiet bookstore as far from LA as possible).

"Mr. Penty–I mean Graham–he helped her with the application, wrote her a really good letter of reference. Pulled strings, I hear. Got her an audition. Her aunt flew out to Connecticut with her. Nailed it, is what I heard. She found out she got accepted during our rehearsals. Couldn't wait to tell Graham."

"It ends well, then?" said Miranda.

Her eyes were tearing up, and not entirely from the fumes at S.J.'s fertilizing emporium. In fact, Miranda hardly noticed the smell now. One can get used to anything, she supposed. A home life bereft of affection, a domineering father, or a sense of suffocation.

"Except it didn't," said Melvin. "End well, that is. Yale and everything. Her dad vetoed it."

"But she's an adult!" Miranda cried. "He can't stop her."

"But he did. Too expensive, he said, even though she offered to get a bank loan, work two jobs over the summers."

That was when I saw her crying, thought Miranda. That was the day her hopes were dashed. Her uncle was comforting her, was telling her not to give up.

Miranda's view of Graham had shifted. He was protecting his niece from an emotionally cruel father.

"She'll get to Yale someday," Miranda vowed. "Even if I have to karate chop her dad into submission!"

Ah, if only life were as simple as a *Pastor Fran* episode. If only the bad guys could be summarily dealt with by a single *Haii-ya!* and a crumpling blow to the shoulder.

Teena had already been accepted into drama school. Whatever tensions and turmoil she faced at home, she hardly needed a one-line death scene on her local stage, however much fun that would have been. And it would have been fun. But worth killing someone for? Hardly. Graham had already gone to bat for her over Yale.

So why would either of them want to kill me?

The answer, Miranda realized, was that they wouldn't. There was no reason for either of them to.

It was then that Susan asked Melvin a crucial question.

"Did Annette Baillie ever spend time in here, alone, with the inventory?"

Melvin laughed. "What 'inventory'? We have an old ledger book that's never filled in"–again, Susan winced at this–"stacks of tins here and there, manure mainly, bug pellets and such."

"So you would have no idea if something had been removed from the store without you noticing?"

It was a rhetorical question; Melvin had already answered it, and the answer was no.

Miranda sighed. Without an inventory list, it was another dead end.

But Susan didn't think so. She leaned toward Miranda and whispered, "We need to talk. Now. Somewhere private."

And less malodorous, Miranda hoped.

Declining a final generous offer of sugar cookies, Susan and Miranda left the store, pursued not by a bear, but by several persistent flies. They buzzed around them like an idée fixe: something you can't quite shake your head clear of.

Susan swatted them away as she had with Miranda's earlier flights of fancy.

"The facts," Susan said, "were right there in front of us all along. Miranda, I know who the murderer was."

Was, not is.

"Let's get out here. I'll explain it all over a bowl of today's soup du jour."

In a corner booth of the Cozy Café, far from any prying eyes or potential eavesdroppers, Susan Lladdwraig revealed the name of the killer with a hushed tone.

"The person who murdered Annette Baillie was . . . Annette Baillie."

Outside, the sky was darkening. The witching hour was at hand. Between Miranda's visit to Edgar in his jail cell, Susan's trove of cozies, and their fragrant visit with Melvin, the day had bled away.

"The *victim* was the murderer?" It sounded strange just to say it.

Susan nodded. "It was staring us in the face the whole time. Who ensured that you always got the chipped glass? Annette. Who knew precisely which glass you would drink from? Annette."

"But why me?"

"Envy? Bile? Who knows. Dead women don't tell tales, but we do know what a vindictive soul she was. Owen's garage. Edgar's bookstore. Haranguing poor Rodney nightly. She even destroyed Graham's life, to hear Denise tell it. She had as many enemies as fans in this town, and why? Because she really was a nasty piece of work."

"And jealous of other people's success," said Miranda with a sigh.

It was something she knew quite well, as all actors do. It was something she fought against within herself. She knew how toxic such envy could become, how septic.

Susan ticked it off. "Means: undetected access to the boric acid at S.J. Fertilizers. Motive: her envious resentment of you. Take you out of the equation and she would be the undisputed star of the production. Opportunity: during the play itself, when she could spike that one glass with poison. She was probably gleefully waiting for you to keel over offstage. Miranda Abbott's final death scene."

"She killed herself... by mistake. Remarkable."

"Hoisted on her own petard," as Susan put it.

"That would explain the silence, and why there were no more follow-up threats or attempts on my life. The person who wanted me dead *was* dead."

Miranda felt elated, but Susan had that same frown on her face. The one that said *We're not out of the weeds quite yet.*

"Problem is, how do we *prove* it?" said Susan. "The real challenge is only now beginning: how to convince the court of Edgar's innocence."

"We go down and we tell them!" said Miranda. "That's how. You saw me switch the glasses! You're a witness."

"That's just it," said Susan. "I could also be called as a witness for the prosecution. Against *you*."

"What?"

"It could as easily have been the other way around. You switched the glasses; you killed Annette. Dead women don't tell tales, true.

But that's the problem. They also can't give testimony or be interrogated. It doesn't make sense for us to free Edgar only to have them incarcerate you in his stead. We have to think."

Miranda wasn't good at thinking–not in a linear way. Hers was an intuitive emotional intelligence. It was why she complemented Susan's more methodical approach so well.

One such intuitive leap had now presented itself to Miranda.

"Who discovers the poison, Susan? During the play. The little green vial conveniently labeled POISON? Who discovers it at the end of Act Seven, hidden in a drawer? I'll tell you who. Mamie Dickens, aka Annette Baillie. Don't you see?"

She didn't.

"Annette expected to waltz out of that theater unscathed," said Miranda. "She didn't *plan* on kicking the bucket. She had to sneak the poison in, and she would have to sneak it out again. But she died, and that never happened. So where is it? Where is the poison? Where did it go?"

Susan's eyes widened. "It didn't go anywhere. It's still somewhere in the theater!"

"Bingo! Hiding in plain sight. Do you know where I would have hidden it?" Miranda asked.

"In the prop marked POISON!" said Susan.

"The last place anyone would look."

Miranda turned to the thickening clouds outside the café window. The streetlamps along the harbor were flickering on. The Duchess Hotel was lit up in a connect-the-dots arrangement of lights, like a starlet's dressing room mirror. Beside it was the ornate glow of the Opera House.

Another leap, but not in the dark. "Susan, do you happen to have a No. 2 Phillips screwdriver on you?"

CHAPTER TWENTY-EIGHT

Ghost Lights

Susan's crossbody purse, flat and square and very sensible, was a quarter the size of Miranda's large amorphous shoulder bag, yet it held twice as many items.

Susan retrieved a roll of screwdrivers and Allen keys from this purse, unfurling them in the booth in front of Miranda like a general laying out his plans.

"What would you like? Phillips? Flathead? Square top? Octagonal?"

A purse as tidy and organized as her ledgers. Miranda was impressed.

"I think this is the start of a beautiful partnership," she said.

"I also have a tire-pressure gauge and a level, if you ever need to check if something is level."

"Just a screwdriver for now. I think he said No. 2, or was it No. 4?"

"I have both."

Susan now slid a pen from the leather loop in her purse that was specifically for pens. (Had anyone ever used it for that purpose before? Like keeping actual gloves in a glove compartment?)

She turned her notebook to a fresh page.

"Okay," said Susan. "What are you thinking?"

Again, Miranda wasn't so much thinking as acting on impulse. And when she explained to Susan, with great enthusiasm and much waving of her arms, what exactly she was proposing they do, Susan balked.

"But isn't that a crime scene?"

"*Was* a crime scene. They arrested Edgar, remember? As far as they're concerned, the case is closed."

"I don't know . . . but breaking and entering . . . seems wrong, somehow."

"Not breaking and entering. Investigating! Look, I did that sort of thing every week on *Pastor Fran* with no repercussions whatsoever."

"Not sure if that applies to the real world."

Miranda played her trump card. "You do care what happens to Edgar, right?"

Of course she did. If they'd arrested anyone else, maybe not. But Edgar mattered. He mattered to the community, and the community mattered to Susan.

"Let's do this," she said.

Miranda and Susan paid their bill and drove over.

After bumbling about in the dark behind the Opera House for a good ten minutes, they eventually found the small window that Burt had mentioned, illuminated by a lone streetlamp in the alley.

The window itself was high up—and disconcertingly narrow. Have to be awfully lean to fit through that, Miranda thought.

Susan slipped in with aplomb, however, after dragging over a bin for them to stand on and then using the screwdriver to loosen the supposedly secure latch, just as Burt had described. As Susan disappeared through the opening, Miranda thought, Sure, easy to do when you're the size of a hand puppet.

She had a tougher time of it. Had to walrus her way in. Managed to squeeze her bust past the frame, but the rest of her got stuck, and she ended up corkscrewing through it with Susan pulling from the other end.

"Damn these voluptuous hips!" Miranda cried as she worked her way in.

Miranda tumbled to the other side with a singular lack of grace, but popped right back up, indefatigable and ready for the fray. Miranda Abbott was nothing if not fearless.

And she would need that courage now. Is there anything spookier than an empty theater at night? It echoed with their voices, their footsteps, their trepidation, as they groped their way through to the backstage area, illuminated mainly by the exit sign glow.

A taped outline marked the ghost of Annette Baillie, which gave them pause. A shiver of ice ran down Miranda's spine.

Small, yellow plastic markers were tented at various spots backstage to flag where items had been removed as evidence. These police markers seemed to glow in the half-light, as eerie as tombstones.

Numbers 1 to 4 had been placed near the taped outline–items that must have fallen or been toppled when Annette fell–and 5 through 7 were on and around the backstage sink, where Rodney would have washed out the jug and glasses, including the one that contained the poison. Those, too, had been removed and numbers left in their place.

"That's odd," said Susan. She had a concerned look on her face. "Over there, by the storage area, where they worked on the set."

This was the workspace where Burt and the others had toiled. It had been spotlessly clean prior to the dress rehearsal, the sets having been erected and the crew told, in Burt's words, to "stand down."

Susan swallowed. A single yellow tent marker had been placed on the floor in front of Burt's work cupboard. "What do you think was over there?"

There were no other tent markers anywhere near it.

"And that number," said Susan. "Thirteen."

"Bad luck?"

"Not that. Look. All of the numbers are in sequence–1, 2, 3, 4– till we get to 7, and then it suddenly jumps to 13."

"So?"

"I have a bookkeeper's mind, Miranda. Why isn't it sequential?" Another perturbed look came over her, and with a flash of insight, she went out onto the stage itself.

Sure enough, markers 8 through 11 were arranged at various points across the stage, the yellow plastic glowing even more eerily under the ghost light.

"That explains it," said Miranda. "They laid down the plastic markers backstage first, and then came out here and put down the rest. Later on, they must have spotted something else, something they missed earlier backstage, and then flagged that as number thirteen."

"Hmm," said Susan.

"I don't know if the numbering of it really matters, though," said Miranda. Her shoulder bag was vibrating, but she ignored it. "I mean, that's not the reason we're here, right? The desk, remember? Where the vial of poison was kept?"

Miranda gestured to the large rolltop desk onstage. The furniture, the coat rack: everything had been left exactly as it was. Even the discreet spot behind the sofa where Graham Penty had been sick had been labeled with a small numbered marker.

Must have scraped up some of that to look for toxins, thought Miranda. Eww.

"But how would they have missed it?" Susan wondered. "The thirteenth clue. Burt left that area backstage completely empty. If something was just lying there on the floor, it would have been obvious. The police would have flagged it on their first pass. But they didn't." And again she said, "Hmm."

The gears were clearly turning, but Miranda's bag was vibrating and she was getting antsy. One doesn't want to skulk around a crime scene any longer than necessary, even if it is, technically, a *former* crime scene.

She crossed over to the desk. Reluctantly, Susan joined her. Something was bothering her; Miranda could tell. Something Susan couldn't quite articulate.

But no time for that.

"This is where Annette–or rather, Mamie Dickens–'discovers' the hidden poison. If I was going to stash the poison, this is where I would put it. Inside the secret compartment within this very drawer!"

With a triumphant flourish, Miranda pulled open the desk drawer and...

Nothing.

There was no secret compartment from which to withdraw a vial of poison. Of course not. When actors produced items from the supposedly secret compartment that was tucked out of sight inside the drawer, they did so through the power of suggestion. They just *pretended* there was a secret panel; they *pretended* there was a hidden compartment. It's what actors do. They pretend.

The stage desk was as sturdy as the real thing, though, this being Burt Linder's handiwork. Anything he built was built to last.

Inside the desk drawer was another yellow police maker, almost mocking them. This was the missing number 12, closing out the set. Miranda considered the sequence of the police markers again:

1 to 7 backstage, 8 to 12 on the stage itself–and that one anomalous number 13, out of sequence, backstage near the work area, like an afterthought.

And inside the deep drawer of the desk: number 12, and nothing else. Other than this single police marker, the drawer was empty.

"They must have taken everything out."

Miranda reached inside to check, ran her hand along the bottom and the inner edges. Nothing. It was empty all the way down.

"Dang it all to heck," she said, channeling her inner Pastor Fran.

Feeling discouraged, Miranda walked out to center stage. Susan joined her.

"I really thought there would be an actual secret panel," said Miranda.

Susan was sympathetic. "If it makes you feel better, Burt wanted to install one, but Judy said it would have caused problems for the actors. What if they couldn't open it in the middle of a performance? So Burt ceded this point. 'Concessions have to be made,' is what he said."

Miranda looked at the darkened theater. She remembered that first audition. Judy's comfy seat in the middle and twelve folding chairs for the actors. No. Not twelve chairs. *Thirteen*. Rodney had had to scramble to place an extra chair on the stage for Miranda.

"I just made it to the audition," she said. "Under the wire. Thanks to you, Susan."

"With only minutes to spare," Susan said fondly.

"Seems so long ago now." Then something twigged. She turned to Susan. "Burt said *concessions*? Is that what he really said?"

Susan nodded. "He said, 'Concessions have to be made, I suppose.'"

"That's funny. He said the same thing to me about an episode of *Pastor Fran*."

And now Susan's phone was ringing.

Unlike Miranda, she didn't need to rummage; her phone was where it always was, tucked in the designated side pocket of her purse. When Susan checked who was calling, she blanched. She showed Miranda: HAPPY ROCK PD.

"What do I do?" she whispered.

"Answer it. No! Don't!"

"I have to answer."

"Don't! Wait. No. Yes, answer it, but be cool."

"Hello, Susan speaking." She listened, said "I see" and "Mm-hmm," and then handed the phone to Miranda. "It's for you."

Gulp.

"Yes!" said Miranda with false bravado. "It is I."

"This is Officer Holly Hinton, Happy Rock PD. I called your number, but you weren't answering."

"Terribly sorry about that. I'm out for my nightly constitutional, a stroll along your magnificent waterfront, and I'm afraid I hadn't thought to bring my cellular phone with me."

"You're walking along the harbor?"

"That's right."

"No. You're not. You're inside the Opera House and you need to come out."

Miranda, bluffing. "An outrageous accusation! What makes you think we're anywhere near the theater?"

"I saw you go in through the window. You need to come out, okay Miss Wiggly Bum? You and your pal. You need to leave. Right now. We've already swept the scene, and the police tape isn't up anymore, so I suppose I can't charge you with entering a restricted zone, but it's still trespassing."

"But–"

"Listen. I'm on the last hour of my last shift of my last night before I start a much-needed and long overdue maternity leave. I'm too tired and too pregnant to go in after you. So you have to come out, okay Nancy Drew? And bring George with you."

Is that who we really are? thought Miranda. Not Starsky and Hutch, not Crockett and Tubbs, not even Turner and Hooch, but just Nancy Drew and her best friend Georgia, aka "George."

"I'll give you exactly four minutes. After that, I will charge you with interfering in a police investigation."

"But—but we were searching for evidence. To help clear Edgar's name! And evidence found is as good as evidence gained. That's what they say!"

"No one says that. Let me guess. You were looking for a vial of green liquid labeled POISON."

"Er, yes."

"And you figured we were too dumb to have looked in the drawer."

"Not the drawer. The secret drawer!"

"There is no secret drawer."

"Well, yes, I realize that now. But still."

She could hear Holly sigh on the other end. She didn't even try to hide it.

"Yes, we found the vial," said Officer Holly. "And yes, there was a green liquid inside. And yes, we sent it to the lab."

"And?" Miranda asked eagerly.

"It showed a high concentrate of triarylmethane dihydrogen monoxide."

"Aha!"

"That's the chemical formula for food coloring and tap water. There was no poison in that vial. And anyway, we already found the source of the boric acid that killed Annette Baillie. We were going to make the announcement tomorrow morning anyway, so you might as well know. It was Carl who did it."

"Carl! I knew it! I was right all along."

"Not the murder, Nancy Drew"–Miranda really wished she'd stop calling her that–"the poison. Carl was the one who discovered it. On our third pass. I was too pregnant and Ned was, shall I say, a little too 'pleasantly plump' to really get under the work cupboard. But Carl? Well, you know how athletic he used to be. Was the star of our high school. Before my time, but the legend lives on. Anyway, he crawls all the way along the bottom. Spots it *waaaay* in the back when he shines his flashlight underneath. Asks me for a coat hook and we pull it out. It was her water bottle. The bedazzled one. That's what caught his light: the rhinestones. She was always leaving that bedazzled bottle everywhere. Anyway. The water still inside was laced with boric acid. She must have kicked it under the cupboard during her death throes."

Number thirteen, Miranda realized.

That was why the police markers were out of order. They'd found Annette's water bottle *after* everything else had been collected and tagged.

That number rattled around in her head.

Thirteen . . .

Something was tugging at her sleeve. Miranda handed the phone back to Susan, then pointed to the darkened sound booth at the rear of the auditorium.

"I'll be right back," she said.

Miranda made her way down the stairs on the side of the stage and then hurried up the aisle, past the seats to the very back. She disappeared through the CREW ONLY door that was next to the main entrance.

•••

SUSAN WATCHED FROM THE STAGE, ignoring Holly's repeated "*Hello? Hello?*" on the phone.

The lights in the sound booth came on.

Susan could see Miranda's silhouette for just a moment before the lights went off again. Miranda then came back out, but instead of walking down to the stage, she opened the auditorium doors. The low lights of the lobby spilled out, then the doors closed behind Miranda–on a muffled thump. What was she up to?

Susan was alone onstage with only the ghost light and the increasingly irate voice of Officer Holly to keep her company. *"So help me, I will lock the both of you up and throw away the key!"* Susan tried to remain calm. But a sudden loud noise from behind startled her. It was the grating sound of the heavy backstage doors.

MIRANDA BURST ONSTAGE, out of breath, nodding–but satisfied–as though having unwrapped something crucial.

"You went all the way around?" Susan asked. "Through the lobby and then in from the back?"

Hands on hips, still panting. "As fast as I could. And as quietly as I could." Miranda held out her palm. "You can give me the phone. Thanks."

"Time's up, Nancy Drew," Holly snapped. "Go get George and go."

"Can you at least unlock the front doors?"

"You got yourself in, you can get yourself out. Same way."

The patrol car was parked in the alleyway, with Holly no doubt watching, amused, as Miranda wormed her way out through the window into the alley. Holly's last official duty as an officer.

After they'd screwed the latch tight again and moved the bin back–under the baleful eye of Happy Rock's finest–Miranda and Susan walked over to the parking lot feeling suitably chastened.

They sat in Susan's car, and Miranda told her what Holly had said, how it was Annette's water bottle that had been poisoned, not the chipped glass.

Annette had been the target all along, right from the start.

"We were asking ourselves who wanted to kill *me*," said Miranda. "The answer is: no one. So the real question is, who wanted Annette Baillie dead?"

Susan was very quiet. "Owen," she said. "It has to be him."

"Except Edgar told me that Owen had already won his case against Annette."

Susan wasn't convinced, though. "Revenge is a dish best served cold. Maybe he still wanted to exact his."

"No," said Miranda. "It's not Owen. We've been looking in the wrong place all along." She turned to Susan with renewed determination. "I want you to drop me off at McCune's Garage. There's someone I need to talk to. I'll meet you back at the bookstore, okay? And Susan?"

"Yes?"

"Be careful. Bring Chief Buckley with you. Just to be safe." She rummaged in her bag. "I have one last call to make, and then we can go."

She dialed Carl's number.

"Officer Carl? Miranda here. Can you pick up Rodney and meet us at the murder store? I'll explain when I get there. I know it's after hours. Susan will let you in."

OWEN MCCUNE'S GARAGE was closed up for the night. There was a light on, but it didn't matter, because Miranda wasn't going to McCune's. She had a different path to follow.

She had to be absolutely certain before she went any further. She couldn't afford another misstep.

Behind McCune's Garage, a gravel lane curved into the forest, shrouded by evergreens under a partial moon. A log cabin at the end of it and a pickup truck parked out front.

Miranda stepped up, onto the front porch, took a steadying breath–and knocked.

"Hello, Burt," she said when he opened the door.

He eyed her warily. "It's late. What brings you out here?"

"I just had a couple of questions. About the set."

"Sure. Come inside. I'll boil us up some tea."

But Miranda stayed on the porch. Didn't go in. Smiled tightly instead. "I'm fine out here, thank you. This won't take long."

"Okay. Suit yourself. What did you want to ask me?"

"You built the entire set, yes? From scratch?"

"Yup. Exactly to scale."

"Exactly?"

"That's right."

"So you would know how it all works? How it fits together?"

"Yup."

Miranda smiled. "Thank you."

"Anything else I can do for you?"

"There is, yes. If you wouldn't mind, could you give me a ride up to the bookstore? I don't have a vehicle, and I need to drop by and pick something up. Would you accompany me?"

"Of course," he said. "Let me grab my keys."

Anything for a lady. He was gallant to a fault, our Burt.

CHAPTER TWENTY-NINE

J'accuse!

Burt was surprised when it was Chief Buckley who opened the door. This was not who he had expected at Edgar's bookstore late at night, after hours.

"Ned?"

"Hiya, Burt!"

Ned was in uniform and on duty, and he beamed at the Deadly Spy of Happy Rock like a schoolboy. Oh right, thought Miranda. The man crush. Let's hope it doesn't get in the way of this.

"Come in, come in," said Ned. "Susan's setting up."

They followed him down the hallway, lined with books, into the main room. Susan had rolled the display tables back to open up the center space. She'd placed five chairs of various vintage in a straight line, with the sixth chair facing them. It looked like the setup for a very intimate book reading.

Murder was in the air, which was appropriate considering where this was taking place.

When Susan saw Burt, she was equally surprised. She came over, whispered to Miranda. "Not Owen?"

"I walked to Burt's from the garage instead," Miranda whispered back. "That way, I could ask him for a ride afterwards. If he'd heard a vehicle, Burt would have wondered."

Burt stood, surveying the room: the heavy desk, the high shelves, the chairs that Susan had lined up for them.

"Expecting someone else?" he asked.

"Why would you say that?" said Ned, hand resting on his holster.

"Simple math. There's only four of us, but there's six chairs."

"Hello?"

It was Carl's voice from the front hall, and he appeared soon after, out of uniform, with Rodney in tow. Rodney, as always, was dressed in drab colors, with his head low.

"Perfect!" said Miranda. "Let's begin. Everyone, please take a seat."

Burt had assumed Ned Buckley would be the one facing them, but Ned sat down next to everyone else.

"What's going on?" Burt asked.

"Your guess is as good as mine," said Ned. "This is like an episode of *Pastor Fran*. I just wish Bea was here to enjoy it."

And, in that moment, it was clear to Miranda that Ned Buckley had an affection for Bea so deep it could almost be mistaken for love. It was also clear that he wasn't taking any of this too seriously.

Miranda chose to stand instead. She addressed them as one might a theatrical audience.

"Good evening, one and all. Let me begin by saying, *thank you.* Thank you for coming out this evening, thank you for–"

"It's late," Burt grumbled. "Think you can get on with it?"

"Certainly." This would normally be where she would thank the sponsors, but there were none, except maybe the bookstore itself, so she pushed on. "I swapped glasses onstage. I had assumed that Annette had been poisoned by mistake when she drank from my glass. Which would have meant that I was the intended victim. But the poison was actually in Annette's bedazzled water bottle, not in my chipped glass. I was not the target of a murder plot. It had been Annette in the crosshairs from the start. So I had to re-evaluate everything I thought I knew. And one name kept surfacing: Denise Penty, Graham's wife."

A murmur from the audience.

"She had *motive*. As she herself said, 'Annette ruined my husband's life. Everything she touches turns toxic.' Toxic. That is how Denise described it. Was she tipping her hand on the method of murder? Denise seemed more bitter about Annette's relentless hectoring of Graham than he himself did. Denise's failed foray at Yale could have also played a part in it. The former Pride of Happy Rock removing the reigning Pride of Happy Rock. There would have been a certain poetic appeal to that. But beyond motive, she also had the *means*. Melvin mentioned that Graham never came in to the fertilizer store to pick up night soil or pesticides because—and I quote—'his wife did all the gardening.' But what of *opportunity*? The killer had to have access to the backstage area. I tried. But it would have been impossible for someone to slip out of the sound booth, make their way backstage, drop poison into Annette's water bottle, then slip back out again and return to the sound booth without being seen—or heard—from several different vantage points and by several different people. It wasn't Denise Penty, even if she had cause to want Annette dead and the means to do it."

The expression on Ned's face had shifted. This no longer felt like a party game. Miranda was zeroing in on something. Or someone. But who?

"Rodney," she said. "Unlike Denise, you spend a lot of time backstage. Practically live there, am I right?"

Anger in Burt's eyes. "What is this? Are you accusing him of something?"

"No. Not him."

Any levity was gone. Things were serious now. Deadly serious.

"You helped out with the auditions, right, Rodney? You put out the chairs for us, yes? The big comfy one for Judy and twelve more for the actors, correct?"

He mumbled in assent, nodded.

"But then what happens? I show up at the very last moment and you have to scramble to find a chair for me, too. That must have really bugged you."

"A little."

"And for that, I apologize. But you do understand that I had signed up according to proper and rigorous protocol–as per the Giant Book of Regulations–and that my fees had been covered before I ever stepped onto that stage to audition?"

"I guess."

"You sound unsure. Here, let me show you."

Miranda crossed over to the rolltop desk, opened the shallow drawer, took out Susan's ledger and receipt book, and held them up to show Rodney, as though they were Exhibit A in a trial.

"My name is listed in this ledger, and a receipt was written for my membership fee. You can confirm that, right, Susan?"

Susan nodded.

Miranda lay the ledger and receipt book to one side, turned her attention to Ned. "The Case of the Missing Pocketbook. Remind me. Who solved that one, Ned?"

"No one, really. It sort of solved itself."

"But that's not entirely true, is it?" She looked to Susan for confirmation. "It was Edgar. That's who found your pocketbook and returned it to you. Is that right?"

Again, Susan nodded. (The pieces were falling into place. Susan could feel it. But what it meant, she wasn't sure.)

Miranda smiled. "Which brings me to you, Burt."

Ned Buckley quietly unsnapped the latch on his service revolver.

"About time you got to me," Burt muttered. "Chairs for the actors and pocketbooks that go missing. What does any of this have to do with–"

"The set," said Miranda. "Edgar wrote his play based on murders that happened right here. In this house. In this very room. And you built the set, meticulously capturing all of it, including this desk, for example."

"That's right."

"It's funny. When Susan and I snuck into the theater earlier tonight, searching for evidence, I was struck by how *deep* the drawer is onstage, and how much shallower the real one is here. Did you make a mistake, Burt? Of course you didn't. You re-created this room *exactly* as it is, right down to the wallpaper. Yes?"

"Damn straight," he said defiantly. "I take pride in what I do."

Miranda tutted. "Pride. One of the Seven Deadly Sins, Mr. Linder." It was up there with envy, the actor's vice. "You were so precise, so proud of your work, and yet . . . the secret drawer. You didn't include that. Because *concessions have to be made.*"

Burt nodded. "Would've tripped the actors up. It's a wooden cleat-and-cog system, with a false bottom. Tricky to work. You have to press the drawer down as you extend it. Let me show you."

"Please," said Miranda, standing aside.

"It sometimes opens by mistake if something gets jammed inside. And then it closes up again if you force it." He wrestled with the front of the drawer.

"When something gets jammed in it. Like a pocketbook, perhaps?" Miranda asked.

"I suppose," said Burt, pulling the desk drawer out halfway.

There were, essentially, two bottoms to the drawer: a top, false one, and a real one underneath it. The space between these two formed a secret compartment. When Burt pushed down on the false bottom while at the same time pulling back on the drawer the rest of the way, the hidden cogs below caught and the false bottom above remained locked in place as the rest of the drawer slid open, revealing its true depths.

"Edgar knew about this secret compartment, didn't he Susan? That's where your pocketbook was. And that's where he found it. Later, he showed you how the drawer worked. You must have enjoyed a chuckle over that."

Officer Carl was shaking his head in amazement. "So Edgar solved that case, huh, Chief?"

"I guess he did," said Ned. "Good on him."

But it wasn't the pocketbook Miranda wanted to talk about. It was the hidden drawer itself. And the contents it contained.

She reached inside and took out a *second* mauve book, this one labeled INVOICES.

"I was looking in the wrong records," said Miranda. "Susan's handwritten ledger contains the names of thirteen actors who auditioned for the play and, if I were to go through the receipt book, I am sure I would find thirteen corresponding receipt stubs, paid in full. But . . ." She opened the INVOICES book. "I imagine *fourteen* invoices were prepared."

Miranda didn't have to look long for the fourteenth invoice; it fluttered out of the book on its own accord. It had been made out to Annette Baillie for her overdue membership fee, as required in order to audition. The invoice had clearly been crumpled up and then flattened out again. Across it, in large angry letters, all caps, was written: I DON'T PAY TO ACT!!

Miranda reached inside the hidden compartment again and, carefully with two fingers, extracted the second dose of boric acid. It was in a sealed packet made out to the bookstore.

There was a long pause.

When Susan finally spoke, her voice was flat. "How did you figure it out?"

"The chairs," said Miranda. "The folding chairs, onstage. You had asked Rodney to put out twelve of them for the actors. Then I signed up, just under the cutoff, so Rodney had to hurry up and bring out another chair–a thirteenth chair. But when Annette Baillie barged in, what did Rodney have to do? He had to go get *another* chair. Annette wasn't late. She hadn't even bothered to sign up in the first place. She just elbowed her way in, onto the stage, and eventually into the play itself. Fourteen actors auditioned that day, including Annette. But there were only thirteen names in your ledger that had the notation 'paid in full' written beside them. Mine was the very last name on the list. The missing name is Annette Baillie's. Shall I check?"

Susan waved her off. There was no need.

"Everyone else paid," Susan said. "She was the only one who didn't. The only one! Same as when she was with the company before. When Annette was the lead last time, she never paid her dues. Never! I asked, I reminded, I sent follow-up after follow-up. She just laughed. It was my complaint that finally got the board to temporarily suspend her membership. All she had to do was pay her overdue fees and we would have waived the fine. Instead, she railed about 'underhanded anonymous henchmen'–singling out Graham–and stomped off in a snit. When she stormed back onstage in the middle of our auditions this year, without even signing up ahead of time or bothering to pay for a membership, it was like the Devil had returned to Happy Rock."

"And the invoice?" Miranda asked.

"She scribbled down that disrespectful answer and threw it back at me. It was rude. And it wasn't just to me! She was tormenting Graham and Rodney, and she was going to take Edgar's bookstore away from him, was going to have it rezoned and shut down. She would have sold it to the highest bidder. Never mind that this bookstore is a community hub. Annette Baillie didn't care about community! She didn't even care about money, really. She cared about winning. It went against everything that the Happy Rock Amalgamated & Consolidated Little Theater Society stands for. She was . . ." Susan seemed to be searching for the worst word she could think of. ". . . *disruptive*. And worst of all, it wasn't fun! Not at all. Usually, it's the highlight of our year, but she soured the entire experience. The play should have been about people coming together to stage a show for their families, their friends, their neighbors, their community. Instead, it was divisive and derisive and mean-spirted. And it was all Annette's fault."

"But we would have got through it," said Miranda. "We were only days away from opening night."

"You don't understand! Now that she'd been cast, she would have played the lead for years to come. Year in and year out. Worse and worse. Denise was right. It was Denise who first put the idea in my head. She said, 'Someone should kill her; the town would be better for it.'"

"But *she* didn't, Susan. You did. You killed Annette over $43.87 in unpaid membership fees."

"It's not the money, it's the principle behind it. Annette Baillie swings in, ignoring the rules, and still gets to take part in our play? It wasn't *fair*. It wasn't fair to me, it wasn't fair to our volunteers, it certainly wasn't fair to the other actors. Everyone deserves to be treated with respect and consideration."

It was what Susan had said to Miranda that first day, when they'd first met. *Everyone deserves to be treated with respect and consideration.*

"You thought they would blame it on her bad heart, didn't you?" said Miranda. "And you expected Rodney to help cover your tracks without realizing it. He was supposed to wash out all of the water bottles at the end of the performance. Is that right, Rodney?"

"Couldn't find Ms. Baillie's," he said.

"She kicked it out of sight as she was dying," Miranda said. She looked at Susan, awareness dawning. "That's why you were so perturbed about that one police marker, the one they had clearly flagged after the first search. You had a premonition about what that meant, what they had found. But you also realized that Rodney had already done you a favor in washing out the chipped glass. It allowed you to steer our investigation toward Annette as our main suspect. Hoisted on her own petard, as it were. *Dead women tell no tales*. You said as much: 'A dead woman can't defend herself.' You weren't my Watson, Susan. You were my anti-Watson, intentionally trying to throw me off the trail."

"Annette *was* responsible," Susan insisted. "She was responsible for her own demise. She brought it upon herself, even if she didn't actually plant the poison. I hadn't meant for her to die so suddenly, at the end of Act One. She was meant to make it to the end. She would have gotten her final ovation. I'm not cruel. I would have given her that. But I didn't realize just how weak her heart was. The dosage I used was meant to percolate through her system slowly in what would have looked like a cardiac attack, backstage, after the curtain call."

Her cozies and the bookstore's DIY section would have taught her that.

It made Miranda think of what Ned had said that first day as well, when he had dropped Miranda off at the bookstore: *Someone like that, surrounded by murder all day? Who knows what they are capable of?*

He had been speaking about Edgar, but he might well have been speaking about Susan Lladdwraig, the diminutive clerk at I Only Read Murder.

Miranda asked, "Why the second dose, Susan? Who was that for? For Judy, who cast Annette even though she wasn't eligible? Or for me if I got too close to the truth?"

"The other one was for me, if I got caught."

Ned rose and softly said, "You read a lot of mysteries, Susan. You know what comes next. *You have the right to remain silent…*"

Susan had been in the wings when Annette died. Which was appropriate somehow, because Susan Lladdwraig had spent her entire life in the wings.

Miranda would visit Susan in jail, would bring her cozies and chamomile. Would visit her afterwards, as well, when she was transferred to the state penitentiary in Salem, Oregon. When reporters caught wind of this, they would ambush Miranda, demanding to know why she was spending time with the very murderer she had helped catch. And Miranda would reply, "Because she's my friend." It was a kindness Pastor Fran had never shown to any of the myriad people she had helped lock up over the years, but then Fran was never as considerate as Miranda was.

When Pastor Fran cracked a case, she simply moved on without looking back: *Maybe down this next road, I'll find a place to call my own. Maybe this time, I'll rest and find a home. Maybe this time…*

But not Miranda.

CHAPTER THIRTY

Opening Night Jitters

Bea Maracle had never seen anything like it. The lassoed "sold out" area of the auditorium had to be expanded, from a hundred seats to two hundred, and then from two hundred to three hundred, until they eventually ran out of rope and had to open up the entire theater, balconies included. And even then, the box office had to turn people away.

"It's Pastor Fran that did it!" Bea said. "All that hoopla has fed ticket sales!"

And she was right.

With the investigation surrounding the play, opening night had been pushed back to late summer. "The show must go on!" Judy had exhorted. Meanwhile, Edgar's arrest and subsequent release had brought with it a surge of attention. By the time the curtains rose, the place was packed.

Teena Culliford's death scene got a rousing standing O at the end of Act One.

She'd truly made the part her own, going throat *then* lamp, a bold choice but one that paid off, to go by the audience's cries of

"The throat! The throat!" So much so that she was chanted back onstage to die again. A continued call began to bring her out for a third death, but modesty prevailed and she chose not to.

When Lord Reginald finally rushed offstage to check on the maid and then came running back out again to announce, "She's dead!" a voice in the back heckled, "No kidding, Sherlock!" to much laughter in the house.

Miranda recognized the voice as that of Holly Hinton, attending her first event since the twins were born and enjoying every moment of being in the audience rather than onstage.

Owen McCune remembered his lines. Mostly. When he did slip up, he was prompted by the audience, most of whom had a better grasp of the script than he did. (Though he did render the phrase "exquisite marigolds and chrysanthemums" as "exhaust manifolds and catalytic conversions.")

Miranda thought, At this point, he's doing it on purpose.

The delays had pushed the opening night past the end of the spring salmon season and, for the first time, Doc Meadows's wife was in attendance. Miranda saw her in the second row, looking up with eyes only for him. Doc's wife watched him throughout the play, never looking away, even during Teena's death scene. Just Doc, and no one else. She was a round-faced woman with dimples and beautiful hair and eyes that shined when she smiled—and she smiled often. A face you could fall in love with, Miranda thought.

When the time came for Doc's monologue, he ignored the staging that had been blocked out for him during rehearsals, which would have had him proclaiming widely to the audience as a whole, and instead stepped to the edge of the stage and addressed his wife directly. Her, and only her.

The crowd went silent as he spoke.

"I hear your laughter in the corridors . . . and in the morning when I wake . . . I am a man condemned. Condemned to love the woman I married. To love her always, dearly, deeply."

Doc's wife looked at him the entire time, tears in her eyes. Next year, the salmon could wait.

Judy Traynor, meanwhile, was in her glory, both as director and as the oracle, with her final line of the play, *"I see... I see... a wonderful community taking root. I see a brighter future for us all,"* met with thunderous approval.

They had brought Seth Jacobson in from the seniors home in Gladstone to watch his grandson step into the role, and Seth himself was brought up onstage at the end for an ovation. He had a walker now, and his gait had slowed, but he was the One True Strongman still. They handed him the dumbbells and he hoisted them above his head one last time with a raspy "Tally-ho."

The Crowd. Went. Wild.

And as the cheers washed across the auditorium, Miranda spotted Edgar in the back row, under the light of the exit sign. A pink glow. A warm smile.

And what of Miranda? What of our star?

The media clangor around the investigation, and her role in cracking it, had thrust Miranda back into a larger spotlight. The headlines were variations of the same, usually rife with superfluous punctuation: *TV's Pastor Fran Solves REAL Murder Case??* Or: *Pastor Fran Cracks True-Life Murder Mystery IN a Murder Mystery!!*

Not "Miranda Abbott," she noted. "TV's Pastor Fran." No matter. She may not have been a real pastor, but she was a real investigator.

The crowd loved her. When she entered as Mamie Dickens, she got applause, when she raised an arched eyebrow at Melvin of the Foam Muscles struggling with the jam jar, she received boisterous laughter, and when she spoke those immortal lines, "Reginald Buckingham the Third, 'tis over, I say! I eschew your lewd advances for the more salubrious airs of Tillamook Bay!" it brought down the house. What those words meant exactly, no one was sure, least of all the playwright, but it was a reference to Tillamook Bay and that was enough. Tillamook Bay was home.

When Miranda came out for her final bow, she was met with applause that was second only to Teena's, the true star of the show, even if she'd only had the one line. Fair enough, thought Miranda. Teena, after all, was the newly anointed Pride of Happy Rock.

She had been accepted into Yale, you see, and the town had rallied to fund a scholarship. She'd moved into Bea's, away from home for the first time. When her father showed up, irate, Ned had escorted him off the property with the warning "I can get a restraining order if have to." "Like I care!" her father had shouted. To which Ned had calmly noted, "Well, you may not, but I imagine Finkel Erdely will. If word should get out, imagine the hoopla. Would hate for that to happen." He never came back.

It was during the final curtain call that a mountain of flowers suddenly separated itself and began making its way toward the stage. A bouquet of bouquets, summer flowers, locally grown: rose-tinted gladioli, feathery white dahlias, a riot of daylilies, and a butterfly froth of buddleia blossoms. The mound of flowers moved from actor to actor, laying the bouquets on the stage, until finally, at Miranda's feet the final bouquet revealed . . .

"Andrew!"

He grinned up at her.

"Everyone!" She turned to the rest of the cast, shouting above the ovation. "My gay assistant!"

She pulled him up onstage, insisted on it, kissed him smack on the lips–Edgar could be jealous all he liked; let him!–held him tight, overjoyed.

"You came!" she said. "I hope that bus ride wasn't too odious. If I ever have to research the role of someone being sent to the gulags, I need only book another ticket from San Fernando to Happy Rock."

"Didn't take the bus," he said. "Flew. First class." His grin grew bigger. "And we're flying back the same way. The two of us. Together."

"But how can you–*we*–afford that?"

"I will tell you all about it later. But for now, know that the sudden boost of your profile caused a massive spike in the value of your *Pastor Fran* collectibles. I sold off a bunch of them, paid myself the back wages I was owed, and saved the rest for you. Put it in a bank account in your name. A very *big* bank account." Then hastened to add, "I kept all the receipts."

"No! No more receipts."

Who would have guessed that her closet full of memories was such a rich trove of nostalgia?

"You even have a rare Nurse Fran doll," Andrew said. "The one where your name was misspelled. I held that one back in reserve. I saw a signed one online going for twelve grand. All you have to do is sign your own Nurse Fran and you can beat 'em to the punch."

She thought of Carl, of his mom and the long-term care she needed.

"Let's hold off on that one, shall we?" she said. "At least till the first one sells. In fact, I may donate mine. Signed, of course. To that talented young lady over there." She gestured to Teena, who was beaming, flowers resting like a sheaf of wheat in her arms. "She's going to Yale to study drama. Could use the help."

"Sure thing," said Andrew. "I'll let her know."

Miranda placed a hand on his shoulder. "But do it anonymously, okay?"

"Sure." He stopped. "Wait. Do you mean . . . *anonymously*, or do you mean–"

"You know. The usual way, with a public announcement: *Donated by Miranda Abbott, anonymously*. I don't want a big fuss about it."

"Of course not." Still Miranda. For better or worse, but mainly for better.

At the reception afterwards, the room was humming with excitement.

"Electrifying news!" Bea said as she hurried past. "Our opening has been so successful there's talk of extending the run! Of holding it over *for a second night*!"

Andrew turned to Miranda. "All of this was for a single performance?"

"Welcome to Happy Rock," Miranda said with a laugh.

Shaking his head in amazement, Andrew went off to find Teena to share the good news–the good *anonymous* news–while Miranda considered the banquet table that was laden with Spaghetti McCune and her own signature homemade lemonade, both of which were untouched. Though she did see several full glasses that had been abandoned after the smallest of sips, apparently.

"Hmm," she said, employing her newly honed investigative skills. "I made more than enough lemonade for everyone. Yet no one is drinking it. What does that tell me? Aha. Clearly a case of opening night nerves. Too giddy for beverages. Or food."

Though the pea soup seemed popular enough.

"Yeah, I know," said Owen McCune, aka Earl Wussex of the Whiskers. He was equally puzzled. "Nobody touched my spaghetti, either, and I made the gourmet version." Meaning he had cut *expensive* hot dogs into it this time, given the VIP crowd that would be attending.

"Regional cities," said Miranda sagely. "Not as sophisticated a palate, alas."

Burt and Ned and Tanvir were in a corner discussing power sanders–or how best to garrote an enemy sentry; it was hard to say–while Harpreet and Denise were going over the costumes for an upcoming school musical. Graham's teen drama would finally be staged. The Yum Yum Tree had been chopped down once and for all and used for firewood.

Holly appeared, her twins side-by-side in a tandem stroller, gurgling away. A boy and a girl, named George and Nancy.

"Always was a fan of those books," she told Edgar. "Probably why I went into law enforcement."

Two more readers had entered the fold.

Melvin sidled up next to Miranda soon after. "You're, like, famous," he said. "All over YouTube and stuff. People are posting clips from your old show."

"So I've heard," she said with a smile. She reminded herself, I really must find out about the royalties on those.

"You're, like, practically a meme now."

No idea what that meant. "Thank you, Melvin. Very kind of you to say."

"I saw that one clip of you. On that parrot show? The one where you're running across the tracks. In slow motion. I watched that one a lot of times. It was . . . really good."

"Ah, yes. My debut performance as–"

"You ever date a younger guy? I mean, Mr. Abbott and you, you're, like, split up or something, right?"

"I beg your pardon?"

"Just saying." He leaned in with that distinct whiff of *eau de manure*. "If you ever wanna get together. Just the two of us."

"I beg your pardon!"

"C'mon," he said. "Let's not kid ourselves. I saw the way you were looking at me when you played the maid."

"I was acting! That was my role."

"Well, you coulda fooled me."

"That's the whole point of acting" she said, exasperated. "To fool people."

"You know where to find me," he said, with the sort of misplaced cockiness that only a would-be teenage Lothario possesses.

As he sauntered off, Miranda heard her name being called.

It was Bea. "Phone call!" she shouted. "At the box office."

Miranda threaded through the well-wishers and the fans to the front-of-house phone. Someone had tracked her down.

"Hey, kiddo! How's my favorite client?"

It was Marty Sharpe, her former agent.

"Marty, why are you calling? You fired me."

"Fired you? What gave you that idea?"

"The part where you said, 'I'm firing you.'"

"You misinterpreted that the wrong way, kiddo. A lover's spat, nothing more. What a story! Pastor Fran solves a real-life murder! This is big, baby. *The Real Has-Beens* called. Suddenly you're a commodity again!"

"I have to go, Marty. I'm at the opening night party with–" She meant to say "the cast," but it came out as "my friends."

"You didn't let me finish. *The Real Has-Beens* called and I told 'em to take a hike! 'She's too big a star for your Reality TV spiral of doom!' That's what I told them. Listen, kiddo. NBC is working on a reboot."

Her heart fluttered. "*Pastor Fran*?"

"*Parrot P.I.!* A *gritty* reboot. They even think they can get the original parrot. They live forever, those birds. The parrot's got a pretty hard-nosed agent, though, so we'll see. But there's talk of bringing you onto the show for a cameo."

"As Pastor Fran?"

"Lord no. They're giving Pastor Fran to someone younger, hotter with the kids. You would play Pastor Fran's older, single aunt."

"A spinster?" she sputtered. "You want me to play a spinster?"

"Not a spinster! An older lady who never married and now lives alone with her cats. *Not* a spinster."

"I don't know, Marty..."

"A window has opened, kiddo. It will soon close. You don't want to miss the boat on this one, or you won't be able to get the brass ring at the end of the rainbow."

Brass rings? Boats? Windows and rainbows? What language was this? Oh yes. She recognized it. It was the language of Hollywood. Desperation and delusion in equal parts.

"That rainbow has sailed!" she said. "Goodbye, Marty."

"Hang up now, you'll regret it!" he snapped.

"Well, your needlepoint portraits of movie stars all look like frogs!" she shouted back.

It was the meanest thing she could have said, even if it was true.

After Miranda hung up, Andrew came over, asking excitedly, "So?"

"Offers are coming in," she said. "Modest offers—but it's a beginning."

"I moved you out of the De-Lux Arms," he said. "I can find you someplace better when we get back. Closer to the Hills, maybe." He was elated. "Miranda Abbott will return with her head high and in style! This is a new chapter. A new beginning."

She smiled. "You're absolutely right, Andrew. This is a huge opportunity, an opportunity to finally be happy."

Death Is the Dickens would indeed be held over a second night, and a third. When the sets were finally struck and the lights turned down, only that ghost bulb would remain, illuminating the stage like an eternal flame, low-wattage and murky, but eternal nonetheless.

•••

THE ENVELOPE ARRIVED at Edgar's bookstore the following week.

Miranda would be flying back to LA that afternoon, and Edgar didn't have a forwarding address for her, so he drove down to Bea's in person, hoping to catch her before she left. He whistled for Emmy to join him, and the golden Lab leaped in through the passenger side of his Jeep.

He suspected it was already too late. Miranda would be gone by now. It was a long drive to the Portland airport, even with Ned at the wheel. He could imagine Miranda urging Ned to switch on his police lights, hit the siren, clear a lane for her, and he smiled.

Bea would know how to get in touch with her. He parked and walked up the steps to the B&B, and Emmy ran on ahead, and there was Miranda, in clamdiggers and a loose shirt, spattered with paint, her hair pulled back, a thick brush in hand.

She was painting the front porch, and when Emmy came bounding in, she said, "Hey, you!"

The dog galumphed back to Edgar, away from the freshly painted section, and Miranda said to her husband–her ex-husband–"Grab a paintbrush. There's a lot of work to do. We're tackling the garden next."

Bea appeared with a pitcher of SunnyD and said, "Hey, Edgar. What brings you here?"

He tapped the envelope in his hand. Hated to ruin the mood. "It's about those papers. The ones Miranda and I signed at the lawyer's office."

"Ah yes, the fainting Atticus Lawson," Miranda said. "He called me Pastor Fran the entire time."

"Oh, how bothersome," Bea said. "Why would anyone confuse the two of you?"

"That's the thing," Edgar said. He cleared his throat.

Miranda knew that habit. Whenever he wanted to avoid something, he would develop a scratchy throat and an evasive gaze.

When *Pastor Fran* had gotten canceled, he'd cleared his throat for a good twenty minutes before he told her.

He opened the letter. "You didn't sign as Miranda Abbott. You signed 'Pastor Fran.'"

She laid the paintbrush across the can. "Did I?" She came over, studied the papers, and said, "I'm so sorry, Edgar. It was a mistake. I wasn't up to anything."

"I know."

"Did he include new papers for us to sign?"

"He said you can initial the change and sign this letter of notification."

She wiped her hands. "Let me grab a pen, then."

But Edgar stopped her. "You know what? Let's just wait on that for now. There's no rush."

"Oh. Well. This calls for something stronger than SunnyD. I just made a big jug of lemonade. Let me grab you some!"

She gamboled off, and Edgar shivered in anticipation.

As did Bea. "You know her lemonade?" she asked.

"Oh, I do," he said. "I know it well."

He looked over at what Miranda had been doing, and he asked Bea, "She does know that you have to scrape the old paint off before you put on the new paint, right? All of that's going to peel away by the end of summer."

"I know," Bea said with a smile.

"And then?" he asked.

"I guess she'll just have to stay and do it all over again."

TMZ BREAKING NEWS!

COUGAR ON THE PROWL?? Is TV's Pastor Fran—a married woman!!— having an affair with her youthful assistant? Pastor Fran (played by Miranda Abot) seems to have developed a yen for boy toys recently. Shocking new photos capture a "dirty weekend" getaway in upstate Oregon when she thought no one was looking, raising disturbing questions about the former star's behavior.

A tightly cropped picture of Miranda kissing Andrew accompanied the story. Photo credit: Finkel Erdely.

AUTHORS' ACKNOWLEDGMENTS

Jennifer Lambert at HarperCollins Canada was behind this project right from the start. Thank you, Jennifer, for your enthusiasm and unflagging support. It's been a lot of fun.

We want to thank Leah Mol at Mira Books, as well, for her keen enthusiasm in launching this series in the United States.

Ian would also like to emphatically state that none of the characters in *I Only Read Murder* are based on actual people he may have encountered during his long career in theater as an actor, playwright, and artistic director. Seriously. (Clears throat.) Not a one.

The authors have noticed how movies and TV shows regularly feature closing credits, but books don't. There is an entire team behind any novel you read, and this is the team at HarperCollins Canada that helped make this one possible. The credits, as it were:

I Only Read Murder

Senior Vice President & Executive Publisher .... Iris Tupholme
Editor in Chief .... Jennifer Lambert
Production Editor .... Canaan Chu
Copy Editor .... Catherine Dorton
Proofreader .... Sue Sumeraj
Cover Designer .... Lisa Bettencourt
Publicist .... Shayla Leung
Marketing Manager .... Neil Wadhwa
Senior Marketing Director .... Cory Beatty
Publicity Director .... Lauren Morocco
Senior Sales Director .... Michael Guy-Haddock
Senior Vice President, Sales & Marketing .... Leo MacDonald
Director, Publishing Operations & Subsidiary Rights .... Lisa Rundle

ADDITIONALLY

Salish Cultural Consultant .... Steve Sxwithul'txw
Southeast Asian Cultural Consultant .... Jagjit Gordaya

In memory of Parnell Hall